# LOVE LUST & Scandalous Hookups

## AN EROTIC DOCU-SERIES VOL. 1

# GIL TU'CHALLA

# COPYRIGHT

# DEDICATION

*To all those, past and present who have allowed me to live life vicariously through your experiences, this Book is Dedicated*

# ACKNOWLEDGMENTS

A special thanks and gratitude to Jahzara for her patience, belief, support and compassion in bringing this book into fruition. Without you I would not have made it to the finish line.

To J.B., Na'Sheed, D1, Pharaoh, Tony Starks aka GunSmoke, FFDiva, Monique, Avon, Zaydia and those who chose to remain anonymous, thank you for sharing your stories.

Thank you Moe, Tanika, Quan aka "S", Beach, Lalonnie, "T", Manny and all those who critiqued, made suggestions, provided advice and encouragement. I listened even when it didn't seem like it. Thank you 2GunzDee for gracing the cover of LLASH.

And to DMG Publishing, thank you for the opportunity

*GIL TU' CHALLA*

1

---

# THE MEAT PACKER

Zaydia McNeil
Bronx, New York
June 1, 2018
FB: Z. Diction

I've always been a sexually carefree person. Well, I actually became carefree after a traumatic experience, but I'll leave that story for another time and place. On this particular day I was on my way over to this dude's house named Kevin. He and I met on Facebook and we had a few mutual Facebook friends. He liked a few photos I posted and slid in my DM (Direct Message). I thought he was sexy. He's a big guy who could have been a linebacker in the NFL. His broad shoulders and slim waist turned me on the first time he sent me a picture of himself in nothing but a pair of boxer briefs. He wore his hair low, in waves, with a trimmed beard. After that first exchange of messages, he and I continued to converse for about a year.

Kevin and I tried hooking up on numerous occasions, but every time we crossed paths the timing wasn't right. Whenever we talked over the phone, he kept it respectable. On this day, he hit me up online inviting me to his brownstone in Brooklyn. I was up for an adventure, so I hopped my fine ass on the IRT #4 train in the Bronx and headed to his place.

When I arrived at Kevin's house, we exchanged hugs and kisses. He was smelling and looking good. We both knew that we wanted each other right then and there, but we kept our desires in check.

Kevin owns an independent record label that I won't name. He's always on the move and super busy, so I wasn't surprised to hear that he forgot about two meetings he had scheduled for that day. In spite of that, he wanted to spend more time with me, knowing that it was a rare occasion that he and I could meet. I could see the fire in his eyes, he wanted me bad. We sat next to each other on the couch. He turned to me placing both my legs on his lap. I was texting my friend Lakye, letting her know what I was about to get into. Kevin said to me, "Don't mind me, keep doing what you're doing. There's something that I wanted to do for a long time now." He pulled me close to him, pulled out my left breast and began to suck on the nipple. That caused my pussy to pulsate as he twirled his tongue around-and-around. We were so in tune with each other because his moans were matching mine, and I knew he was enjoying my double 'DD' cups. He came up to kiss me, and in between kisses he kept saying, "Damn, I've waited a long time for this." He had a decision to make, take this pussy now and cancel at least one of his meetings, or miss the opportunity to enjoy me...

Looking into his eyes, I could read his mind. He got on his knees and grabbed both my thighs, pulling me to the edge of the couch. He began kissing my inner thighs and crotch through my jeans. "If you had on a skirt, you'd be in trouble," he said, as he got up and sat on the couch next to me, contemplating whether he should leave or stay. He looked at me "I want to taste you before we leave." I smiled and replied, "If you do that we'll never leave, and you will miss at least one of your meetings."

"Nah Ma, I got dick control, I can have a lil snack now and save some for later!"

"Okay, if you say so." I replied.

He stood, taking my hand, leading me into his bedroom. We entered the room and he laid me on the bed. He took off my jeans and started kissing my stomach, proceeding slowly to the hem of my panties. He slid them off me, then said, "Open up wide for me." I did just that, spreading my legs, allowing him to caress my soft buttery thighs. He proceeded to taste me, whirling his tongue in and out of my pussy like it was a snack. Damn! He was doing his thing. My vagina was beginning to soak his beard with every flicker of his tongue. He licked and sucked up every last drop of my juices. Then he concentrated on my clit. I arched my back, moaning in pleasure as he ate me just the way I liked. It felt so fucking good. I closed my legs, squeezing his head between my thighs to let him know he was hitting my spot. He responded by spreading my legs wider, pulling me closer to him, then resumed eating me as if I was his last meal. His tongue felt so good, I let out soft moans, grinding my crotch into his face. Then he started to finger me, sliding two fingers into my tightness… My soft moans encouraged him to slide another finger into me. My shit is tight, but it could stretch and expand for the right touch, and he had that touch.

Kevin briefly came up for air to say, "Damn, this pussy taste so fucking good." I looked down at him and watched him eat me out. Then he slipped another finger into me, stretching my walls further and going deeper. I closed my eyes, laid my head back and let out another moan. I didn't realize how good that shit would feel until he squeezed his thumb into me. This motherfucker had my pussy so wet his whole hand was inside me. I fucking came in a rush. I grabbed his head and pulled his mouth into my clit. He sucked on it while fucking me with his entire hand. This was literally a hand job.

"Cum for me!" He said in between licks of my clit. Then, just as I was about to reach another orgasm, he stopped and said, "Your pussy tastes good as a motherfucker Ma!" He stood up, kicked off his sneakers and started taking off his clothes. I'd never seen anyone move that fast before. He went back to eating me out. I smiled to myself, knowing from the jump that this was going to happen.

Kevin was acting like he hadn't had pussy in years the way he was finger fucking me and sucking on my clit. When he came up to kiss me, his dick was more than ready to infiltrate my walls. While looking me dead in the eyes, he slid on a condom. The smirk on his face told me that he could read my mind. I wanted that dick just as bad as he wanted this pussy. Grabbing both my legs he pulled me into him and entered me. The first stroke took my breath away. He wasn't lying when he said he was getting me prepped and ready for him. My insides were already stretched to its limits after having his whole hand in me, but his huge, juicy, fat, long dick stretched my pussy more. And Kevin knew how to work my middle.

He started off slow, just giving me the head, and that shit was phat.... Inch by inch he went deeper inside me. Once he reached my bottom he paused. I started to feel the pulse of his dick inside me. No lie, his dick filled every inch of me. Then he started to stroke me, slowly picking up the pace, going balls deep. I matched his every stroke, his balls smacking against my butt cheeks. The look on his face was priceless. He started slowing his pace, not wanting to cum just yet. After catching his composure, Kevin started up the pace again, but this time he was going harder, fucking me like an animal. And what turned him on was how I met his strokes with mine.

"Turn that phat ass around," he said. I didn't hesitate to get on all fours to assume the position. Doggy style is my favorite.

He slid his dick in me nice and slow. I looked over my shoulder so I could see his facial expression as he fucked me from behind. He started biting his bottom lip watching my ass bounce every time he stroked into me. Then he closed his eyes as if he was in some sort of trance. I started throwing it back, going faster and harder. The intensity of how I was giving it back to him snapped him out of his trance. He placed both his hands around my waist and started fucking me fast. The pounding was so hard, my upper body was over the edge of the bed, but that didn't faze me. Being the pro that I am, I placed both my hands on the floor as if I was in the pushup position. Still fucking me hard, that shit felt even better in that position. I was moaning and making all sorts of sounds. "Fuck me, fuck me hard. Fuck me harder!" He pulled me back onto the bed and started fucking the shit out of me.

He was pounding my walls and I was loving every single moment of it. Then I brought my torso as close to the bed as possible, arching my back into a curve so that my ass was poking up for him to go even deeper. The force and intensity of his strokes were so hard and fast, his balls were slapping against my clit, and every time they hit my clit, a million sensations went up my spine. I didn't think he could go any harder or faster, until he shifted into a higher gear. "Oh my God, oh shit, oh shit!" I said, moaning and panting. Sweat was dripping down my body. Then my body went into convulsions. I started shaking, my pussy was speaking in tongues as he drove his big phat dick in and out of me. His strokes were long, pulling all the way out of me, then driving into me like a battering ram. I felt his dick in the pit of my stomach. And just when I thought I would pass out, he made one last thrust into me and exploded.

We both collapsed on the bed drenched in sweat, and fully exhausted. After a few moments we regained our composure. A knowing smile spread across his face. He was satisfied, and I was happy to have been able to give him such pleasure.

"That shit was good Ma. If I had more time, I know it would have been even better," said Kevin. I was thinking to myself, "Damn, this nigga got some good dick!" We took a shower together and ate some lunch. He rescheduled the first meeting and was able to make it on time for his second meeting of the day. We made plans to meet up again, and I headed back uptown.

My pussy was sore for days after that encounter. I don't know why I gave my friend Lakye all the juicy details, because for several days all she kept asking me was, "When you gonna hook up with that dude Kevin again?" I don't know why she didn't just come out and say she wanted to hook up with him too. Shit, a closed mouth won't get fed. If she had asked, I would have hooked up a threesome!

2

———

# THE JUMP!

## WHEN TWO ARE BETTER THAN ONE

Zaydia McNeil
  Bronx, New York
  June 1, 2018
  FB: Z. Diction

After a long day of work, I arrived home and surprisingly, I wasn't tired. I jumped in the shower and felt refreshed, but a little bored. I was sitting on the couch watching TV when my phone goes off. I'm wondering, "Who could this be calling me?" I looked at the caller I.D. and see the name 'Rich' pop on the screen. I let it ring for a while because this dude is a cocky motherfucker who swears he's God's gift to women.

To his credit, Rich is fine with a caramel complexion, 6'2" tall with an athletic build. He played professional basketball overseas. His acne was prominent on his face, but aside from that he had sex appeal, plus he exuded confidence. He and I met online, and although he wasn't the typical man I would date, or even fuck, no matter how good he looked, we hooked up from time to time.

7

I answered the phone, "Hey Rich, what's up?" He responds, "What's up sexy? What you doing tonight?" I roll my eyes cause knowing Rich, he has something planned. "I ain't doing nothing, I say sounding bored, because I truly am. "You feel like chilling with me tonight? I'm over my brother's crib. We can hang, watch TV and have a few drinks." He asks. I'm saying to myself, "I know this nigga got something up his sleeve. Anytime you hang with Rich something seems to pop off."

I don't really want to go all the way to Harlem in the projects where his brother lives. I have never been to his brother's place. Usually I'd give Rich a hard time just to spite him, and to let him know that he doesn't have a hold on me like he has on his other women. I'm my own woman, I don't belong to him, and even if I did, nothing would change. But since I'm bored, I tell him, "Yeah, I'll come through and have a few drinks with you."

I get dressed, slip on a pair of tight jeans, a sweater and a pair of Milano Timbs, I love heels. I jump in a cab and head downtown to 116th Street and Park Avenue in Harlem. Rich meets me in front of the projects and escorts me to his brother's building. The apartment is on the ground floor and to my surprise it's clean. Most men are very sloppy and dirty. Rich's brother enters the room, and he's fine as hell. He's an inch or two shorter than Rich but more muscular. I can tell that he works out. Rich introduces us, his name is James, and as I shake his hand I'm thinking, "You can get it, and trust you would want more." Then it dawns on me, "This is why Rich wanted me to come over. He wants to have a threesome with me and his brother!" I smile and silently say, "Hmmm, if that is to be the case how could I say no!"

His brother excuses himself to the back and Rich and I get comfortable on the bed. We talk about our day and things going on in our lives. Rich offers me a glass of Hennessey and I take a few sips.

Although Rich is cocky and borderline conceited, he's

sensual and attentive. He gives me a full body massage which I needed badly. If he had stopped talking in my ear, I would have fell asleep. He turns to me and says, "Lay on your back," and begins to kiss me while fondling my breasts through my bra. He slowly makes his way down to my pussy. I moan in reaction to his touch. I allow him to unbuckle my belt, then the buttons on my jeans. I lift my butt as he removes my jeans and panties. My pussy is soaking wet. He has this devilish grin on his face because he knows it's due to him, plus the Hennessey, adding to my arousal.

Rich begins eating me out, but the television is distracting me. The BET Awards is on. I don't understand why men like to watch TV while having sex. That shit is a turn off to me, and my pussy will get dry in a hurry. I decide to return the favor. I tell him to lay back on the bed. I remove his Jordan's from his feet, then pull his jeans down. His boxers come next. I work my tongue from the tip of his dick down the shaft. I come back up and swallow him whole, gripping his dick with my tongue and the roof of my mouth. I know I'm doing my thing by the sound of his moans and how his hips are rotating. I make sure I use a lot of spit, lubricating his dick because I like to deep throat. I want that shit to touch my tonsils. In no time I got him ready to fuck. Rich is squirming cause I'm sucking on his dick with vigor.

I don't want him to cum just yet, so I lay off him. He slips on a magnum condom. I wouldn't consider him a magnum man, but hey I guess it works for his ego! He says, "Get on your knees. I want to hit it from the back." I position myself on my hands and knees. Rich gets behind me and grabs my waist with his left hand while placing his dick inside me with the other hand. His dick fills my pussy and I moan with pleasure. My pleasure is soon interrupted by the sound of Maxwell who's performing in the BET awards. I couldn't help but watch him sing after he'd being gone from the music scene for years. I'm such a huge fan. And just when I'm about to tell Rich to turn off the TV because it's a distraction, his brother walks in on us.

"Damn, yaw started without me!" His brother says. I'm shocked and a bit embarrassed. I almost forgot his brother was there, but another part of me was thinking, "If you want to join us, I don't mind!" But instead I blurt out, "Oh my God, I'm so sorry you're seeing us like this." I say to Rich, "Why don't you turn off that TV and the lights." James agrees with me, but Rich is protesting, "Come on Zay you know I like to see everything." James shakes his head, lights candles for us, then turns off the TV and the lights. I thank him, and he says, "I'm going to take a shower." As he heads to the bathroom I'm thinking, "Damn I wish I could join you!"

After James leaves, Rich and I get completely naked, we resume fucking doggy style, and I'm throwing it back at him, giving it to him as hard as he's giving it to me. The sound of our bodies smacking against each other fills the room. Then he starts smacking my ass real hard. I look over my shoulder and I tell him, "Smack it, yes smack it harder, harder, yes, yes, smack that shit, smack my ass, yes, just like that, smack it." We're going at it like two animals in the heat of lust when I look up and James is standing there wearing nothing but a towel wrapped around his waist. His body is nice with cuts in all the right places. He had definition in every ab. I wanted to suck on his nipples if he'd let me. Then he walks over to me while Rich is still fucking me from behind. James opens his towel and I come face to face with his dick. I don't hesitate to grab it and swallow him whole right then and there. Now I got James in my mouth and his brother Rich in my pussy, and they're both fucking me at the same time. I'm in heaven.

I begin to suck James off, giving him this award-winning head game cuz they don't call me the Head Doctor for nothing. I know he's loving my mouth by the way he's gripping the back of my head and moaning. He's fucking my face, his dick hitting the back of my throat causing me to gag. Saliva is dripping off my chin and I'm working his dick with my mouth.

Rich is fucking me from behind, smacking my ass over and over again, fucking me harder while I'm still sucking James' dick. After a while I sense James is about to cum in my mouth because his knees are buckling and he's moaning and holding my head tight. He pushed his dick deep into the back of my throat. I felt the explosion from his balls erupt into my mouth. He came so much his semen filled my mouth and overflowed down the side of my cheeks.

After regaining his composure James lies on the bed. I climb on top of him. I'm not a rider, but for this special occasion I make sure I perform well. I grab James' dick, guiding it inside of me. Of course, protection is used. James' dick feels so fucking good inside me that I get lost in the pleasure and forget that I'm actually riding him and riding him well.

Rich gets behind me, and while James is in me, he tries to put his dick in my ass. Now I love anal sex, but on this day, I wasn't about to allow Rich's cocky ass to get his way completely, so I tell him, "No, you're not fucking me in my ass." He leans forward and kisses me, "Come on Zay!" I look at him over my shoulder and he knows I'm not having it. Defeated, he stands up on the bed and gets in front of me, and I start sucking his dick while I'm riding James. I'm amazed at myself because I'm able to suck Rich's dick and ride James at the same time without missing a beat. We stay in that position for five minutes or more. James leans up to suck on my breast, while palming my ass and stroking up into me.

James and I switch positions, so he can fuck me from behind. I get on all fours, and while James and I switch positions, Rich gets off the bed and takes a chair and positions it at the foot of the bed. I begin throwing it back at James. He's staring down at my ass as it jiggles like Jell-O every time my ass bounce against his pelvis.

While James is still fucking me from behind, I crawl to the foot of the bed. Rich grabs my face and starts kissing me. I'm so turned on by the way he looks into my eyes and says to me, "Fuck him, fuck my brother like you fuck me. Give it to him, like you give it to me!" I start throwing it back at James so hard that he has to hold onto my waist to control how hard I was giving it to him. Rich says, "Yeah just like that. Fuck my brother, fuck him" Then Rich puts his thumb in my mouth, and I started sucking on it, but I wanted to suck on something else. Rich says to James, "Fuck her, fuck her harder!" Then he asks me, "Do you like the way he's fucking you?" I tell him yes in an erotic voice. James fucking me feels so good. He's giving it to me harder and faster the way I like it. Then Rich places a pillow under himself so I could suck his dick. I'm so happy that both of them are enjoying me. Fucking two brothers at the same time is a first for me. I feel like I have so much power. I'm loving every moment of it.

I start jerking Rich's dick and sucking his balls at the same time. Then I go back to sucking his dick deep in my mouth. While I got Rich's dick in my mouth, I start throwing it back at James because I want him to never forget this night. James is trying hard not to cum, I could tell because he slows down in between strokes. I slow my pace down with him. While still sucking Rich's dick, James reaches his orgasm, rolls over and says, "Damn, I couldn't hold it anymore, that shit was feeling good."

James climbs off the bed, and Rich takes his place, it's now his turn to work my pussy over. We start off fucking in the missionary position. I wrap my legs around his waist to pull him deeper into me. Its feeling so good, I begin to grind my hips in sync with his. Then we switch to the doggy-style position. Rich starts to give me deep, long strokes just the way I like it. I bring my torso down close to the bed, poking my ass up in the air so he could go even deeper. I know he's loving it because he starts going faster, and harder. I tell him to fuck me, fuck me harder. Then I ask, "You like this pussy?" He answers, "Yes." Rich is fucking me real hard, but I can take it. I close my eyes cuz he's beating the pussy up. When he finally reaches his orgasm, we both collapse on the bed drenched in sweat.

While we both lay on the bed, James joins us, and we talk. James lets me know how good the pussy was, saying, "Yo, I couldn't hold my nutt that shit was feeling so good, that shit was crazy." I could tell by the look in his eyes that he wanted to hook up again, but without his brother. Rich cuts into our conversation and says he has to go. So I get up and head to the bathroom to clean myself off. That's when I realized we were in a studio apartment. So, Rich planned this shit, and wanted the three-some to pop off! I look into the bathroom mirror and said to myself, "Touché!" and started laughing.

We all get dressed and as we're leaving James is walking next to me. We exchange small talk and I know he's feenin for my number but before he got a chance to ask, Rich quickly inter-venes steering me to his car and opening the door for me to climb in. What a hater! Rich and his brother talk for a minute, then Rich climbs in behind the wheel. As we're talking Rich gets horny again. He couldn't believe how crazy the episode was. He was shocked that I fucked his brother. I didn't care how he felt about it. Either way I enjoyed myself and the look on his broth-er's face told me that he enjoyed it too.

On our way back uptown Rich begins to pull into a parking spot.

"What you doing?" I ask him.

He grabs his crotch. "Damn, that shit was crazy, I'm getting horny again thinking about it."

"No, take me home." I reply.

"Come on Yo, why you acting like that?" he asks.

"Rich, I'm tired, take me home or let me out. I can catch a cab." He looks at me all seductive thinking that would change my mind. I stare back at him with that, "Don't play with me look." He gets the picture and pulls back into traffic. Twenty minutes later we pull up in front of my apartment building in the Bronx.

"I don't want to go too long without seeing you again," he says. I look at him and give him a smirk like, "whatever!" He wraps his arms around my waist and palms my ass, then kisses me. "I'm serious, I want to see you more often."

"That's totally up to you. You're the one who's always busy. Give me a call when you're free," I reply. I pull away ending our embrace, leaving him standing on the curb. I know he's staring at my ass while I'm walking away. I look over my shoulder as I enter my building and see the lust still in his eyes.

I know Rich wished he could have gotten the booty again but you gotta play cocky motherfuckers like Rich that way, leave them wanting more!

Rich and I continued hooking up for a while, then one day, while trolling on my home girl's Facebook page, I noticed Rich in a picture with a nice-looking woman. Curious, I dug deeper and realized that the woman in the picture was on my friends' list. I clicked on her page and there he was, hugged up with her. Wow! They were engaged to be married.

A few weeks later on a chance encounter at an event my home girl was hosting, I met Rich's fiancé. She seemed really nice, and now I felt bad about fucking her man all this time. I could no longer fuck Rich with a clean conscience. Don't get me wrong. I wanted to... But like I said, every time we hooked up Rich had something crazy up his sleeve... Another story for another time.

On occasion Rich will slide in my DM feenin for this pussy and mouth, but I always decline. I feel sorry for his fiancé. Rich is and will always be a dog in heat that no woman can contain, not even me the Head Doctor!

3

---

# TRICK OR TRAP

**DARRIUS HOWARD, AKA NA'SHEED**
Madison, Wisconsin
September 2015
FB: NA'Sheed

EVERY TIME I THINK ABOUT THIS STORY I LAUGH AND SHAKE MY head. My name is Na'Sheed, I'm from the west side of Madison, Wisconsin, the second largest city in Wisconsin. It's considered a college town, but like every major city in America it has its underworld elements. My homies and I were considered hustlers, so in essence we were a part of that world.

My big homie Rated-X, we called him X for short, is a few years older than me. A big dude who stood 6'4" tall with long dreads. X was known for simply being a freaky dude. He was eating pussy in junior high when the rest of us were jerking off to Black Tail magazines.

The homie hit me up on the celly (cellphone) early one Friday morning. "What's up Sheed? You ready to take that trip to the City my nigga?" I was in bed lying next to my girl. She was still asleep so I turned to my side and spoke low into the phone. "I'll be ready after I make a few runs." We agreed to meet up at his baby mother's.

It was still early, so I made something to eat, got dressed and headed out the door. I made a few rounds but wasn't done yet, so I headed to my cousin Tonya's house who was X's baby

mother. The plan was to drive out to Chicago and meet up with the plug (supplier), by 10p.m. that night. We had a few hours to burn so I rolled up a blunt and we played Madden 12.

X's phone kept pinging, so I paused the game while he returned the text. That's when Tonya came in the room beefing. "Why yaw smoking in here? You know that shit ain't good for the

baby." She glared at X. I put the blunt out and said, "My bad cuz, I figured it wouldn't bother him down here in the basement." She rolled her eyes at me and turned her attention to X. "I need some money for some formula." X looked up from his phone, "You always need money." Digging into his pocket, he peeled off a few big faces and handed them to Tonya. As soon as she left the room, he turned to me and said, "You know that chick 'Black' from The Circle, over there on Park Street?" I started going through my mental rolodex of people I knew from the south-side. I replied, "Dark skin, long hair with a piercing on her cheek bone right under her eye?" X started smiling, "Yeah that's her. She just hit me up on Facebook talking bout she wants to hook up."

I knew this was coming: X was always getting side-tracked by pussy. "Come on my nigga, we ain't got no time for that," I said, un-pausing the game. But of course, Mr. Rated X had a one-track mind. Completely ignoring me, he continued to exchange texts with this chick. Then he glanced up from his phone, "She said she got a buddy for you!" My mind was racing for plausible excuses to duck out of this double-date shit when he said, "It's only 3p.m, we ain't gotta be in the City until 10p.m."

His mind was made up, debating with him would be a waste of time. "Her friend better be cute!" I replied. We made arrangements to meet up with them at 7p.m. and resumed playing the game.

An hour later I got hit up for a few sales, so me and X headed out to make our rounds. At around 6p.m. X got another text from Black. "My home girl can't make it. Her guy is at the crib and she can't get away."

X texted her back, "So what you tryin to do? Cause my homie still with me." Black seemed to be down for whatever, she texted back. "I don't care, I'm still tryin to kick it!" When X told me what she said my dick got harder than a motherfucker. Although I normally didn't mess with dark-skin girls I was always down for a Jump (tag team). She agreed to meet us at the Best Western near East Town Mall. That was convenient for us because afterwards X and I would jump on the beltway and head straight to Chi. (Chicago).

We were done trapping. I was sitting in the passenger seat counting the $14,000 I had for the re-up when we pulled up in front of the Best Western Motel. Black was already there standing in the lobby wearing an all-white denim suit. "Go pay for the room, I'mma grab something from Popeyes real quick," X said. I jumped out of the truck and headed to the motel lobby. Black recognized me immediately. I had done business with her cousin a couple of times. I never paid her much attention and was thinking to myself that I should have. She was looking good. Her body was well put together. She had wide hips and a nice heart-shaped ass. Her breasts were a decent C-cup. She wore her hair straight. It was long, silky, and reached her shoulders, and it looked like it was all hers too. We exchanged greetings and a quick hug. Then she asked me, "Where' s X?"

"He went to grab us something to eat." I replied, sliding her a $100 bill for the room. I watched her strut across the lobby towards the reservation desk. Damn, that body was crazy! She had on a pair of heels and strutted like a runway model. Come to think of

it, she reminded me of Naomi Campbell but thicker. Her skin was smooth with no bumps or blemishes. She was definitely a pretty black chick.

Moments later she came back with the key and led the way to the room. I texted X the room number as we entered the room. Black turned to me and said, 'I'mma freshen up real quick," and headed to the bathroom. I grabbed the remote on the nightstand and clicked on the flat screen TV. I was laying on the bed with my feet kicked up channel surfing when Black emerged from the bathroom wearing nothing but a pink thong.

"You can watch TV at home," she said with this knowing look. She didn't have to tell me twice. I immediately jumped up and started taking off my clothes. The sight of her smooth black skin had me mesmerized. The pink thong and bra were a perfect contrast to her complexion. Her stomach was flat without a stretch mark in sight except for a few on her thighs. The only visible flaw was the black mole under her right breast. It was hard not to stare at that shit!

We both climbed on the bed. She motioned for me to lay on my back. She pulled my boxers down to my ankles then came up and took me in her mouth. That shit felt so good I grabbed the back of her head, forcing her to deep throat me. She gagged on my dick, while I held her head in place. I closed my eyes enjoying the feeling of having my entire dick stuffed down her throat. Then I released my hold, allowing her to do her thing. She was working her mouth like a porn star trying to make me cum quick. I wanted to see what that pussy was hitting on, so I pulled her off me and told her to turn around. She giggled as if reading my mind, knowing that I almost ejaculated prematurely. She assumed the position and I got behind her. Her ass was nice and tight but not hard. I spread her butt cheeks to take a peek at that asshole. Her pussy lips spread apart and she was so pink inside I automatically thought of that saying, "The blacker the berry, the sweeter the juice!" I was tempted to eat her from behind, Not! I'd leave that shit to X. His freaky ass would eat any stray bitch in heat.

Soon as I slid inside her I knew her pussy was good. It was hot, wet, and tight. A perfect combination. She moaned, looking over her shoulder. We made eye contact and I thought to myself, "You do this on the regular don't you?" I started fucking her hard, and she must have liked it that way because she closed her eyes breaking eye contact with me. I decided to concentrate on the view of my dick sliding in and out of her wet pussy. Her juices soaked me. I don't know if she came or not but her juices started to foam turning white. She started throwing it back. Her ass cheeks smacking and bouncing with every thrust. I'm saying to myself. "Damn! I should have been fucking dark-skin chicks..."

𝕏 𝕏 𝕏 𝕏 𝕏 𝕏

Pulling into the drive-thru, X received a text from Sheed. "Room 1102!" A broad smile came across his face. He placed his order at the drive-through window, giddy with anticipation. After paying for his food X headed to the Best Western. He parked his Escalade around back near room 1102 and grabbed the bag of Popeyes Chicken before exiting the truck. As he's locking the door the Nike bag in the back seat catches his attention. "Damn! I almost forgot," he admonished himself.

Rated-X had been feenin to link up with Black for months. Since the first time he sent her a direct message on Facebook they'd been flirting with each other online. Black kept reminding

him that he had a woman, and he joked about knowing her baby's father. He knew fucking with Black could lead to some drama, yet subconsciously the thrill of him getting caught up in some crazy shit motivated him to do the dumb shit that he did.

Those thoughts were racing through his mind when he entered the motel room. It took him a complete second to register the scene unfolding in front of him. He assumed that the party wouldn't start until he arrived, but to his surprise, it had started without him. X stood there

watching his lil homie stick dick to the chick he'd been feenin to fuck for months. He shook his head, then smiled, shrugging his shoulders. "Fuck it!" He thought, placing the bag of food on the table at the far end of the room, and slid the Nike bag under it.

"Damn, I see yaw didn't wait for me!" He said, stripping naked, and climbing on the bed. X positioned himself in front of Black, lying on his back. She buried her face between his legs, giving X her mouth to enjoy, while Sheed fucked her from behind.

Black licked the tip, then the sides of X's dick. Stroking it with a firm grip, she lubricated it with plenty of spit. She relaxed her jaw muscles, opening her mouth as much as she

could to accommodate his girth. She was determined to get his entire dick down her throat. "Oooh, oooh shit," X moaned, palming the back of her head. "Yeah, suck that shit, suck that dick girl," pushing her head down further, forcing her to swallow him whole. She gagged and he held her head in place, while he fucked her mouth.

Na'Sheed was sliding in and out of Black at a steady pace. Whenever his dick slid out her pussy and re-entered her, it would make farting sounds. "Damn this pussy wet." He kept

telling himself. He stared at his dick going in and out of her. He spread her cheeks to get a better view of her asshole. "I should fuck this bitch in her ass," he thought, but instead he slid a thumb in her butt.

Na'Sheed and X were lost in sexual bliss, and neither one

noticed the room door crack open. Two men entered wearing Halloween masks. The first one to enter the room stepped behind Sheed, placing a gun to the back of his head. "Bitch nigga don't move. You know what it

is!" Sheed froze, his dick instantly going soft inside Black's pussy. X was oblivious to what was going on. His eyes were still closed until he sensed someone standing over

him. He opened his eyes and jumped up in surprise. Black pushed him back on the bed while the second gunman pointed his gun at him.

"Where that bread at?" The first gunman said. Sheed pointed to his jeans crumbled on the floor. "Black, check them pockets," the first gunman gestured with a nod of his head. She proceeded to go through their clothes retrieving $14,000.

"Grab your shit, let's go." The first gunman said to Black. She started to get dressed. As they were about to leave, he noticed the Nike bag.

"Hold up! Black, check that bag under the table. That's the bag he had on Facebook counting that 30 bands." She ran and grabbed the Nike bag from under the table and handed it to the first gunman. He shook his head up and down after glancing inside. X blurted out, "Ant, that's what we on?" The first gunman took his mask off shaking out his dreads. He replied, "Yeah! It's me. It is what it is, you gonna have to catch up with me in the streets." The two gunmen kept their guns pointed at Sheed and X while exiting the room. "That's what you get for trying to flex on Facebook nigga!"

After Black and her accomplices left the room, Sheed and X looked at each other and burst into a fit of laughter. "Man, I can't believe Black set us up like that!" X shook his head in disbelief.

"If you would have listened to me in the first place and stuck to the plan we'd be on our way to Chi, but no you wanna go hook up with a scandalous hoe. You owe me 14 racks (thousand) nigga."

"Whatever, you were with it too!" X replied…

One week later in a Marriot Hotel room across town, Na'Sheed and X were chilling with a local thottie named Sabrina. Sheed and X were live streaming themselves counting $60,000 in cash from a Louis Vuitton bag.

On the south-side of Madison called the Circle, Black and her baby's father Ant were lounging on the living room couch enjoying a night of Netflix and chilling. Ant grabbed his phone, checking for messages. He noticed a recent post from X's Facebook page. He smiled, then clicked "LIKE."

# 4

# NEVER TRUST A BIG DICK ON THE GRAM

**Soroya Jones**
Harlem, New York
Sunday, May 5, 2013 @ 8:45pm
Social Media: Instagram
Screen name: SosexyRoya

We all got that one follower on Instagram that you never met in person. You both like each other's posts, laugh at each other's comments. It's almost like you're in a relationship, and nobody knows but you and that person. For me that was bk_brisk. He had a caramel complexion, stood about 6' tall with waves spinning with a half-moon part. That signature Brooklyn Nigga style! I'd been hooked on his pictures since day one. His body was cut up all crazy. He wore Cartier frames with a Rolex on his wrist. By all accounts he was the man of my dreams. Only problem, he was in most of his pics hugged up smiling with a light-skinned chick.

One night I got the balls to hit him up in his DM. "I'm no home wrecker or anything, but I'm so into you."

He replied back immediately. "LOL, what you mean?"

"You and your girl look happy, but I wanted you to know I'm feelin you."

He laughed and replied, "That's my sister."

A bitch was relieved because for a second I thought I had to step on someone's toes to get what I wanted. We exchanged numbers and talked for the next two weeks. During our discussions I found out that bk_brisk was only 21 years old. It wasn't a big deal, but I definitely had some age on him. He seemed to have his shit together though. He drove a black Lexus coupe, and lived in a studio apartment in one of those new luxury high-rises in Flatbush, Brooklyn.

One Friday afternoon we made plans to meet up later that night. I jumped my ass in the shower and got this pussy all the way together, because I knew what it was hitting for. I put on my brand-new red lace Vicky set. Bra had my titties sitting up pretty, boy shorts had my ass poking out looking super right. I looked over my shoulder at the mirror and could see parts of the butterfly wing tattoo spread across my ass. I slipped on a mini dress and headed out the door. I always get catcalls whenever I wear form-fitting clothes, and that night was no different. After jumping in my ride, I put Brisk's address in the GPS. It gave me the directions and an estimated arrival time of 23 minutes. I jumped on the FDR Drive at 116th Street and Pleasant Avenue and headed south towards the Brooklyn Bridge.

Traffic was light and it took me no time to get to my destination. Soon as I pulled up in front of his apartment building, I gave him a call. Several minutes later he met me downstairs wearing a white tee and basketball shorts. He greeted me with a hug, and I could feel his dick print on my thigh. In my head I'm saying, "Oooh God!" But I played it cool.

We stepped into the lobby, which was modern, and plushed out in soft burgundy carpeting with silver highlights. The elevator was chromed out and mirrored. I couldn't help looking at my reflection, watching Brisk take sneak peaks at my ass. The elevator raced up to the 22nd floor. His apartment was nicely laid out. I said, "Nice place you have here."

He responded "Thank you," then asked could he get me something to drink. But before I could answer he had a glass of Henny in my face. As I'm sipping on my drink, he's taking off his shirt. I wanted to say, "Hold up nigga, you moving way too fast… and who said we was fucking?" But the sight of his fine ass physique had me tongue tied. I couldn't resist him, so I went over and kissed his juicy lips. I had my tongue all down his throat. His hands went straight down my back to my ass. He palmed it like a basketball. My dress was super short, so he pulled it up to my waist, and slid his hand inside my boy shorts. I felt his finger slide down between my butt cheeks. I let out a moan and pressed my body closer to him. "Damn your ass is phat!" he said. Then he helped me slip out of my mini dress. Brisk stared at me in amazement. "Damn, your body is crazy!" Then he pulled my titties out my bra and started sucking on them. My pussy juices started flowing like a faucet. I reached over to grab his dick through his basketball shorts. I was shocked, it felt like a third leg. In the back of my mind, I'm like, "Shit is too big, too wide, it won't fit." But the freak in me pulled his shorts down and put my plump lips around his dick and started sucking that fat shit. I couldn't get it all in my mouth but what I could do was cover it with saliva.

Once I got him wet with my saliva, I took him in my mouth slowly and gradually proceeded to speed up the tempo, sucking his dick until I damn near choked. But my ego wouldn't allow me to fail and before I knew it, I was deep throating all that shit. I looked up at him and his head was tilted back in pure ecstasy, he was enjoying it. Then suddenly, he got up, grabbed me, then threw me on the bed. My heart was racing as he pulled down my panties and started eating my pussy. He sucked both lips gently together, then began to suck on my clitoris. The sensations sent me squirming, but he held on to my waist pulling me deeper into his mouth. I could feel myself about to climax. I never had my pussy licked like that before. I came all over his lips and he continued to suck up my juices.

"Turn around, I wanna hit it from the back!" He could have told me to bungy jump out the window at that point. I didn't hesitate, allowing him to bend me over on all fours. He starts to put his big, fat, long dick in me. That shit was abnormal, my pussy was soaking and all he was able to get in was the tip. He begins to penetrate deeper, going back and forth. I scream, "Ouch, it's too big!" He bends over and whispers in my ear. "I'm sorry, I'll be gentle." He takes his time, and it's so sensual the way he's stroking me, going in and out, deeper with each stroke. As he's fucking me, he's kissing on my neck and grabbing my titties at the same time. The lovemaking is so intimate, it's as if we're in love. I couldn't hold it any longer and came like a bursting dam. As I'm cumming he's getting more turned on. He flips me onto my back and starts to suck the cream right out of my pussy.

Then he begins to fuck me in the missionary position. He's sexing me so good, I wrap my legs around his waist, push my pussy closer into him and meet his every stroke. I sense him coming to a climax as his strokes become more intense. He's digging deeper with his thrust and I know he's about to explode. He's breathing heavy and panting like crazy. "I love it, I've waited for this, ahhhh your pussy is so good," he kept repeating as he's reaching his orgasm.

"Can I cum in your mouth?" I was so caught up in the moment that I answered "Yes," in an erotic voice. He took his dick out of my pussy and stroked his dick with his hand. I had my mouth open ready to receive his load. He exploded, cum splashed all over my face and mouth. I felt crazy slutty at that moment with his hot sperm in my mouth, and all over my face.

Then Brisk brought me a washcloth and helped me clean my face. He ran the shower and guided me to the bathroom where he washed my body. It was at that very moment when I knew age was nothing but a number. We laid down and I ended up falling asleep in his arms.

I was awoken by an alarm at 6a.m. "Hey Ma, you got to get dressed and get ready to go, my girl is on her way home from work," he said. I had the stupid face. I was in disbelief and pissed off. But I played it cool. In the back of my mind, I couldn't believe I let Brisk's young ass fuck me all sorts of ways and dismiss me. I put my clothes on and headed for the door. This clown had the nerve to ask when he'd see me again. I laughed and made my way towards the elevator. I pushed the down button and when the door opened, there stood that light-skinned chick in all his Instagram pictures. She greeted me with "Good morning!" I had a smirk on my face and replied, "Have a good day Ms. bk_brisk!"

I jumped in my ride and headed back uptown. From that day on I never dealt with any young boys again, and vowed to never trust a big dick and a smile…!

# 5

# P.O.F KITTY

**MARLON DEWITT**
Summer, 2019
Location: Alexandria, VA
Plenty of Fish: dreadhead_88cash

MY NAME IS MARLON DEWITT, BUT MY USERNAME IS dreadhead_88cash. The ladies call me Tongue Soldier by the way my tongue stands at attention when it's digging in some pussy, just like my dick. LOL… Let me stop.

It's Thursday night around 9:30p.m. and I'm sitting in the house bored as fuck listening to NBA Young Boy's Trap album, smoking loud (marijuana) while killing these dudes online playing 2K19. For me the weekend couldn't come fast enough. My girl Melissa was flying in from Miami for the weekend. But I couldn't wait that long, my dick was throbbing, and I was feenin to find some pussy to get into. My buzz kicks in and I'm hungry as fuck. I look down at my crotch to see my dick standing at attention in my joggers. That's when I get a notification from my POF account. Ain't nothing wrong with Plenty of Fish, they got some bad chargies on their platform.

On the real, I don't really need POF to meet women, I'm on it for fun. Out on these streets I be flossing on these joints (women). I'm 6'4" tall, 190 lbs, with long dreads and plenty of tattoos. My shoe game and clothing stay on flame. Hands down I'm the fashion Don. Chicks see this slim physique and make assumptions, then become shocked when I will fold a big girl like a pretzel and dagger her pussy to convulsions with this 8-inch, banana-shaped dick.

When I checked my phone the POF notification pinged 15 times. It's a tall, slim chick I've been trying to get up with for a minute. She liked 15 of my pictures. She was trolling at that hour, so I checked her page. I could tell by her pics that she had 'GPP', good pussy potential. I wasn't the only one sending heart emojis, I noticed a lot of dudes on her page doing the same. That didn't matter to me though. I'd been craving for new pussy for the past two weeks. So, I slid in her inbox. Her profile name read 'Independent-Climax...' The name alone intrigued me.

Ms. Independent Climax was scantily clad in most of her photos, but the one of her wearing a black see-through body suit, red bottoms and a Gucci belt securing her slim waist caught my eye. Her legs were long. Her hair weave looked like the expensive type all the Instagram models were wearing these days. This slim chargie could be a winner. I didn't hesitate to go straight at her...

"Cute and sexy how are you doing?" I asked.

"Hey." She replied with the blushing emoji.

"Ms. Independent Climax, what's your real name, and can I get your number?"

"Nikki," was her response, and immediately she sent me her number. I texted her from my number I give all my thots, and side joints.

"So, what you doing tonight, you lit?"

"Who is this?" She asked.

"Damn lil momma, how many niggas you got on your line? This is Dreadhead."

"Naw, my bad, I don't be answering people texts like that. Plus, you didn't give me a heads up of who you were."

"Well, let's meet up, unless your man got you on a curfew?" I asked.

"'No man here, just trying to get into something fun. I've been sipping on Cîroc, getting lit," she replied.

"Ahight bet! Where you stay? I'll come scoop you up." And just like that I got the address and all her info. I told her that I'd meet her in an hour. I got myself straight, sprayed on some Creed Aventis, grabbed my keys, then jumped in my S550 Benz.

Forty minutes later I pulled up in the hood of south-east D.C. I'm no fool, I pop open the stash box and lay my Glock 40 on my lap just in case this chick tries something crazy. As she approaches my car, I'm checking the selfie she got posted on her POF page, comparing them to the chick I see walking up from my rearview. Her complexion is lighter in her picture, but it's her and not a catfish situation.

She walks up to the car smiling. Her teeth are all white, no gaps and straight.

"Hi, it's me Nikki." I greet her in return and told her to call me soldier. She climbs in the passenger seat and I pulled off, jumping on Route 295 south, heading downtown to the water-front. Once there we head to the Crab Cake Café. After dinner we head to the pier where I parked my car. We're chopping it up (talking) while watching the boats sail by. It's a nice summer night, I glance at my watch, it's 11:45p.m. Nikki turns the radio to her favorite station, and City Girls is playing.

I lean my seat back to recline and watch Nikki move her body to the music. She's talking but I'm not listening. My mind is on sex and I'm ready to fuck. I lean over and start kissing her. Then I take her hand and place it on my dick. Nikki starts rubbing it. My dick was already hard, but her touch got it stiffer. She unzips my fly and pulls my dick out. I'm watching the expression on her face. I can tell she's intrigued by my hooked dick. I recline back into my seat and tell her to taste it. She drops her head down into my lap and begins sucking me off.

Nikki moans taking this Captain Hook dick to the back of her throat, choking on it briefly. I looked down at her mouth moving up and down at a steady pace. Without missing a beat, she places her two hands around my dick and begins twisting it while staying in rhythm with the up and down motion of her head. "Damn lil mama, you're a champ!" I compliment her which seems to turn her on. She begins sucking with more eagerness and intensity. She gulps my entire dick to the back of her throat swallowing all 8 inches. I couldn't help letting out a grunt. Her mouth felt so good I decided to name her "Big Gulp," like 711's drinking cups.

I take her hair and shift it to one side to get a better view. She's sucking me, making loud slurping sounds, and grabs my balls, rubbing them at the same time. "Damn, this bitch got a mean mouthpiece on her," I thought. I guide her head to pick up the pace. Soon I feel myself about to explode. She must have sensed this because she pulls back just in time. My sperm had almost reached the top. Nikki still has her hand wrapped around my dick. She squeezes it real hard, then spits on it and begins to jerk it. I stop her and tell her to climb in the back seat. I smack her ass and tell her to strip.

Nikki did as she was told stripping down to her thong. I climb out of the car with my dick hanging out my fly. I open the door and order the slim freak to get on all fours facing me. I'm standing at the back door. Nikki takes my dick into her mouth and resumes sucking without using her hands. She rocks her body back and forth, sucking me faster and faster with the rocking motion of her body. I begin to move my hips back and forth to meet her mouth, feeding her more and more dick with every motion.

Nikki pauses, grabs my dick and smacks it across her lips. She takes it back in her mouth, back out again teasing it with her lips. I inadvertently let out a moan and say, "Damn your mouth feels so good!"

Nikki looks up into my eyes and winks at me like a porn star, then resume sucking my dick. I reach into the door jam and grab a bottle of Moet that I keep in my car. I take a swig to the head and think "Damn this bitch can suck my dick forever!" I tilt the bottle and poured champagne all over my dick and her head. She froze… momentarily stunned, and looked at me with a "What the fuck?" expression on her face.

"Lil momma don't worry, I'll get your hair done!" After hearing those words, she grips my dick even tighter with those cherry red lips of hers. I pull out my phone going live on IG. I made sure I didn't show her face. Then I lean in the car, reaching over her back to smack her on the ass, then I cut my live.

I pull my dick out of her mouth and tell her to hold that position. I walk around to the other side of the car, open the back door, then squat down until my face is parallel to her ass. I slide her thong to the side, take the same Moet bottle and pour champagne all over her ass. I put the bottle on the ground and begin licking champagne from her pussy. My nasty ass didn't stop there, I spread her butt cheeks and stick my tongue deep in her asshole, going in and out. I alternated back and forth from her asshole to her pussy. I'm nibbling on her clit and slide two fingers in her pussy. Lil momma tried pulling away, but I wrap one arm around her thighs pulling her back into my mouth.

I was really feeling nasty. I slid my tongue back in her asshole as deep as it would go and begin to vibrate my tongue while humming at the same time. Nikki couldn't handle the feeling, she was moaning, trying to squirm out of my grasp. I take my tongue out of her ass and place my thumb in it while blowing hot air into her pussy hole. I grab the Moet bottle and pour more champagne down her ass crack, allowing it to run down to her pussy where I catch it with my tongue. Still holding her waist, I slide the bottle into her pussy. I start fucking her pussy with the bottle. After a minute or two I replace the bottle with my tongue and slide my thumb

back inside her asshole. I remove the hand I have wrapped around her and slap her ass hard as she erupts into an orgasm.

I stuff my face back into her ass and resume licking her pussy. My thumb is still in her ass. She's grinding her ass into my face, and begins to moan, "Oh, oh, ohiii!" That shit brings the beast out of me. I slap her ass hard, leaving a palm print.

"You want this dick?" I ask her.

"Yes Zzaddy, put it in me!" She moans. I slap her ass again repeatedly, "smack, smack, smack!" I take the Moet bottle and start fucking her with it again. After 8-9 strokes with the bottle, I remove it and stare at the gaping pussy hole before sticking my tongue back inside her, rubbing her clit until her insides begin to contract. That excites me, so I start rubbing her clit faster with two fingers, and slide my thumb in her ass. She's cumming so hard it squirts out like pee. I take off my shirt to wipe her pussy with it.

I smack Nikki on the ass and tell her to step out. She crawls out the back seat. I grab her by the waist, place her on the trunk of the car and spread her legs wide like an eagle. We start kissing. I whisper in her ear, "You a bad bitch!" She wraps her arms around my neck, and I say it again "You a bad bitch." I guide my dick to the entrance of her pussy. Inch by inch, I go deeper with every stroke. I don't stop until my balls smack against the crack of her ass. I kiss her on the neck, and nibble on her ear.

"You like how my dick feel inside you?"

"Yes, yes, it feels so good," she whispers back into my ear. I pull all the way out then thrust back hard inside her. She gasps, digging her nails into my back. I pull completely out of her again. Then I look into her eyes, "You want this dick inside you?"

"Yes please, oh yes, I want it," she moans. I tease her with the tip, rubbing her clit with it...

"Tell me you want it."

"I want it Zzaddy... give it to me," she begs. I ram my hooked dick deep inside her. She yelps in pain like a wounded puppy with every stroke of my curved dick.

I'm hitting her G- spot with every stroke. Nikki is pulling me into her. I grab her waist and begin pounding that pussy.

I lean her back against the back window of the car, spread her legs wide like an eagle. I look down at my dick as it goes in and out her pussy. Her legs are so long and smooth, I get this uncontrollable urge to lick them. I glance back down between her legs and stare at the movement of her pink, fleshy insides going back and forth with each stroke.

I pull my dick completely out of her, bend down and begin licking her pussy. After a few licks, I slam my dick back inside her. I'm fucking her hard and fast in that position with her legs still spread wide for at least 50 more strokes. It's humid outside, sweat is pouring down my back. It feels so good that I forgot we're outside in the open. Good thing Nikki and I were the only ones parked at the pier.

While I'm in the pussy I'm thinking, "This lil freak got some good pussy, plus it taste good like Honey Nut Cheerios. I may need to keep her on rotation!"

I reach down between her ass cheeks and stick my middle finger in her ass. With my dick still going in and out of her I rub her clit with my right hand. Nikki soon erupts into another orgasm. I pull out of her, place her feet on the ground, turn her around and bend her forward against the trunk. I take my middle finger and hook her mouth like a fish and enter her from behind. "Take this dick bitch." I say going in and out of her. Then I grab her by the waist turning her around to face me. I pick her up and wrap her legs around my waist. I put my back against the trunk and start drilling up into her going deep inside trying hard to bruise her pussy. I'm going harder, faster, and my legs start to tremble. I give her one last pump then exploded inside her. I place her feet back on the ground and we both stand there drenched in sweat, staring at each other.

"Girl, you got some Torch Pussy!" I say popping my trunk and handing her a fresh white t-shirt. She blushes, and replies "I never fucked a dude with a hooked dick before. That shit was hitting my spot." I chuckled, "Oh yeah!"

We hopped back in my ride. I dropped her off where I picked her up from. Before she climbed out of my car, I slid her $750. For a new outfit and hairdo.

"Make sure you hit me up tomorrow!" I yelled out the window, then peeled off, burning rubber.

I headed straight to the 24-hour carwash/detail shop. I had to get ready for the weekend, my girl's plane was due to land in a few hours.

Thanks to Nikki leaving those scratch marks on my back my weekend was a bust. Don't get it fucked up though, after my girl flew back to Miami, I hit Nikki up and took my sexual frustrations out on her. Lets' just say this 8-inch hook did some deep anal excavation the second time around. Nikki started calling me "Captain Hook!" from that point on.

6

# A CURIOSITY TURN FETISH

CIARA MICHELLE
Location: Washington, D.C.
Social Media: Black Planet
Username: _plushpinkz_
Summer, 2014

EVERY RELATIONSHIP GOES THROUGH TESTS AND CHALLENGES. Long distance relationships are one of the most challenging. But nothing compares to the challenges faced in an incarcerated one.

My name is Ciara and my man at the time name was Lamont, but went by the name "Low." However, I never called him Low. He was Lamont to me.

Lamont had been incarcerated for some years when we met. We were introduced by my home girl Kay-Kay. She was the leader of our all-girl crew, "The VIP Honeys." Our crew included me, Kay-Kay and 15 other females. We all partied at the GO-GO clubs in Washington, D.C. together. Our names stood for "Very Important Pussy." Trust me it's a D.C. thing. A lot of people wouldn't get it unless you grew up in the District of Columbia.

The day I met Lamont I was tagging along with Kay-Kay and her BFF Donna to the D.C. jail. They were visiting Kay-Kay's dude Ricky, and his friend Lamont. Yes, you read it correctly, they were visiting two guys in jail.

Donna was there to visit Lamont. Although Donna was a part of our crew, I never considered her a friend. She and I never really clicked. She was a few years older than me, but I was harder than her, which is why I had no problem scooping Lamont from her bougie ass.

On the real, she had no business being a part of our crew. She couldn't fight, and thought she was better than the rest of us. But she was Kay-Kay's best friend, and if anything popped off, I would still have her back. I would never stand there and let her get jumped. I also heard her pussy was trash, and she acted too good to perform during sex, laying there like a dead fish.

The day Kay-Kay asked me to tag along with Donna to visit their dudes at the jail I didn't have any plans, so I said "Okay." While Kay-Kay and Donna waited on their dudes, I sat there in my own world thinking of an outfit to wear to the GO-GO club that night. All the guys walked into the visiting room at the same time wearing blue jumpsuits. I glanced up then went back to my thoughts, but it was something about the way Lamont walked into the visiting room that caused me to pay attention to him. Donna got up and walked towards the visiting booths and sat in the one Lamont was in. I thought to myself, "He's actually kind of cute!" I looked him dead in the face and watched his body language. I wondered if he'd seen me rolling my eyes to the top of my head because I knew Donna was boring him to death. I looked over at Kay-Kay's booth and compared Lamont to Kay-Kay's dude who looked geeked out like a junkie, all crusty and dry.

During their visit I kept looking at Lamont while Donnas'

back was turned to me. I'm shaking my head from side to side silently saying to myself, "If you only knew. And why were you wasting your time talking to that dumb bitch?"

I'm not a hater, I just hate the fact that Donna thought she was too good to breathe natural air. A real stuck up for no reason type of bitch. I don't know where their conversation went because out of nowhere Donna turned around and asked me if I wanted to talk to him? With no hesitation I said "Okay!" But in my mind, I was nervous and didn't know what I was going to talk about. I walked up to the booth and waved a greeting, smiling, letting him know it was all good. I sat down, picked up the phone and wiped it before speaking into the receiver.

I started off cracking jokes, teasing, and throwing shots at Donnas' dry ass attitude.

I opened up my giddy and bubbly personality to him. I could tell he felt the same way I felt about Donna as I did by the way he laughed and smiled shaking his head. He kept saying, "You ain't right, you're crazy as hell MA!"

I immediately picked up on his accent. He certainly wasn't from D.C. Only New York dudes spoke the way he did, calling me "MA!"

After the visit I asked Kay-Kay if Lamont and Donna were together? She said she didn't think so. I definitely wanted him, so I sent a message through Kay-Kay and her boyfriend telling him that I liked Lamont and wanted to write him. I knew after receiving the first letter from Lamont that he was different. I wanted him for myself but he was playing hard to get.

Lamont had been scorned during his incarceration. He conveyed to me that in the past people had come and gone, and it was better for him to simply be friends with a woman as opposed to trying to maintain a romantic relationship behind bars. I was determined to have him, and my bubbly personality and realness eventually won him over.

Lamont introduced me to phone sex and mental stimulation,

along with sensuous and creative ways to get sexually aroused. He got me into sex toys. I got myself a dildo, suction cup dildos, clit bullets and anal beads. We learned how to connect intimately over those telephone lines. I would moan in his ear as I deep rode those dildos. One time it got so good I took the anal beads and slowly inserted them in my ass one at a time while I rode the suction cup dildo. It felt so good that I craved to cum while he was on the phone with me. Lamont had me addicted to him on a higher level. One that went beyond the physical, it was mental.

𝔁 𝔁 𝔁 𝔁 𝔁 𝔁

I was also cool with another group of girls called "SHAKE EM UP HONIES!" They were telling me about this website called "BlackPlanet." I never heard of it or knew anything about online dating, and to be honest with you at that time I really didn't care. My relationship with Lamont was blossoming, and despite him losing at trial, being found guilty of a leadership role in a drug conspiracy, I was determined to stand by his side.

Lamont was extradited back to New York to fill out the remainder of his state time. Six to eight months later I began to notice a change in Lamont's attitude. I began feeling disconnected from him. Whenever he called it didn't seem as if he was into me. Our discussions centered on tasks he needed me to complete. Our love life had turned dry. There was no more intimacy or love in his voice. We barely spoke about seeing each other anymore. Keep in mind we were now hundreds of miles apart in a long-distance relationship, on top of the physical barrier of prison that separated us. He was physically incarcerated, and I was mentally incarcerated. In essence we were both doing time together and Lamont failed to realize I was locked up with him.

Week after week I begged Lamont for attention, some affection, but he gave me nothing. I finally got fed up and said, "Fuck it!" I decided to create a "BlackPlanet" account. I wanted some attention, and since my man wasn't giving me any, acting like a selfish bitch, popping slick out the mouth, I got on some selfish shit as well.

I started trolling and checking out different male profiles when I came across this tall, light-skin, slim Jamaican dude's profile. He lived in New York. I thought to myself, "How ironic, Lamont was from New York as well." He looked sexy as fuck. His username was "Webcatcher_24." This dude was a real pretty boy and I had to catch myself because I was already having thoughts of infidelity. My hormones were on 10. I hadn't had sex with a man in over two years. Lamont was keeping things spicy with phone sex, but since his mind had been on everything other than my needs, I was in the head space of being fucked.

I started liking his pictures, commenting, just letting it be known I was interested. He sent me a message.

"Where you from?"

"Maryland!" I replied. "And you?"

"New York."

He asked me questions like, "What you do for fun?" I was in a sassy mood, so I replied, "What's that?" He jumped straight into "As sexy as you are you must have a man?"

'Yes, I'm engaged."

"Oh, okay! So, what you like to do for fun?" He asked.

"Whatever comes to mind," I said.

I started laughing to myself because I knew where his questions were leading to, "I like being creative, and I love sex toys." I added.

He was intrigued. "Really, I've never done toys before."

"First time for everything," was my reply.

Two weeks later I got a message, "Hey beautiful, what you

up to for the weekend?" I'm not going to lie and say I wasn't feeling the attention, because I was. I replied, "No plans."

"Come see me. I'll pay for tolls, gas and a hotel room. Oh, you can bring your sex toys too. I'll watch you have fun with yourself."

"I'll get back with you," I said.

I ignored his advances for the next month. I was fighting for my relationship with Lamont, but it seemed like he either didn't care, lost interest in me, or simply took for granted that I'd be there no matter how bad he treated me. Our relationship just seemed one-sided and I was tired of it. Lamont had a way of saying things that made me feel like shit. He was pushing me into the arms of another man and didn't know it. Its only so much neglect a woman could take. One day I finally said, "Fuck it!" and decided to take that plunge. I hit up Webcatcher_24 and said, "I'm about to make a stop at the toy shop, then hop on I-95. I'll be there in 4 hours." I packed my crotchless panties, then headed to 'Lick Em Dry' adult exotic store to grab a few toys, before jumping on that highway. I purchased some Grey Goose and headed up to New York City. I was gunning 100 mph in a 70 mph lane on I-95 north, smoking on a blunt.

Lamont hadn't called the entire day. He was probably pissed at me for not setting up the appointment to get married. The New York Department of Corrections allowed married couples to have conjugal visits. I guess subconsciously I was having doubts. I loved Lamont, but at that time I wasn't feeling valued, loved or secure in our relationship. My friends and family were in my head, they thought it would be a big mistake marrying Lamont. "He's locked up, what can he do for you?" That was their view, not mine. I believe if he would have called me that day I would have turned back, or detoured pass the Bronx and headed all the way up to Dannemora, New York to visit him, instead I pulled up to a motel in the Bronx, with no panties on.

Webcatcher_24 met me in the parking lot. We greeted each

other with warm hugs. "Wow you are much prettier in person," he complimented. I smiled, and we entered the hotel not making much conversation. We rode the elevator up to the 8th floor. I stepped out and he followed close behind me.

"Brownin, how yuh batty round suh?"

I replied, in the same Jamaican accent and dialect, "Den ah suh di ting set!" We both bust out in a fit of laughter.

Soon as we stepped into room 810, he slaps my ass and says, "Easy Phatness!" Little did he know I was nervous as hell. Remember, I hadn't had sex in a minute. I stripped down to my bare titties, pussy and ass, while he sat on a chair rolling a spliff. To calm my nerves, I took a few shots of that Grey Goose.

"Pum Pum phatter than a quarter pounder," he said, as he took a long draw of the weed, looking me up and down. The liquor had me feeling right, I took the initiative and walked towards him, taking the palm of his hand and pressing it against my warm, plump pussy. He says, "It nuff don't it?" Squeezing it and using his fingers to part my pussy lips, he starts fingering me. I took the spliff from his hand and started smoking it while he continued to play in my pussy. I pushed him back onto the chair and decided at that moment I wanted to give him some dome. I got down on my knees between his legs, and reached inside his pants to check the width and length of him. His dick was an average 7 inches. It was kind of skinny, but okay. It would do!

Webcatcher_24 was not circumcised so I decided to clean him myself. I got up and went into the bathroom. I soaped up a washcloth, returned to the room and cleaned his dick while he lit up another blunt. After cleaning him off, I took his entire dick in my hand and sniffed it. I was back on my knees between his legs. Slowly and seductively, I used my pink lips to lock around his dick. His eyes widened as I began to suck on it. Webcatcher leaned over and grabbed his spliff, while my mouth and jaws pressed tight on the tip of his dick, stroking it with my hand. I could tell he was enjoying it by the moans and lip-sucking sounds coming from him.

Slowly I went up and down, up and down on his dick with my mouth. For about five minutes I worked him, watching him as he enjoyed the feel of my mouth. I paused and leaned up for a shotgun, then resumed sucking his dick, but this time my tongue made its way down to his balls. I took my time, licking them softly with gentle care. Webcatcher moaned, "Suck it, suck it babes. Oh, fuck yeah, your lips feel so fucking good on my dick." Those words did something to me, arousing me. It caused me to suck it harder, and better.

I took another shotgun from his lips, then took another sip of Grey Goose and swallowed his entire dick until it reached the back of my throat.

Webcatcher started grunting and let out "Mi Mumma Bumbo Rass Claat. Brownin your mouth powerful babes!" I laughed and continued sucking him off, wrapping my tongue around his dick, sliding up and down like it was a popsicle. Up and down I went, glancing up to check his facial expressions. He was still smacking his lips, and I noticed the tears running down his face. I stopped, "Am I being too rough?" He was looking me dead in the face when he replied, "No babes, continue!"

I got up and went in my overnight bag and pulled out a silver egg with a remote control connected to it. I directed Webcatcher to lie on the bed. He complied and I bent down and started sucking his dick again. I took half his dick in my mouth, positioning my body across his, laying on my side. He took the egg and inserted it inside me while rubbing my clit. I take him deeper in my mouth to the back of my throat. I hold him there and begin vibrating my throat on his dick and rubbing his balls at the same time. He moans, so I rub his balls faster, and force his dick deeper down my throat, gagging as it goes past my tonsils. That's when he started snapping his fingers. I picked up the pace and speed, he's still making these smacking sounds with his lips. He's getting louder and louder, rubbing my hair, which lets me know it's feeling good to him. I'm whining on the vibrating egg inside me. I can feel him about to cum so I let off and say to him "Trust me okay, I got you, trust me, you will like it."

He says, "Okay!" I take him back in my mouth and while I'm sucking him, I pull out my toy bullet. He didn't notice me grab it while I was sucking his dick.

I take my tongue and lick all the way down the underside of his dick until I reach his balls, then I lick under his balls and follow that line underneath his balls to his ass, testing to see how far he'll let me go. I go back to sucking his dick and place the bullet at his ass. He flinches, and I tell him "Relax, I got you, I won't put it in, I promise!" I place the vibrating bullet between his ass cheeks and resume sucking his dick.

Webcatcher_24 starts to breathe hard and heavy, then he begins to moan. I could feel his dick vein pulsate and throb. I move my head up and down faster and faster. I arch my ass in the air as I'm sucking him, he inserts three fingers inside while the egg is still inside me. The feeling is uncomfortable, but I ignore my discomfort and continue sucking him off. I'm determined to make him cum. I grip his dick with my jaw muscles tighter and tighter. I feel him busting off in my mouth. I continue to suck him until I get it all out of him, then I run to the bathroom and spit his cum into the toilet.

After rinsing out my mouth I return to the room and lay on the bed beside him. Webcatcher wasn't into eating pussy so we get straight to fucking but before we do, I grabbed a condom and slid it on his dick. I laid in the eagle position while he fucked me. His sex game was a 4 on a scale of 1 to 10. I wasn't tripping off his sex game. What had me intrigued was his reaction to how I sucked his dick. I never had a man react the way he did. The fact that I brought tears to his eyes solidified my skills. I wanted to freak him out, do things to him that no other woman had ever done.

While he's lying on his side, I start to suck his dick again. We shifted our bodies until he ends up on all 4's and I get behind him pulling his dick back between his legs. I'm sucking him from behind and blowing hot air in his ass at the same time. He starts throwing his ass in my face as I sucked on his balls and rub them. I begin sucking his dick and balls at the same time. After a while I push him onto his back, climb on top of him and start to ride his dick. With his dick in me I slide his legs up and place mine between his and begin riding him in the fuck position, feeling his dick shift inside me. I'm working my pussy muscles, gripping his dick tighter and tighter, riding it rough, gliding his dick in me. I stop, pull off his condom and go down on him, slurping up his dick like a tasty cone. Then I paused to grab some whip cream I had in my bag. I spray it all over his dick and suck it off. It didn't take long for him to cum. I take his dick out of my mouth and placed my tongue at his ass crack and jerked his dick faster and faster. Cum started pouring out his dick and he screams, "PINKS, PINKS, PINKS!" I go back to sucking his dick, going harder, roughing it up, spitting, kissing and jerking his dick.

"Cum inna mi mouth. Fuckah yuh!" I say to him, and grabbed the dildo and started fucking myself with it while I'm sucking the cum out his dick. I stand up and place his fingers in my pussy, then I rub my clit until I cum on his fingers. He sits up on the bed and just stares at me not saying a word. I walk to the bathroom and he continues to stare at my ass and blurts out, "You fucking bad!"

The next day I'm sober. I look over at him in the bed sleeping. The liquor wore off, the weed high is gone, and I begin feeling bad. I gather my things and leave him in the bed sleeping.

I had betrayed Lamont. That's all I kept saying to myself. I couldn't go back to him now. It would feel different. How could I face him? I'd promise to never cheat, and never leave him.

Those thoughts ran through my head as I headed back home to Maryland. Although I felt bad about cheating on him, another part of me felt liberated. When I got home, I replayed my encounter with Webcatcher over and over again in my mind. Then I made the decision to write Lamont a Dear John letter ending our relationship. I wanted to hurt him, and I did. He said in his reply, "If you truly want to end us, face me, tell me to my face!" I never did. I stop visiting him. I knew I crushed his heart, but I was tired of that mental love.

My one-night stand with Webcatcher_24 turned into a 13-year on and off sex affair. A story for another time and place. My curiosity had turned into a fetish! A fetish I put over the man I loved. Eight months later when I finally got up the courage to write Lamont again, asking for forgiveness, he was in another relationship engaged to be married. I was crushed and from that day on I never fully gave my heart to another man.

# 7

# A LATE NIGHT CREEP

**DE'ANDRA BONDS, AKA BADAZZ**
  City: Bronx, New York
  Summer, 2016
  FB: ThaReal BadAzz

PEOPLE USE THE TERM "STREET LEGEND' TO DESCRIBE themselves. That's what lames do. I let the streets do the talking. What I will say is, I'm well known, my homies got mad love for me, the ops call me a problem, and the chicks label me a hoe. That's because I ran through most of them and a few of their friends. So, it was inevitable for me to broaden my horizons.

After throwing up a profile on Facebook, I started meeting different females online. One in particular was a Puerto Rican girl named 'Lizzie' who I connected with a few weeks after posting. She liked all the pictures I posted. I viewed her page and was feeling her pictures too. She had a pretty face, long black hair, and a nice body, not to mention her breasts were super big. I thought they were fake, but she assured me that all her assets were real.

We started vibing online, just getting to know each other. Months went by before I thought about linking up with her. Thinking with the head between my legs, I shot her a direct message on Facebook. "What's up Pretty Lizzie? I 've been thinking about seeing you. If you free, come check me." The first time she came through we chilled at my brother's crib in the Bronx. We talked, laughed, and one thing led to another. But, it's not what you think, we only kissed. I knew she was feeling me. Who wouldn't though? Lol…Like I mentioned earlier, I smashed damn near every shorty in my hood, chicks were feeling my swag!

After our first encounter Lizzie and I talked on the phone nearly every day. She was staying at her home-girl's house in Harlem. One night she invited me over. Living the lifestyle I lived, I had to stay on point. Meaning at all times I was security conscious. As a golden rule I never traveled outside of my hood to visit a female. These broads will have you walking into a project lobby full of grimy niggas looking for a victim. Good thing her friend didn't live in the projects though, because for the first time ever, I decided to break my golden rule and accepted her offer.

It took me 45 minutes to reach my destination. When I got off the #6 train at 103$^{rd}$ Street and Lexington Avenue it was 11p.m. I called Lizzie and she arrived at the train station five minutes later. She was all smiles and looking cute in a pair of True Religion jeans and a shirt to match her baby blue and white Nike Air Max. We hugged and she gave me this peculiar look feeling the bulge in my waist band. Although I sensed no petty larceny in her heart, you could never be too careful, plus I stay strapped. That shit is like an American Express card, "I never leave home without it!"

The lobby was well lit and empty. I could tell it was one of those newly renovated buildings because everything was clean and modern. We rode the elevator to the 7$^{th}$ floor and proceeded down the hall to her friend's apartment. Lizzie had her own key. We entered the apartment and she introduced me to her friend 'Kiana'. I looked her over, she was slim, dark-skin with glasses. She stood 5'3" tall and was holding a newborn child in her arms. After we exchanged a few pleasantries, Kiana excused herself to the back.

Lizzie and I got comfortable on the pullout couch in the living room. I asked her could I smoke. She said "Yeah, but you gotta do it out in the hallway." We both stepped into the hall and got lit off that sour diesel.

We went back inside and got comfortable on the couch. She turned on some music and dimmed the lights. I was feeling the effects of the weed which gave me the munchies. I got up and headed straight to the kitchen for some snacks. Lizzie followed behind me. "You're pretty comfortable I see!" I turned to her and said, "You're pretty comfortable yourself." She blushed.

Lizzie had slipped out of her jeans and shirt and was wearing a pair of boy shorts, tank top with no bra. I couldn't help staring at her big breasts with the nipples poking out. She poured herself a drink. I was hungry and shorty was looking like a late-night snack.

I grabbed her waist from behind pulling her into me, we rocked back and forth with my dick growing stiff rubbing against her butt cheeks. She turned to face me, and we started

kissing. My hands explored the contours of her body then resting between her legs. She was soaking wet.

"Stooooop," she moaned, grinding her hips into me. "Not in the kitchen," she said, pulling away from me. I had visions of that R. Kelly song, 'Sex in the Kitchen' and was tempted to bend her over the kitchen table, but since we were visitors, I kept it respectful and followed her back to the living room, watching her butt jiggle with every step.

"I got to take a leak," I said. She pointed to the bathroom. I stepped in and closed the door behind me, then sniffed my fingers to see what that pussy was hitting on because you never

know. Good thing for her it smelled like Avian Water, because if it smelled like a sewer that would have been the last time she saw me.

The apartment was pitch black when I emerged from the bathroom. I had to feel my way back to the living room. When I finally reached the couch she asked, "What took you so long?" I chuckled, then replied, "Why, you missed me?" She scooted closer to me then whispered in my ear, "Hell yeah!" The sound of her voice turned me on. We both got under the covers and started tongue kissing. The heat emitting from her body was so intense it had my blood boiling. I started sucking on her neck while my hands headed south, pulling her panties off. She spread her legs and let out a moan when I slid two fingers inside her. Her pussy was on Dorney Park. I finger popped her while rubbing her clit with my thumb. She started to rotate her hips to let me know I was working her spot. I told myself that I needed to get in that pussy immediately. I slid the magnum on and went in missionary style.

Lizzie arched her back when I entered her…she wrapped her legs around my waist and just held me there. I started to grind into her slowly, savoring the feel of her tight walls. After a couple of minutes of slow grinding I started to pick up the pace. I took her legs and placed them on my shoulders, I wanted to go deeper. She was so wet her pussy started speaking Chinese, you'd think she was stirring a bowl of macaroni… her moans stimulated me. She started sucking on my earlobe, sending a million sensations up my spine. I was about to nutt…so I slid up out of her. I needed to regain my composure.

"Turn around, I wanna hit it from the back." I got behind her, grabbed her waist and started giving her them long, deep strokes. She moaned, "Oooh, ooh this feels sooo good. Ooh,

ooh I can feel it in my stomach!" She was moaning so loud I

knew her friend could hear us. I started fucking her harder and faster. The sound of her butt cheeks smacking against my body

filled the living room. SMACK, SMACK, SMACK, SMACK, SMACK! We were working up a good sweat. That's when her friend stepped out of her room and headed to the bathroom.

Lizzie froze, looking back over her shoulder. "Oh my God, stop, she's gonna hear us." I laughed to myself, shorty was fooling herself if she thought her friend didn't hear all that noise we were making. I slowed my pace to appease her. After Kiana went back to her room, Lizzie and I went back to doing our thing. I started to really drill into her. She was moaning and trying to crawl away from me. I grabbed her waist with one hand and her shoulder with the other to hold her in place. "Where you going? Stop running, stop running!" I was in beast mode now. Her head was banging against the couch. With nowhere to go, she had no choice but to take this dick pounding.

SMACK, SMACK, SMACK, SMACK, SMACK, SMACK! I was relentless. Sweat was pouring from our bodies. "Ooh, ooh, ooh, oooh, ooh," she moaned over and over again. That's when her body started to shake, she was coming, and I knew it. I kept fucking her, harder, and faster, I was trying to hold my nutt, but it was feeling too good. After a few more strokes I exploded, collapsed on top of her, and we both fell asleep.

I awoke the next morning to find Lizzie and her friend Kiana in the kitchen cooking breakfast. I could tell they were talking about me when I entered the kitchen because they started giggling like little schoolgirls. Her friend kept giving me the side eye. Looking at me like a piece of meat. I could read her thoughts. She wanted a sample of what Lizzie got the previous night. That's when it dawned on me. I had two willing females. If I was thinking correctly, I could have tried my hand on a threesome...SMH.    I left them in the kitchen giggling and stepped out into the hallway to smoke a lil Cush. Afterwards we all ate breakfast together, then I dipped. That was the first time but not the last time Lizzie and I hooked up.  She became a regular, one of the girls I had on rotation until her feelings got involved. I had to constantly remind her I was on my Joe & Big Punn shit, "I'm not a player, I just crush a-lot!"

# 8

# ADDICTED 2 THE GRAM

**Jessica Durvey**
Cleveland, Ohio
Summer, 2019
Instagram: Jessie_Jay

My last boyfriend accused me of being shallow. He said I lived in an alternate universe, all because I stayed glued to my phone. I will admit that I have an obsession with Instagram. My app is on automatic login so when I wake up, I get my notifications instantly. I'm on it when I'm at work. I'm on it when I'm sitting on the toilet. When I can't sleep, I just roll over and click on my Instagram app. One time after sex, I rolled over and logged online, that was it for my boyfriend. He was done with me after that!

There is one thing I will say about myself. I don't accept random new requests. I mean if you and I accepted each other at the same time, or if I knew you and we have mutual friends, then cool it's all good, but otherwise it's quiet.

One boring day I finally decided to ween through my

requests to identify fake pages and stumbled upon a request from Richsway118. I clicked on his page and surprisingly I knew this dude. He and I met a year before during CIAA weekend. Nice dude, we simply lost contact. Well actually the timing was off, I was involved with my boyfriend at the time. Although he and I flirted via text, when I purchased a new iPhone I deleted his contact. But now that I was single, I accepted his friend request and he jumped in my DM.

"Hey pretty lady, how are you? Long time no kick it. Shoot me your number." I smiled and sent it to him. He called me right away and got straight to the point.

"Damn girl, how you ghost me like that? I've been trying to connect with you for a minute. I sent you a request like six months ago." I apologized and began to ask him several questions to find out his head space. He said he was no longer married and wanted to take me away for a few days. Those words brought back memories. He was always offering to take me on some out-of-town trip. But I always declined.

Back story, he had a wife and I had a man. Before I had a chance to give him an answer he blurted out, "I'm booking you a flight right now, give me a few minutes and I will send you the information." I could hear him clicking away on what I imagined was an iPad or laptop. A half hour later I received the itinerary for a round-trip ticket from Cleveland to Atlanta that upcoming Friday. I'm not gonna lie I hadn't traveled in a minute, so I'mma make sure this getaway was lit. I was like, "Bet!" Smiling from ear to ear. I wasn't sure what he had planned in Atlanta, but what I did know about him is that he's a music producer. Rap music to be exact. He's from Jackson, Mississippi, a real country boy. Later that night he called me and told me he got us a cabin on Lake Lanier for the weekend and had all intentions on spoiling me… Shit I was all for the attention he was willing to give me. Friday couldn't arrive sooner.

I arrived at Hartford International Airport and texted Richsway to meet me at gate 18. He replied, "I'm already here, come outside." I walked out the sliding doors and there stood Richsway118. I stared at this dark chocolate, medium built, Yo Gotti look-alike with a mouth full of gold. He greeted me with a bear hug, lifting me off my feet, and while I was in the air, he leans in to kiss me. I'm a little shocked and embarrassed by the public show of affection because I wasn't used to it. I look around subconsciously. People glanced at us but were more or less preoccupied with their own affairs. Richsway holds open the passenger door to a candy apple red SRT. I climb in and he jumps behind the wheel and pull away from the curb. "We got plenty of time before we head out to the lake, let me take you to the mall." I look over at him and smiled, shaking my head, okay!

We pull up to Lenox mall and he's the perfect gentleman, opening my door and giving me his hand as I climb out. He took that moment to stand behind me hugging and pressing his hard dick against my ass. I reached back and grabbed his sack, and he laughed. Richsway grabbed my hand and led me into the mall. We took the escalator to the second floor and proceeded to the Louis Vuitton store. At the counter I noticed two boxes gift wrapped. I thought to myself, "Somebody's going to be happy to receive those gifts." The salesclerk greets Richsway with a smile and says, "Good Afternoon Mr. Wilson, we have everything ready for you" and nods towards the two gift wrapped boxes. Richsway looks at me and says, "Those are for you babe." I turned to him and gave him a big hug and kiss. My boxes were placed in a big shopping bag. I took it from the salesclerk and asked him if there was a lady's room I could use. The salesclerk smiled and pointed me in the direction. I turned to Richsway and with my eyes, directed him to follow me. Moments later I opened the door to the lady's room and pulled Richsway into the restroom with me.

I couldn't open his belt buckle fast enough. I unzipped his fly and pulled out his dick. It was super wide, around 7 inches long. I couldn't wrap my entire hand around it. My mouth watered as I squatted down and began to suck him off. My mouth was full of saliva and his dick stuffed my mouth until it was hitting the back of my throat. He pushed his hips forward holding the back of my head. I gagged in reflex but caught a rhythm. I was able to deep throat him steadily. He started moaning loud, so I tapped him on his leg to be quiet.

All that dick stuffed down my throat had my pussy wet as hell. He must have sensed it because he stood me up, then unzipped the back of my bodysuit and proceeded to slide the top of my bodysuit down past my waist, exposing my titties, ass and all. He begins sucking on my breasts and grabs my pussy with his right hand. He whispers in my ear, "Damn, your pussy is hot" and slid one finger, then another inside me. I moaned and squirmed out of his embrace. "Stop, the people are gonna catch us." He pulled me into him and whispered, "Don't worry about that, we're good," and resumed tongue kissing me and finger fucking me at the same time.

I went with the flow pulling his pants down to his ankles. He pushed me into one of the bathroom stalls (thank goodness for LV's clean ass establishment), then spun me around to face the wall. He kneels down and spreads my lips from behind, sticking his tongue inside of me. Damn, this man had a super long tongue. I never had a tongue reach so deep into my pussy. It felt like a slithering snake exploring my insides. He started spinning his tongue super-fast inside me like a tornado. Then he took my clit into his mouth and sucked on it real hard. I lost control, my knees shook then buckled. I was cumming in his mouth. He sucked and slurped even harder. I was about to faint, then he spared me, letting go of my clit. He fumbled in his pocket and pulled out a condom. I took the condom from him, bent down and put it on the tip of his dick with my mouth. Gently I eased the rubber down his chocolate dick. I got up then faced the stall wall, and bent my slim thick ass over so he could slide his dick into me. I let him lubricate his dick with my pussy juice. After 10 pumps I reached behind him, pulled his dick out, and pointed it into my ass. Richsway slid his dick into me. It hurt but yet it felt so good. The more I moaned the deeper he went. The more he pumped the wetter my pussy got, the easier it became to take the dick. I started throwing it back and bouncing all over his dick, he wasn't ready for all that action. He started grunting, "Oh shit, oh shit" under his breath then he was cumming. My nasty ass bent down, took the condom off and had him finish ejaculating in my mouth. Now he's moaning like a bitch and his legs starts shaking.

After I sucked the life out of him, I spit his cum in the toilet, wiped my ass and cat clean, pulled up my bodysuit then washed my hands and mouth. I'm in the bathroom mirror fixing my makeup when I catch Richsway staring at me in disbelief. I turn around and tell him to fix himself up. I grab my gifts and gesture for him to lead the way. As we exit the Louis Vuitton store I'm smiling, and the salesclerk returns my smile with a knowing one. I say to myself, "I definitely earned these gifts and vowed to check my DMs more often."

We went to dinner then headed out to the lake. The cabin was really nice. High oakwood ceilings, a fireplace. Really classy. I was in the shower when I thought I heard yelling. I said to myself, "What the fuck?" I stepped out the shower, slipped on a robe and was shocked to see Richsway restraining some hysterical woman. She was screaming, "Where she at, where she at motherfucker? You think I wouldn't catch you? Where the bitch at?" I'm no punk but I was definitely a little caught off guard and out of my element. I dipped into the bedroom and locked the door behind me. Let's just say I barely made it home without getting my ass whooped by a hysterical wife and her home girls. Mr. Richsway obviously wasn't divorced. This nigga left me at the cabin with Uber fare and said "I'll explain every-thing later." Later my ass!

I flew back to Cleveland on the next flight smoking, wondering to myself how did his psycho, fatal attraction wife locate us way out at Lake Lanier in Atlanta? Damn, a bitch needed to be more careful next time because these men ain't loyal!!! Fucking Instagram Niggas!!!

9

# WEST L.A. LIFE

**Pharaoh Luciano**
Social Media: Twitter
Date: June, 2013
City/State: Los Angeles, California

"To live and die in L.A. is the place to be!" were the words from the Tupac song bumping through my speakers while I sat behind the wheel of my deep red Dodge Challenger. Like usual, the sun was shining in California on this summer day. Twenty minutes earlier I had got a text from my brother-in-law informing me of the graduation BBQ for my niece being held at Dockweiler Beach. Lucky for me my hair was already cut, all I needed to do was get dressed. The drive to LA from Bakersfield where I stayed would take me 90 minutes to 2 hours tops.

The BBQ was chill, mostly family and friends. I chilled with my niece listening to her speak excitedly about her plans for the future, her attending UCLA to study neurosurgery.

After the BBQ I got a text from my nephew Dinero. Dinero is only three years younger than me. He's the person who introduced me to Twitter back in 2010. Me being new to Twitter back then I poked around here and there so most of my followers were associated with him.

My nephew and I frequently traveled back and forth between LA and Compton, which is how I became familiar with a lot of his associates in the Rap scene. Jerk movement, New Boyz, YG, Tyga, Joe Moses, The Rangers and more. I got cool with Nipsey Hussle, rest in peace! Not all the rappers were jerks, but the movement helped propel them.

On the day of the BBQ Dinero texted me telling me to shoot over his crib. By this time (2013), my Twitter page was lit, and the likes got me on my shit. I'm trolling on my TL and all the baddies from the LA area was showing me love. Since I was in LA, I decide to tweet on my wall my current location to see who takes the bait and comment. One cute dyme tweeted back with the kiss emoji. I let her know I was trying to pull up and take her out to eat. She DM me her number and pinned me her location. Moments later I pulled up to her place. She scoped out my ride from wheel to wheel then invited me inside while she continued getting dressed. She introduced me to her mother which I thought was weird, but moms had a good vibe about her. As I waited on the couch, she appeared out the back wearing a tight ass Body Con dress and Red Bottoms. I nicknamed her Ms. West LA, who smelled like blooming sweet flowers. We jumped in my ride, I turned to her, "Do you introduce every man you meet online to your mother?"

"Only the ones I go out with, shoot I don't know you, you could be a serial killer. Moms need to know who I'm with just in case," she emphasized with sass, bobbing her head, rolling her neck and eyes. I chuckled and put the car in gear, easing out onto the road. She put the directions in the navigation system to a Mexican restaurant in Inglewood, which was located on a street that ran through Queens St. and Manchester.

At the restaurant, she ordered some authentic tacos for us

which were pretty spicy but good. Then she says, "Big Buddha told me to tell you wuz up!" I looked at her from the corner of my eyes while I'm chewing on a taco. She giggles and says, "I checked your followers and saw his link, so I hit him up. That's my homeboy, he told me you were good peoples and I should fuck with you." I shook my head and allowed a smile to crease my face. "That's wuz up, give the big homie a shoutout for me." Big Buddha is a Treetop Piru. He's YG's big homie. I met Buddha at YG's 'Toot it and Boot it' video shoot in the summer of 2010.

After crushing a few tacos shorty ordered us a few rounds of Patron shots. She challenged me to go toe to toe with her. I'm not a big drinker so I was like, "What the hell I'm game." I tilted my head back and took two to the head. Ms. LA followed behind me by downing two shots of tequila. Before you knew it we had crushed 10 shot glasses of hard liquor. I took one hard look at shorty, paid the bill and said, "Let's bounce."

By this time, I'm checking to see what Ms. LA's next move would be while we headed back to my ride. Watching her ass jiggle from left to right I instantly felt my dick rising in my pants. She turns to me and says, "I know you're not driving back to Bakersfield like that?"

"Yeah, I'm good!"

"Naw, you may as well get a room," she said, shaking her head. I'm a lil buzzed and thinking that long drive through the mountains may not be a good idea. "Yeah, you're right I'll get a room for the night," I reply. She perks up, "If it's cool, I'll stay with you cause it's still early and I don't have any other plans for the night." At that moment it dawned on me Ms. LA was trying to let me sample that pussy. I chuckled, "Sure we can defiantly hang out tonight." Little did she know I was going to be feeding her all this Patron dick the entire night.

"Let's get some more drinks," she suggested. I'm in total

agreement because I'm about to burn dat ass up. As we head to the liquor store, I noticed she's directing me past a whole bunch of stores. My radar instantly turns up and I sober up. So, I asked Ms. LA, "Where the fuck you about to take me shorty?"

"A blood hood obviously!" She responded, assuming from my many Twitter associations I was blood. So, I had to correct her. "Naw baby girl I'm cool with all the Damus' on Twitter off the strength of my nephew Dinero." Her eyes lit up at the mention of his name.

"Dinero is my partna. Damn, I wish I'd known that cuz we could have hooked up a long time ago." I told her I'm a gangsta from Bakersfield, she replies "Cool!" Then we headed to a liquor store in a hood that's cool with "Gangstas." I respected that and appreciated the fact she wasn't some naïve goofy chick who wasn't aware of LA gang politics.

We pull up to the store in the Eight Trey's hood, grabbed some Patron and made our way to the tellie. As I'm driving, we pass all the mainstream hotels, motels, Quality Inn, Marriott, Best Western, LA Quintana's, etc. "What's wrong with these?" I gesture with a wave of my hand. "I know a really good hotel, don't trip," she says excitedly. I glance over at her in the passenger seat. I'm thinking to myself, "What's up with this chick, is she trying to hangout and chill, or get smashed?" I know females play games. I'm not trying to get caught up like Pac, so I play it cool and decide to see which way this whole situation would play out.

We finally pull up to a motel near Stocker and Labra. I pull to the drive-through window situated at the front of the motel, which has the rates posted on the sign near the window. I looked over at shorty and gave her this look like, "you sure you want to stay here?" The rooms were rented by the hour, day, and week. I pay the room rate for the night and pull up around the back where the parking lot is situated and all I see is nothing but foreigns, from Benzes, Beamers, Audis, to muscle cars, Camaros, Chargers and Mustangs, just to name a few. I'm thinking this is where the young money bag boys bring their bitches, or where hoes bring their tricks, either way I'm here, trick or treat.

We get in the room, the place got so much red it hurt my eyes. It had that old 70s, 80s porn theme. I looked at the room décor and for a moment, expected Ron Jeremy to come out a back room. Ms. West LA went to freshen up in the bathroom, I grabbed the remote and started channel surfing. I clicked through the regular FOX, ABC, NBC stations and settle on the 24-hour porn channel. It was time to get the mood right and settle the unanswered question floating through my mind, "Was she trying to smash or not?"

Baby girl stepped out the bathroom and sat on the bed next to me. She poured herself a cup of Patron and started watching the sex scene portrayed on the TV. I took a couple of swigs then placed my cup on the nightstand. I decided to make the first move. I leaned over on her side of the bed, she turned to me and we started kissing.

New pussy always excites me, my heart started beating faster in anticipation as my hands went on an exploration of her body.

Ms. West LA's caramel skin felt hot and soft under her blouse. Her breast sat perfect in the palm of my hand. I can't tell you her bra size except to say those were some nice, perky titties. I twirled, pinched and flicked her nipples to erection.

After removing her top, I sucked on her nipples which were nice and swollen. She helped me remove her bra. Her skin was on fire when I pulled her into my embrace. My hands traveled below her waist, palming her ass, then I unbuckled her belt, unzipping her jeans. I dug my hand down her pants between her legs. I slid two fingers in her pussy. She moaned and ground her hips into my hand. After a few finger strokes, she stood up and wiggled her 5'7" tall, slim thick frame out of her dress. I took a sneak sniff of my fingers; baby girl was 100. I smiled and stared at her body. She walked up to me while I sat up on the bed. I kissed her stomach and ran my hands up the back of her legs until I reached her butt. I slowly pulled her boy shorts down her waist. She stood naked in front of me for a moment before I pulled her onto the bed. She straddled me as I wiggled out of my jeans and boxers.

I got to keep it 100 with you, I normally slap on a magnum, but that night I was caught up in the moment, the liquor and the feeling of her warm skin against mine had me on fire. She grabbed my dick and inserted all 10 inches into her. Her pussy walls seemed to massage my dick with every stroke as she rode me like a pony, "Genuine!" She was lost in the throes of ecstasy with her eyes closed, moving her hips into me. The head of my dick was hitting her cervix. Sweat glistened off her Rihanna forehead. I knew she was near her climax when she started biting her lower lip, so I wrapped my hands around her waist pulling her down to me. I started driving my dick deep into her pussy repeatedly as fast as I could. All you heard was the slap of hips and balls beating against her. She started moaning louder trying to wiggle free from the pussy pounding I was giving her, and as she came, I fucked harder and faster into her, making her orgasm more intense.

After a few more strokes she relaxed, and I allowed her to catch her breath while she laid on top of me. I could feel her pussy muscles contracting. After a few moments I flipped her on her back and began to grind into her missionary style. They say missionary position leads to a deep level of intimacy. I can agree because when we stared into each other's eyes I felt an emotional connection to her that I wasn't expecting, but when her nails started to dig into my back it was time to change positions.

I put her in the doggystyle position and was amazed at how well she was throwing her cute ass back at me. We went through every position imaginable. I nutted inside her at least eighttimes that night. We were both exhausted when we finally fell asleep.

The following morning, I awoke to a hard dick and the sun's rays seeping through the part in the curtains. I rolled over and climbed between shorty's legs. She woke with a gasp. This hard dick had her reaching a morning orgasm in no time. She rode me again and I ended the marathon plunging balls deep into her from behind.

By 9:00a.m. we had taken a shower together, gotten dressed and was exiting the hotel room. As I pulled out of the parking spot, she told me to pull up to the lobby. She stepped out and ran inside. She emerged moments later with a small package in her hand. "What's that?" I asked, nodding towards the small plastic bag on her lap. She reached into the bag and pulled out a single DVD case. "This the video of us getting it on last night." I looked at the DVD then back at her and replied, "Get the fuck out of here!" The shocked expression on my face must have amused her because she couldn't stop giggling.

"Yeah, it's definitely a home video. Couldn't you tell by the theme of the room? Its set up like a porn set."

"Shit, I need a copy of that!" I said, pulling off the lot. She smiled and replied, "No I don't think so. I'm not trying to have my business blasted all over social media."

"Shit, how I know you won't post it yourself?"

"We could both view it together," she replied. I told her to keep it until I saw her again.

After dropping her off I jumped onto the freeway heading back to Bakersfield. We continued chatting on Twitter, exchanging texts. I was waiting to hear her hit me with, "I'm pregnant!" I splashed up in her at least eight times that night. Although I don't claim anything but West Side Gangsta Carnation Tract, it could've been a possibility, despite it being a one-night stand. We would've needed a test because if I smashed on the first night, how many others did too? The pregnant thing never came up, and although I never got a chance to see that video, me and West LA still kick it till this day. My LA Freak Thang is what I call her. Ms. West LA!

10

---

O.A.D

**MEGHAN PALMER**
   Oxon Hill, Maryland
   June, 2019
   FB: All_Ds_nosilicone

WHEN IT COMES TO HOOKUPS, I GOT STORIES FOR DAYS. ONE-night stands, affairs, and even a few love triangles I could write a book about. I keep my personal business to myself though. Not that I care what the next person thinks about how I move, especially women, most of them got a whole graveyard full of skeletons in their closet. I keep my shit discreet because I don't plan to live this freak life forever. Eventually I want to settle down with a husband, have a few kids, but right now I got this itch that I can't seem to stop scratching.

I wonder if I'm simply addicted to sex. I love dick, but I play with pussy too. Anyway, enough psychoanalysis of my sexual appetite, let me tell you one recent story.

I'm self-employed with a mail order business. I'm in my home office reclining in my chair, wearing a lace nightgown exposing my pointy nipples. They've been stiff ever since I got out the shower. I stare down at them, "These girls need to be sucked on!" I logged onto Facebook and the post on my timeline said, "Ladies drop a selfie if you sexy and you know it!" I wanted to get out of my element, so my courage jumped in and I exposed my phat caramel ass and took a few pics. I clicked select, upload, and posted onto the comment section. I got 23 likes and 4 comments of my super thick brown frame; My 44DDs were evenly proportioned with my thick thighs. I look like an oversized hourglass from the front. Oh, did I mention this tractor trailer ass I have behind me! Whoever get this ass better make sure he sits a glass on it, and sip from it!

Ten minutes later, ping, ping, ping, my Facebook notification is going off like crazy. I click to see the comments. Hmm, should I reply or ignore? I scroll through and decide to click on a dude named Shooter's profile picture. He hit me with, "What's up beautiful I like your picture, can I meet you?" I hit him back, "That's what's up! Send me your number so I can pin you my location where we can meet up." Forty-five minutes later I pull up on the Iverson Street entrance of this hookah bar. I do a breath check, pass, pussy check A+, then dab on some Issy Miyachi perfume and I'm good to go. Five minutes later Shooter pulled up beside me in a white-on-white 750 BMW.

"Hey goodie hop in!" I leave my car parked and we head up Greenbelt Road. We stop at the Maryland Live casino. After arriving we walked around a bit, played the roulette table, blackjack table, then we slid off into the stairwell.

The casino was packed so no one paid us any attention. We immediately started kissing each other, and I grabbed and squeezed his dick. His hand is in my shirt, squeezing my breast, then he pulls one out. I gasped, it felt so good. I pulled the other one out so he could suck on both of them. With his face buried in my 44DDs he started using his hands to lift my skirt up. By the time his hands reached down to my pussy it was drenched.

He yanked my thong down to my ankles, and I stepped out of them... He looked at me and I stared back at him and said, "Get the fuck down and taste this pussy river."

When it comes to sex, I know what I want, and I'm not shy about it. He complied as I knew he would, and began sucking, making slurping sounds while eating my pussy. I cock one leg up on the arm rail and started fucking his face. He pushed his tongue deep in my pussy and started vibrating it until I felt myself about to explode. He stopped in the midst of me cumming in his mouth, looked up at me and said, "Bitch bend over in 6:30 position." Without a second thought, I did what I was told.

Shooter took one step lower so his face would be parallel to my ass. Then he spread my ass cheeks apart and started sucking my pussy from behind. I wiggled my ass on his face while he was spitting and blowing bubbles in my pussy. Damn I almost forgot we were in the stairwell, but that didn't stop us. He kept sucking and licking on my pussy then found his way to my asshole. I looked back at him with a devilish grin and said, "Plug all holes!" He looked at my ass again and realized I had a tattoo of flames circling the outer rim of my asshole. "You such a nasty bitch," he said, smacking my ass before sliding his thumb in it. "Ohhhh fuckkk, plug this ass... mmmm spit in the hole," I moaned in an erotic husky voice. He stood up, slipped on a magnum condom and stepped up several stairs to slide his dick inside me. There was no gradual build-up of momentum, he immediately started fucking me hard and fast. The more he pounded the more my ass shook back on him in waves. I held onto the rails as he picked up his pace, speed fucking my pussy. He spit in my ass and slid two fingers in it. In and out, in and out, faster and faster he went. I felt his dick growing harder inside me. I stopped, turned around, took the condom off and started sucking his dick. I used one hand to hold his balls while I sucked and pushed his dick to the back of my throat. He grabbed the back of my head to force his dick deep down my throat until tears came to my eyes. I twirled my hand around his dick, and I sucked more and more and more until his legs began to tremble.

The box of magnums was on the step next to me. I reached for another one from the box, while still sucking his dick. I ripped the pack open and placed the condom on him. Then we stepped up to the next landing and I pushed him to the floor. I hopped on the dick and started riding it. With every movement, I made sure his dick hit every wall inside my pussy. I start contracting my vaginal muscles. My back was to him, so I spun around on his dick to face him, I placed both hands on each bar rail and bounced up and down, then grinding on it, making it rub against the inside of my pussy. He sat up, grabbed each ass cheek, and starts pounding my pussy harder and harder. I started losing control and balance as he kept pounding up into me. Just when I thought he was pulling out to bust his nutt he slides his dick into my ass. We both let out a moan... "Ahhh!" He's fucking my ass, working it and I'm playing with my clit while biting down on my bottom lip. He thrusts faster and faster. I matched his pace rubbing my clit and pussy at the same time. I feel my body shaking, I cum so hard it squirts on his stomach and onto the floor. He's still stroking up into me for 5-6 more strokes before exploding into my ass. We rush to get ourselves together thinking at any moment somebody will walk in on us. I looked at him and said, "Damn that dick got me right."

Shooter and I headed out the stairwell and back into the casino. We both go into separate bathrooms to get ourselves freshened up. We chilled at the penny slot machines for another 30 minutes, then approached the counter to collect our winnings before calling it a night. After leaving Maryland Live casino, we pull up next to my car back at Iverson Mall. We hugged. "Hit me later cutie!"

"Facts Boo!" I replied, then I got in my car. I checked my phone. I blocked him from my contacts just as I was pulling off. "Nigga please, I'm not trying to be your Boo, you met me and ate my ass on the first date!"

My moto is One And Done! I checked my inbox. "Oh shit!" Another sexy dude messaged me. I was on to the next sexcapade. Like I told you, I got this itch that I can't seem to stop scratching…It's O.A.D. Baby, ONE AND DONE!

# 11

# IT'S A DOGGY DOG WORLD

**Tony "Gun Smoke" Starks**
Social Media: Tagged
Username: Polo2x
City: Bridgewater, Massachusetts
Year: 2016

I'm not going to lie and say I wasn't familiar with social media, it was 2016, who wasn't? But prior to my release from behind the wall (prison), I wasn't a big fan. Too many people I knew caught cases from the things they posted on social media. Mindful of that, I kept my activities on the web limited, limited to chasing ass that is!

Early in the evening of spring 2016, I was riding shotgun with my kinfolk (homie) down an unfamiliar street. My cell phone was pressed to my ear as I spoke to this Yime (pretty girl) I met on Tagged. "Yeah, I see it, I'm out front, come outside!" I said to her, pulling up in front of the address she texted me earlier.

Kinfolk pulled into the driveway of a ranch-style home in a tree-lined suburban neighborhood. "Are you staying the night?" kinfolk asked me.

"Naw I ain't staying, I'll call you when I'm ready to stab out?" I responded.

"You got the blick right?"

I gave kinfolk a look like, you can't be serious! "Come on gun smoke, you know me, I wouldn't slide over here without the slammer."

"Just making sure," he replied.

The front door to the blue house swung open and I was glad to see the woman standing in the doorway matched the pictures she texted me along with the ones posted on her profile page. Not really my type, light skin, but it was something about her smile and pretty eyes that attracted me. She stepped out of the doorway and into the glare of the setting sun. Her grey eyes mesmerized me for a moment, then I took in her entire body. She wore a blue denim skirt that hugged her hips, and a tight black belly hoody that pressed against her large breast. She was on the thick side but wore it well. Her brown, shoulder length hair complimented her eyes and skin tone. I was wondering which one of her parents were Caucasian, because she was obviously bi- racial.

"Damn Bro where you find her at?" Kinfolk said, checking her out from behind the wheel. "Baby girl looking like a snack, something like a banana moon pie." He added.

"On Dawgs!" I concurred, rubbing my hands together in lustful anticipation. "I'll hit you later," I added, stepping out the car.

Her username was Yellow Diamond, and that's what I called her as we greeted each other with a hug. "Just call me Diamond," she said with a smile, showing off her pearly whites with a slight gap in the front. I thought her gap fit her perfectly. We stepped inside the house and she locked the door behind her. I looked around checking out the layout of the crib. To my right was the living room, straight past the living room were stairs that I assumed led to the bedrooms. Beside the stairs was a hallway that was gated. I wondered what laid beyond the gate. Then I heard barking, which sounded deep and menacing. I immediately slid my hand in my pocket and wrapped a finger around the trigger of my .25 auto, I looked at Yellow Diamond

suspiciously thinking "If this bitch thinks she got a lick, she and whomever got another thing coming."

Yellow Diamond saw the expression on my face and reading my mind she smiled and said, "I'm dog watching."

"This isn't ya spot?"

"No," she said, strolling into the living room, taking a seat on the couch. "Come sit down." She patted the space beside her. I hesitated for a moment, not sure if I should sit on the love seat closer to the entrance or beside Yellow Diamond on the large couch which was close to the hall. Feeling the Steel in my pocket, I felt reassured and sat next to her.

Directly in front of the couch was an oak coffee table, and sitting on it was a five-gram bag of weed with a chrome pipe and lighter. My first thought was, "This bitch is a weirdo, and probably grew up with a whole bunch of white people, cuz we don't smoke weed out of pipes in the hood." I looked at her and said, "You smoke out a pipe?" Clowning her on the low, but she didn't seem to realize it.

"Yeah, rolling up takes too long," she replied, with this innocent smile like she never had it hard her entire life. I wondered how that must have felt, to live without hardship. Then I asked her, "Where you get that smile from?" She shrugged her shoulders innocently. "You got some sexy lips too." She blushed, and I knew I had her.

"So," she said, still blushing, "you smoke?" Reaching for the pipe and sandwich bag on the coffee table.

"You betta know it!" I replied with a devilish grin. "Good," she said, while applying some weed from the bag into the pipe.

"I don't smoke out no pipe ma. We don't do that where I'm from- no funny shit!" She looked up from the bag of weed and asked, "Why not? The pipe is so much better. You get the full effect of the bud, and you could actually taste it." My face was still screwed up. I shook my head, "Pipes are for geekas."

"For who?" Shawty was definitely not from the hood. I didn't feel like going into hood lingo and philosophy, so I said, "Nobody! Go ahead and do ya thing, I'mma roll something up." I pulled out a pack of backwoods, sweet of course, removed a cigar, and a bag of sour-diesel and twisted up a blunt. I lit my blunt, took a long pull and sat back on the couch. "So, this what you do?" I asked, blowing weed smoke into the air.

"What you talking about?"

"I'm talking this!" Gesturing with a wave of my hand. "This is what you do for work, watch dogs?" She chuckled, "Oh no, I'm just doing a friend a favor. He and his wife went on a trip for the weekend. They'll be back Monday." Me, being the suspicious person that I am, slid my right hand in my pocket, wrapping my finger around the pistol trigger. I don't know if it was the effects of the weed, but I started to listen intently thinking I may have heard the creak of a door opening, a footstep, or breathing.

"Why you all the way over there? Come a little closer I don't bite." I glanced around, then scooted over to where she sat. "All the time!"

Yellow Diamond looked over at me seductively, "You funny!"

"And you're sexy."

"You like what you see?" She asked, licking her lips.

"I can show you better than I can tell you!"

"Boy you crazy. Come here let me give you a shot-gun. I want you to try my bud." Yellow Diamond leaned towards me, cupped her hands around my mouth and blew her smoke into it. I inhaled the stream into my lungs. She watched me intently, taking in my reaction. "All weed baby!" she said with a knowing glint in her eyes. "How does it taste? Good huh?" I couldn't lie I nodded my head in approval. "Yeah, it has a good taste, but I think it would taste better on your lips." I leaned forward and kissed her, then sucked on her bottom lips which tasted like honey.

The taste of her lips aroused me as she slid her tongue in my mouth and we started French kissing with our tongues dancing in unison. My hands explored her soft, juicy curves. With expert precision, I unzipped her hoody. She had no bra on underneath revealing her full, yellow breasts. Her nipples were hard, cinnamon brown. I cupped one in my hand, caressing it, plucking and slightly pulling on her nipple. She let out a soft moan, her body was like a combination lock and I had just figured out the first digit.

Our tongues unlocked, and Yellow Diamond licked her lips seductively, savoring the taste. I leaned in kissing her neck, making a trail of kisses down to her breast. I took one into my mouth, sucking her erect nipple. The scent of myrrh rose from her flesh, I inhaled, taking it in.

"Mmmhh," she moaned, "you just get right to it huh? What are you doing to me?"

"What you want me to do to you?" I replied while feeding off her breast.

"Take off those pants!" She didn't need to tell me twice. I took off my trousers with the quickness. I love a woman that knows what she wants and isn't shy about getting it. I watched as

Yellow Diamond slid out of her denim skirt. I stared at her succulent thighs and was glad to see her pussy was just the way I liked it, bald.

Yellow Diamond sat at the edge of the couch then reclined back and parted her legs, revealing her pink pedals that glazed with her creamy juices. I thought to myself "She's ready!" I contemplated eating her pussy, glazed donut is my favorite. I battled with the thought for just a moment and decided to roll a condom on instead. I just met this chick! Ain't no way I was putting my tongue in her. Instead, it was my dick that entered her body.

I went in slow, not stopping until I reached the depths of her ocean. With her eyes clenched tight, she cooed in pure delight.

Her moneymaker was soft as velvet wrapped tight around my weapon like a glove. I looked down at her face and thought "I'm bout to perk-dick you!" I placed my hand on her knee spreading her thighs further apart, then I palmed her titties. I started stroking in and out of her slowly making sure she felt every inch of me. She held on to the arm of the couch with her jaw clenched tight. "Fuck" she blurted out biting down on her bottom lip. I picked up the pace, she reacted by clenching her legs together. But that didn't keep me from plunging deep inside her. She looked up at me, her eyes pleading for mercy. I gave her none, increasing my pace.

"Daddy I'm cumming, I'm cumming, oh daddy!" I stared down at myself plunging in and out of her. Her cream glistened on my dick. I could feel her cum juice rolling down my balls. "Wait, wait!" she said placing her hand flat on my pelvis.

"What's wrong?"

"Nothing, that was amazing," fanning herself with her hand... "Pass me my pipe, that calls for a hit." I leaned back and grabbed the pipe and lighter, handing both to her. I watched her take a hit. I couldn't help having visions of a fiend taking a hit from a crack pipe. Then she offered the pipe to me. I shook my head declining the offer.

"Come on now, you're no fun, loosen up, smoke with me." Again, she offered the pipe to me. Don't ask me why I accepted it. I normally don't succumb to the flesh, but those pretty eyes, soft luscious body, and the fact that my dick was impaled in her juicy pussy didn't help. I felt funny, and uncomfortable taking a pull from a pipe, but I had to admit, the effect of the weed was instant, and the taste was completely different. This was the epitome of that Young Jeezy song "All we do!"

Yellow Diamond and I continued to pass the pipe back and forth until the weed was consumed. By then I had slid out of her and was sitting on the couch beside her. After she took the last pull of the pipe, she looked over at me and smiled, then said, "Now come over here and get back in this pussy."

I watched as she stood then strolled over to the end of the love seat and bent over the arm poking out her ass. I got up off the couch and positioned myself behind her. I grabbed a handful of her ass cheeks and entered her. The feeling was amazing. The view from behind captivated me. There is nothing that could compare to the sight of a woman's ass bouncing and shaking during sex in the doggy-style position. The sight, the sound of our bodies smacking, the scent of sex and weed in the air, all consumed me. I was in the throes of pure debauchery. Throwing all caution to the wind, I yanked off the condom and reentered her raw. The pussy felt 10x better, wetter, hotter. At that moment I doubted I'd be able to pull out. Then I heard the loud bark of a dog. The dog's bark had a heavy base to it, so I imagined it was big, mean, and vicious, but I ignored it, concentrating on the sight of my dick pounding in and out of Yellow Diamond.

"Smack my ass!" she exclaimed. I didn't hesitate. I pulled her hair as well, digging her back out. She wailed "Oh I'm cumming, I'm cumming!" This fueled me to fuck harder, faster. I could sense her reaching multiple orgasms as her body shook and she continued to moan, "Oh my God, oh my God, I'm cumming, please don't stop, please don't stop." I was trying my best not to, but I could feel the eruption creeping up from the depth of my loins. I was enjoying this Pink Panther, savoring the sensations. I held on for five more strokes before pulling out and splashing on her back and ass cheeks.

Yellow Diamond got off the couch then got on her knees, directly in front of the coffee table. She looked over her shoulder at me and smiled. I walked over to where she was and began packing the weed pipe with some of my sour diesel. I took a hit of the weed pipe and passed it to her. I sat back on the couch rubbing and stroking my dick back to erection, staring at Yellow Diamond, hoping she'd get the hint. I wanted her lips wrapped around my stick. I love a good slice of pie, but I'm weak for a girl with good head. She took another drag at the pipe. Obviously, she didn't get the hint, so I slid up on her and started playing with her violin. Still bent over the coffee table she started to moan at the touch of my fingers stroking her clit. I stared down at her plump, yellow ass cheeks and caught a glimpse of that brown eye. It was glistening with sweat and my cum. It looked so inviting I decided to try my hand and positioned my dick dead center. When my dick head touched the entrance to her asshole she jumped forward and yelled, then looked back at me angrily.

"My bad! I apologize." Grinning, I proceeded to redirect my aim into her pussy. I had her on all fours and this time she was throwing it back at me. Her ass bounced and wiggled off my stomach every time our bodies connected between strokes. Our sweaty bodies smacked against each other's. I could hear the dog barking in the background but the sound of Yellow Diamond's moans and ass slapping off my pelvis drowned out the barking. I was in the throes of ecstasy when out of nowhere I got this funny feeling in my gut. I instantly glanced over my shoulder and jumped in fear and shock. I looked around searching for my pants. I needed to get to my gun. Staring right back at me laying on his stomach was the biggest Mastiff I've ever seen. The dog stared at me lazily as if to say, "Nigga do ya thing, don't let me bother you, I'm just tryna watch." I relaxed and bust out laughing. That's when I realized the dog was back there laying in the cut watching us fuck the whole time. That dog was just like me, he wanted to see Yellow Diamond get fucked doggy style! I gave that dog a show. We were like kindred souls. My only regret was not bringing him a bitch Mastiff to get his nutt off…!

12

# A DIRTY LITTLE SECRET

Zaydia McNeil
Bronx, New York
Summer, 2018
Instagram: @zaydiction

Some things are better left unsaid. Some secrets should never be shared. This story is a prime example; yet here I am running my mouth digging up shit that should stay buried. But, these sorts of stories are usually the juiciest, and a juicy secret won't remain one forever.

I got this home girl, her name is Lakye. She and I have been friends since grade school... she's like my day one. We've been through mad shit together, shared our most intimate secrets with each other, and did some crazy, scandalous things together.

Lakye has another close friend, her name is Gweyn. They became close friends during the time I attended college in upstate New York. I'm not the catty or jealous type. We all got cool and hung out a few times during my Christmas and spring breaks.

Layke used to tell me about Gweyn and her then boyfriend Joe. I never met Joe but heard a lot about him and the tumultuous relationship Gweyn shared with him. The chicks he had on the side, the aborted pregnancies, etc. So, imagine the look on my face when Layke told me she had invited him to the club with us one night. I stood there giving her the side eye.

"When did you and Gweyn's ex become besties?" I asked with a hint of sarcasm.

"They ain't together anymore!" Was her reply as if that made it okay.

"Bitch you scandalous." I replied. Her excuse was, "It ain't like he's her baby's father. Plus, we just friends." I gave her a look like "whatever bitch!" I knew from that point on, I had to keep my eye on Lakye cuz if she would fuck with Gweyn's ex-boyfriend, she would fuck with one of mine. Bitch was breaking the girl code.

That night we all met up downtown before heading to the club. It was me, Lakye, Angela, Dwayne and Joe. It was my first time meeting Joe. He's dark skin, slim and stood around 5'11" tall. He wasn't bad looking. In fact, he was handsome in a rugged sort of way. Yet he didn't give me the impression of a thug.

The club was lit. We all had a really good time. I could tell that Lakye and Joe shared a deeper level of intimacy by the way they touched each other in the club that night. We partied and danced until around 2:45-3:00 in the morning. Angela and Dwayne slid off together, so me, Lakye and Joe hailed a cab and we headed uptown.

I'm not gonna front, alcohol gets me horny, and I'd been drinking all night so I was a lil tipsy, we all were. In the cab Lakye and Joe started kissing. The sight of them tongue kissing got my juices flowing. To keep my hormones in check, I looked away and started staring out the window. When we came to a red light, I glanced over at them. Lakye was sucking Joe's dick like a tasty lollipop. Damn, the sight of his dick in her mouth got me hornier. Don't ask me why, but I leaned in on him and we started kissing. I let out this moan as he massaged my breasts. I had on this tight spandex dress. His left hand made its way down to the hem of my dress. Next thing you know my thong was pulled to the side and Joe had two fingers sliding in and out of me.

The sound of my moans and Lakye sucking Joe's dick filled the confines of the cab. The driver couldn't keep his eyes on the road. Every time I glanced up he was watching us through the rearview mirror. I spread my legs wider, giving him a sight to remember. The cab dropped us off at Layke's apartment in the Bronx. We go upstairs into her apartment to wind down and freshen up because I needed to pee from all that liquor I drank. We got some more drinks and started listening to the radio. Hot 97 be turned up on weekend nights. It felt like we were having our own intimate little after party.

We got into a game of strip poker. Now I don't know a thing about poker, and I couldn't tell if Joe was cheating or not, but I was stripped down to my bra and thong after a couple of hands. Joe got up from the table and starts sucking Lakye's titties. My home girl Lakye got some big ass titties. She's 5'9" tall with a cute Monica hairstyle. She ain't got no big ass, but she got big thighs. Before you know it, they both head to the living room couch. Lakye starts giving Joe head. Her ass is all poked up in the air. I get behind her and start rubbing her pussy from behind. Now mind you, I never touched my best friend in this way before. It felt weird, but exciting at the same time. I crouch down behind her and start eating her pussy while she's sucking Joe's dick, we're literally running a train, lol. I spread Lakye's butt cheeks and insert my middle finger into her ass while sucking on her clit. She's moaning and starts sucking his dick harder and faster, which tells me she's loving it. Then she slides up and starts kissing him. I'm still eating her from behind but before I can bring her to a climax, she climbs on top of Joe and starts riding him in reverse cowgirl position.

The sight of her bouncing on his dick is such a fucking turn on. Her big titties are bouncing up and down, and she's moaning "Daddy, Daddy, Daddy!" I'm laughing inside like "What the fuck?" Hearing her call Gweyn's ex "Daddy" is weird to me. Plus, this is the first time I ever witnessed my friend having sex. I get in front of them and start rubbing Lakye's titties and her clit while she's riding Joe. She reaches her first orgasm that way. When she climbs off him, I grab his dick and start sucking her juices off it...Yeah, I know that's some freaky shit, but fuck it, blame it on the alcohol!

I'm not bragging, they literally call me the "head doctor," because when I suck a dick, I try to suck the soul out a man and Joe was no exception. I start sucking the side of his dick from the head to the base while massaging his balls at the same time. Then I work the tip, sucking it real hard making these slurping sounds. He's moaning, "Oh shit, oh shit," as I gradually deep throat him, trying to swallow the whole dick if I can. It must have been too much for him to handle because he stopped me. I guess he didn't want to cum that quick.

Lakye gets up from the chair. She was sitting there playing with her pussy while I was sucking Joe off. She takes his hand and guides him to the love seat. They start fucking in the missionary position. I grab Lakye's right ankle, lifting it up to expose her pussy so I could rub her clit while Joe's fucking her. I start cheering them on saying, "Yeah, get it, get it. Hit that shit, hit that shit. Get it!"

They switch positions. Lakye gets on her hands and knees, Joe gets behind her, and starts fucking her doggy style. Lakye is moaning that "Daddy" shit again, but I can't blame her cause Joe is giving it to her. He's crushing it, fucking her hard with long deep strokes. He got her pussy farting and everything. Their bodies are sweating making that smacking sound. I'm sitting on the chair playing with my pussy. It's like looking at a live porn movie. I'm so turned on. Watching them fuck is amazing. Then Joe looks over at me while he's fucking Lakye from behind. He gestures me over to him. Now he didn't have any hold on me like he had on Lakye, I just met him, but being caught in the moment I found myself getting up off the chair and making my way over to them.

He's still fucking Lakye when he pulls me towards him and starts kissing me. Then he tells me to lay in front of Lakye. I get in front of her, lay on my back and spread my legs. I swear I never did this before, and I never considered allowing my friend to eat my pussy, but here I lay with my legs spread parting my pussy lips to allow my friend to eat me out.

That shit was feeling so fucking good. I grabbed the back of her head pulling her face deeper into me, grinding my clit on her mouth. I nutted so fast, the sensation was incredible. Every time Joe drove his dick into her, her mouth grinded into my clit, it was like a chain reaction. Lakye's body started to shake. I knew she was busting another nutt. She collapsed between my legs, then rolled off the couch. Joe must have thought that was his cue to get in between my legs, but I wasn't having it. His dick was fresh out of Lakye's pussy. I was not about to let him fuck me raw with Lakye's pussy sauce on his dick. Plus, I just met him. Yeah, I know I sucked his dick raw, fresh out of Lakye's pussy, but that's different, a bitch got a lil morals.

I closed my legs and told him no, "You not fucking me." He had a shocked look on his face, but I wasn't budging. He slid off the couch and got on the floor next to Lakye. He rolled her onto her stomach and started eating her from behind. Then she got on all fours. He spit on his dick then rubbed the tip against her asshole and started to fuck her in the ass. I was beginning to have second thoughts about him fucking me because I love anal sex. I'm the anal queen. The sight of him going in and out of her ass was making my pussy cream and pulsate.

I got on the floor with them, repositioning myself in front of Lakye's face so she could eat my pussy some more. After around 10 minutes of that, I came three times. Lakye came, then Joe bust his nutt in her ass. I got up off the floor and headed to the bathroom to wash myself off. When I went back into the living room Lakye and Joe were laying there in the 69 position. I thought, "Damn Lakye you a freaky bitch, sucking your own ass juice off his dick. Lol." Hey to each his own. I got dressed and called a cab. I left them there on the living room floor going at it again. I ain't gonna front, that was a memorable night, and once again I proved to myself that I got the bomb ass head game. I caught Lakye looking at me sideways when I was sucking Joe's dick. I don't know why. She ain't got nothing to worry about. I don't want him, well maybe his dick every now and then, but other than that she could have him all to herself.

The sun was rising by the time I got home. I was exhausted, but before I jumped in bed, I logged onto my Instagram and just as I expected, Joe requested to follow. I clicked accept and went to bed. But the story didn't end there....

# 13

# THE ASIAN PERSUATION

**JOHN B.**
Occupation: Recruitment Officer
Location: Fremont, California
Social Media: Tagged
February 2016

YOU MAY BE WONDERING, "IS THIS JOHN B, THE SINGER?" AND IF I told you I was, would you believe me? Probably not, but for the record, I'm not that John B…my real name is John, and my last name begins with the letter 'B'. Due to my line of work I've chosen to refrain from revealing my full identity.

When I was in the Armed Forces, I was a Public Relations Officer. In my civilian life I transferred those skills to the position I hold now as a Recruitment Officer for a modeling agency. I also manage the talent that I personally recruit. My work involves a great deal of networking on social media platforms such as Tagged, Plenty-of-Fish, Facebook, etc.

On an average day I message at least 100 women. I will log onto a site like Tagged, click on a particular city, starting with a city close to me. I will start at the top of the list of women featured in that city. Each day I would message 100 women until I've messaged every single woman from that city. Then I would move on to the next surrounding city. If a particular woman happens to catch my eye, I'll message her once a day until I receive a response.

While going through a list of women from Stockton, California, a cute Vietnamese woman named Saunta caught my attention. For three weeks, I messaged her until I got a reply.

Saunta was 25 years old at the time. She stood 5' tall with long auburn hair that hung down to her ass. She had piercings on her cheeks.

We texted back and forth, exchanging small talk. I asked her if she had kids. She didn't. Her goal was to become a model. I told her she would do great in the urban modeling scene. I gave her some advice and we continued to kick it.

Our small talk piqued my interest, and one day I decided to meet up with her. Now I have a thing about visiting a woman at her home. After a bad experience on a first date where the woman's ex-boyfriend tried to assault me at her home, I no longer visit a woman's home, especially on the first date. So, on this day I cautiously drove to Stockton to pick Saunta up. When I arrived in front of her residence, she was accompanied by her friend named Lisa. Now, if Saunta was a dime, her friend Lisa was a roll of quarters. Lisa had this exotic look about her. Her eyes were completely slanted like cats' eyes. She was shorter than Saunta, around 4'11" tall. Her hair hung down to the middle of her back. Her breasts were a nice B-cup, stomach was flat, and when she stood straight you could see the gap between her legs. Her ass fit her body perfectly. She was a beautiful sight to behold.

After being introduced, Lisa and I shook hands and I felt this sudden wave of sensual energy that went through my entire body. At that moment I lost complete interest in Saunta. My mind raced for a good reason to invite Lisa on our date. After a few moments of contemplation, I simply asked, "Would you like to join us?" She smiled displaying pearly white teeth, glancing over at her friend. Saunta shrugged her shoulders and said, "I don't care!" I was thinking, "How can I get this sexy lil thing alone?" I opened the passenger door for Saunta and the rear door for her friend. I got behind the wheel deciding I would dump Saunta on my cousin Cliff.

My cousin Cliff wasn't the most attractive man by any means. He was a little overweight, couldn't dress worth a shit, but what he lacked in looks and charisma he made up for financially. I turned to Saunta and said, "You'll love my cousin Cliff. He's single, no kids, owns several rental properties and lives alone in a four-bedroom house." I was bigging him up. Occasionally I would look at Lisa through the rearview mirror, saying a few things, trying to engage her in conversation.

I had a change of plans and decided I would take these two hotties to my cousin's house. But I couldn't just pop up on him unannounced, so I made a pit-stop. I pulled into this mini-mall and headed to the liquor store where I purchased some Hennessy and texted my cousin, letting him know I was on my way to his house with two exotic Vietnamese women. He returned my text immediately, "Bet!"

The drive out to the suburbs took 20 minutes. Cliff was all smiles when I arrived at his house. I introduced him to Saunta, and Lisa. We all went into the living room where I left Saunta and Cliff, and asked Lisa to help me in the kitchen with the drinks. Lisa and I engaged in small talk. She told me that her parents immigrated from Laos and knew Saunta's parents from Vietnam, and that she and Saunta were more like sisters than friends. I complimented her on her exotic beauty, causing her to blush. After getting the glasses and pouring the drinks we headed back to the living room.

Saunta and Cliff were lounging in front of the big flat screen

TV on top of the fireplace. I was tempted to throw on a porn movie but decided against it. I rolled up some weed, and we all sat around smoking and drinking. Once Shaunta and Cliff seemed to be lost in their own conversation, I took Lisa upstairs to one of the bedrooms.

"Take off your shoes and relax." I told her, and she did just that, lying on the bed. I switched on the TV and climbed on the bed beside her. I'm bold, and I figured since I got her upstairs alone, she was down for whatever! I slid close to her and started rubbing her pussy through her pants. Her crotch was warm and moist, and that turned me on, causing me to kiss her. She puts her hand in my pants and begins to rub my dick. I knew then that she wanted to have sex. I got up, "Hold on I got to use the bathroom." I took a quick leak, then headed downstairs to check on Cliff and Saunta. I wasn't surprised to find both of them sitting in the living room drinking and watching Netflix. I went back upstairs. Lisa's clothes were strewn on the floor. She was laying naked under the covers. I walked towards the bed and pulled the covers off her then got between her legs and started eating her pussy. Lisa gyrated her hips, moaning and pushing my head into her. I turned on my back and she climbed on top of me attempting to ride me, but I wasn't through yet. I turned her around so her ass was facing me, and started eating her pussy in the 69 position. She grabbed my dick and put it in her mouth and began sucking it.

I know for most women the clitoris is the most sensitive part of their body, I took hers in my mouth and began sucking on it. In less than a minute she came, squirting on my face. Her cum soaked my neck and portions of the pillow. I popped her on her ass so hard it sounded like a thunderclap. "DO IT AGAIN!" I told her as I resumed sucking on her clit. Within a minute she reached another orgasm. I smacked her ass again telling her, "DO IT AGAIN!" And like before, within another minute she reached another orgasm.

I was enjoying the taste of her cum and kept smacking her ass hard every time she reached one telling her to "Do it again, do it again!" She must have reached 30 orgasms that way, because I ate her pussy for 30 minutes and smacked her ass at least 30 times.

Lisa rolled off me and onto her back, and I positioned myself on top of her, then grabbed her feet with my hands and pushed her legs back until her knees were parallel to her armpits. I positioned myself in a squatting position directly on top of her and started fucking her like I was squatting. As I'm going in and out of her a thick white coat of cum soaks my dick. It's so thick it looks like mayonnaise. Lisa is biting her lip and her eyes are rolling to the back of her head. Seeing this I begin to bounce in and out of her faster and faster. After a few minutes I let her legs go and lay on top of her. We start making love in the missionary position. Lisa is built so small I'm trying to get all my dick inside her but couldn't. Her pussy just wasn't deep enough.

We switch positions by laying on our sides. We're slow grinding and I'm kissing her trying to savor the moment because the pussy was good. After a few minutes of slow grinding, she rolls me onto my back and aggressively spreads my legs, grabs my dick and starts sucking me off. She looks up at me as she tries to deep throat me, gagging on my dick. Saliva stretches from her lips to my dick as she takes my dick out of her mouth. She wipes the saliva off her mouth, and starts to jerk my dick, licking the side then taking me into her mouth again until she gags, all while keeping eye contact with me. The sound of her sucking and gagging on my dick almost brings me to an orgasm.

After five minutes she climbs on top of me in the reverse cowgirl position. She bends forward. Her ass is facing me, and I watch as she inserts me inside of her. Her juices lubricate my stiff dick. It glistens in the light. She begins to work her hips up and down. I watch her ass bounce and my dick stretching her pussy going in and out of her. She moans, talking in her native tongue. The sight of her hips and petite yet thick ass bounce and twerk on my dick is something to treasure. I know she's about to reach her climax as she picks up the pace of her thrusts. Her moans become more intense. She grabs my feet and begins to suck on my toes. Then she screams, shivers and collapses in a state of pure ecstasy.

I lay back staring at her ass and the flow of her thick, white cum soaking my dick. I roll her over to her side. Her head faces the foot of the bed. I lift one of her legs to my mouth and return the favor, sucking her toes while I fuck her. She's panting, "Go harder, go harder." Until I bust my nutt.

Lisa and I get it on that entire night until the early morning. I get up and head downstairs to check on Cliff and Saunta, Cliff is snoring and Saunta is sound asleep. I quietly wake her. I hold out my hand, she takes it, and I lead her up the stairs to the bedroom where Lisa laid. I tell her, "Take off your clothes!" She looks up at me, then looks at Lisa on the bed. "Take off your clothes!" I say with a little more assertiveness. She hesitates, and before she says a word, I put my finger to her lips to "shush" her. She removes her clothes and I guide her onto the bed, and we both get under the sheets.

I could feel the rapid beat of her heart as our naked bodies touched. She was both nervous and excited. My plan was to have an early morning orgy, but first I had to get my fill of a threesome before I'd allow Cliff to join in on the fun...

# 14

# NEVER SAW IT COMING

**BRITNEY PERRY**
Bronx, New York
Summer, 2018
Social Media: Facebook
Screen Name: TherealBritneyPerry

I WAS AT WORK SCROLLING THROUGH FACEBOOK WHEN I GOT A new friend request from a dude named Mikey-Mike. I looked at his profile and it says we have 13 mutual friends. I start looking at his pictures because clearly if he requested me, he must know who I am because I don't have a picture on my profile page, so I accept him. Soon as I do, he hops in my inbox.

"Thanks for the add sexy!"

"You're welcome." I replied and left it at that. He hits back, "I've been wanting you for some time. No lie I've been in love with you since the first time I saw you at Shana and Dave's baby shower." Now I'm looking at my phone with my face screwed up. This dude is clearly joking because Shana's baby shower was three years ago. I hit him back, "You must have the wrong person."

"Your name is Britney, right? 5' 5" tall, about 150 lbs, slim thick, with a cute ass, pretty pecan tan complexion, Indian hair and a birth mark on your left inner thigh?"

That threw me off. Only a few people could know about my birthmark. You'd have to be a stalking peeping Tom otherwise.

"I'm Dave's cousin. Ever since the baby shower I've been trying to connect with you." He added.

"Well clearly it wasn't that hard to find me, you could have asked Dave for my info."

"I did, but Shana said you had a man and wasn't playing matchmaker. Plus, me and Dave fell out over some bread. I haven't spoken to him in over a year and a half." My response to that was, "Oh!"

We started texting back and forth. I pull up his pictures. He's dark skin, 6' tall, nice build with a low fade and beard. His eyes were chinky and he had a radiant smile. I was intrigued by him. His beauty stimulated me, and I was bugging on the fact that he was interested in me to the point of stalking.

"Let's cut all this small talk, slide me your number so I could hear your voice." I smiled at the phone when I read those words. He was taking charge and I liked that. But still I wasn't giving in. I told him I was at work and that he should send me his number, and I'd hit him once I got off.

I couldn't wait for 5 o'clock to come. I called him on my way home. He answered on the first ring. "Hey beautiful, I thought you would never call." I laughed, blushing at the same time.

"I told you I would call after I got off. So, what's up?" I asked, feeling all giddy like some schoolgirl. "I wanna take you out for dinner tonight, and I'm not taking no for an answer!"

Dude was really confident. "You know I have a saying in this don't you?" I replied, holding back a smile. "Just say yes, the rest is up to you." I couldn't hold back my smile. I replied, "Bet, it's a date."

He asked where could he pick me up? I told him I stayed on 180th and the Grand Concourse. He said he was in Connecticut at the moment but would be there to pick me by 8p.m.

As soon as I got off the phone, I called my home girl Meika because they were mutual friends on Facebook. I asked Meika for the low down on Mike, and surprisingly enough she had nothing bad to say.

"He doesn't like people."

"What?"

"Exactly what I said. He doesn't fuck with too many people. He gets his money and stays out the way. I'm not sure if he has a girl." Then she paused, "Why you ask?"

"No reason." I answered. If I ain't learn nothing I learned to keep my shit to myself. I got off the phone with her and tried to figure out what I was going to wear. It was the beginning of September, so the weather was perfect. Not too cool, and not too hot, it was just right. I decided on a gold spandex dress and my strappy sandals. It hugged my curves in all the right places. My 36C-cups were sitting up nice and perky. I didn't wear any panties because the lines would show under my dress. Plus, I like to let my cootie cat breathe, and my ass jiggle all over the place when I walk. And if Mike was head over heels for me like he said he was, his ass might be in for a treat.

8p.m. rolled around, and like clockwork I got a text from Mike saying he was outside. I got downstairs and exited my apartment building, a cab was double parked out front. When I got closer to the curb there's a red Ferrari 458 Spider parked beside it with a super handsome chocolate man standing holding the passenger door open. I was already horny from not having sex for a while, seeing that ride really turned me on. I approached the vehicle and Mikey kissed me on the lips. I stood there in shock. He gestured for me to climb inside his Ferrari, taking my hand as I climbed in. He got behind the wheel and before putting the car in gear he looked over at me and said, "Damn, you look even prettier than I remember!" I blushed like some shy, bashful chick. He pulled into traffic, and all eyes were on us. It's not every day you see a red Ferrari on the Grand Concourse in the Bronx. I was enjoying the moment. Mikey didn't waste time with the small talk, he starts talking about our first encounter three years ago. "I was the dude who helped set up the DJ's equipment at the baby shower. I saw you over there helping with the decorations. Remember you almost fell from the chair while hanging the banners?" I looked over at him trying to picture it in my mind. He could see from my facial expression that I was slowly coming to that recollection. "Yep, I was the one who caught you in my arms. That's when I saw the lil birthmark on your inner thigh. I know this shit sounds corny, but I knew I had to have you. I was in love from that moment on."

If he was running game, he was good. He recollected too much detail for such a short encounter some three years ago. As I'm sitting beside him, looking at his profile while he focuses on the road in front of him, he reaches over and gently touches my thigh and pushed my dress up getting a glimpse of my birthmark. His touch made me flinch. It had been months since I had sex, and the fact that Mikey was saying all the right things made me super sensitive. I was horny as hell and my pussy was pulsating in heat.

"Where are we going?" I asked him, trying to gain some control of my hormones.

"I made reservations for us at this restaurant downtown called 'Del Frisco's' for 9p.m. Have you ever been there?"

Actually, I had, but I didn't want to spoil the mood for him, so I responded, "No, is it nice?" He smiled and replied, "Very, you're gonna like it!"

I was mesmerized by his whole aura. His YSL cologne was

intoxicating. When we stopped at a red light he reached over and touched my leg again, this time his hands went a little higher. My dress was already short, not to mention I had on no panties. He felt the moisture between my thighs and said, "Oh, someone's excited!" I was so embarrassed, but at the same time hornier. Then without provocation he grabbed my pussy and I let out a moan. Damn, my pussy was betraying me.

"I see you've been needing some attention," he chuckled. This negro was a psychic or something?

"You clearly searching for my attention touching me down there," and we both laughed. Mike looked over at me, "You don't have a clue of what I'm about to do to you!" I thought, "Oh yeah!" and told him to keep his eyes on the road.

We were merging onto the Major Deegan Expressway when my hormones got the best of me. I reached over and pressed the release button on my seatbelt, then leaned across the center console to reach between his legs. His dick was harder than a metal pipe. I smiled, "Someone's standing at attention!" He couldn't do anything but laugh. I wanted to give him a hand job, but his Versace belt was in the way. I proceeded to unbuckle the belt, then went to the buttons of his white jeans. He scooped his ass up making it easier for me to adjust his pants so I could get to that dick. I pulled it out. His dick was slim, but long. I wrapped five fingers around it, and felt it pulsate and bulge harder. His chocolate dick looked like a king-size snickers bar, veins and all. To myself I'm saying, "Fuck this hand job, I wanna suck it."

Mikey's watching me in amazement as I take him into my mouth. I gesture for him to focus on the road. My mouth begins to water with lust. The extra saliva does wonders, and I know exactly what I want to do. I don't know if it's the fact that I haven't been fucked in months, or simply the excitement of being in that moment. I lean over and position myself better so I could take more of that dick in my mouth.

The wind is blowing my hair. I feel the car swerve, so I tap his leg, reminding him to focus. Then Mikey takes his right hand off the steering wheel, placing it gently on my head forcing me to eat that dick up. I relax my throat and feel the tip reach my tonsils.

I'm slobbering, smacking and moaning, putting on a show for him. My pussy muscles are contracting forcing moisture down my legs. I start sucking a little harder, and a lot faster. I knew I was putting in work when his leg jerked forward and locked up. I immediately slowed up, easing off him. I looked up over the dashboard and noticed we were on the Westside Highway heading south. We needed to get there safely, so I told him to pull over as soon as he could.

Mikey took the 72nd Street exit and pulled over to the pier. We faced the Hudson River looking over at New Jersey. The sun had fallen over the horizon, so there were no inhibitions for either one of us. Mikey reaches over and slides his finger into my pussy, then he's sliding another one in me. I jump out of my seat. Then he starts kissing me. I'm caught up in the rapture as he whispers in my ear, "I want you right now!"

"Where, right here, right now?" He shakes his head. I'm unsure as to how this would work, a Ferrari isn't known for its leg room. Mikey shimmies his pants down to his knees, slides his seat back as far as it could go, then tells me to climb on top. I climb over the middle console and position myself on top of him in the bridge position. He inserts his dick into my wet vagina. I close my eyes and tilt my head back in pleasure as the head breaks through the entrance. The deeper he goes the more I moan. Then he pulls my dress over my head. I'm practically naked underneath and he glances over every inch of my body. I stare down into his eyes while I bounce up and down on his long, stiff dick. I let out a sensuous moan when he grabs my titties and starts sucking them. I'm steady riding him as he sucks on my neck. All I could think was, "Thank God for the dark tints."

The windows begin to fog up. Mikey is starting to huff and puff, breathing faster and faster. I don't let up, picking up the pace, because the harder he breathes the more I'm turned on.

Mikey then grabs me by the waist with both hands and gives out one, two, three hard strokes, then explodes inside me on the fourth one. His hot sperm sends a stream of warm sensations through me like an electric shock wave that triggers my orgasm and we cum together.

Mikey is still holding me tight by the waist grinding into me, I can feel his sperm flow out of me, we had made a mess everywhere.

After a few moments I got my thoughts together and was no longer dick-ma-tized. I realized what just happened. I reached for my dress and slid it back over my head and tried to fix myself as best as I could, climbing back into the passenger seat. Mikey looked over at me.

"What's wrong?" He asked.

For me, reality had set in. I done sucked this man's dick, done got fucked in the car, and had the nerve not to use protection. I sat there with his semen seeping out of me. I dropped my head into my hands in shame.

"Baby what's wrong?" I looked up and cut my eye at him like, are you serious?

"You don't have nothing to worry about," he said while proceeding to adjust his pants. Then he opened the driver's side door and walked around the car to open my door. "Oh God, I know this nigga ain't about to put my ass out on the Westside Highway?" He put his hand out, gesturing for me to climb out. I get out, stand in front of him adjusting my dress and fixing my hair. He kissed me on the forehead and spoke with such care and thoughtfulness.

"What just happened is what I've wanted since the first time

I laid eyes on you. This is not a one-night stand, or a fling. This is forever." I couldn't believe what I was hearing. I looked him in the eyes and said, "You don't even know me."

"I loved you from the first time I saw you. Before I knew your name. What just happened solidified it for me." I felt relieved but I didn't know if he was running game or not? At that moment I didn't care. I wanted to believe him. We hugged, and I kissed him with all the passion in my soul. After a moment, he glanced at his watch and said, "Okay, we need to hurry before we're late for dinner."

I couldn't believe this was happening. It was hard to believe that I'd gotten this lucky.

When we arrived at the restaurant Mikey was greeted by the maître d. It was obvious he'd been there frequently. We were led to a table against the window that overlooked the Hudson River. Mikey was the perfect gentleman, recommending the best choices on the menu. He then offered to suggest the best wine to me. I was loving his energy. After ordering our entrées I excused myself to the ladies' room. He stood with me, and to my surprise led me to the restroom.

When we got there, he grabbed my waist and escorted me inside. "What are you doing?" I asked, as he pushes me into a stall and reaches under my dress, then grabs my pussy. My knees start to buckle at his touch. He bends me over and I brace my right leg up on the toilet and place my hands on the bathroom stall. Mikey's behind me opening his jeans, they fall to his ankles. He slides his pointer finger in my pussy and his thumb in my asshole. I look over my shoulder with a "hell no" expression on my face.

"Chill, relax babe, it won't hurt" Once again he has me willing to try anything with him. He eases his thumb in my butt. I clinch up and blurt out, "Ouch, that hurts!" He removes his thumb and squats down behind me. He palms both my ass cheeks and spreads them. I let out a moan when I feel his tongue slither in my butthole. He begins to twirl his tongue inside. I couldn't believe this was happening in a restaurant bathroom and how good it felt. I've never been in this type of situation before. I was enjoying it. I let out another moan when he reached for my clit with his finger. His tongue feels so good. I find myself grinding back into his face. Mikey knew I was ready before I knew it myself. He stands up and slides his dick in my booty. I screamed cuz that shit hurt. I was still a virgin back there. He covered my mouth and held me tight, slowly stroking in and out with the tip of his dick. After a couple of strokes, it started to feel more like pleasure, and less like pain. I didn't realize he was all the way up in me until I felt his balls slap against my clit. We both caught a rhythm and was matching each other's strokes. Within moments I was shaking and erupted into an orgasm that ran down my leg. My orgasm must have caused a chain reaction because Mikey pumped into me three more times and it was over, he bust his nutt all in my asshole. I didn't realize a woman could have an anal orgasm.

At that moment I was no longer ashamed. I turned around to face him. Looking into his eyes I said, "Nigga you stuck with me now!" We both burst into a fit of laughter. Mikey grabbed some tissue and cleaned me off, then cleaned himself. We washed our hands and proceeded back to our table. He joked about that being the best six minutes he ever spent in a bathroom. We laughed, then he grabbed my hand and got all serious, gently kissing it. He looked into my eyes and said, "You're mine now!" Long story short and a whole lot of sex later, Mikey became my husband and I am forever grateful for social media because that's where I met my soul mate.

# 15

# SHORTY FROM THE BEAN

**D1**

Spring, 2016
Bronx, New York
Instagram: @D1_SITCHED

As far as technology is concerned, my generation has benefitted more than previous ones. Take for example smartphones, I can't imagine life without one. Think about it, technology has made life's tasks easier and the world smaller. I can connect with someone on the other side of the planet by simply logging on to the Internet. Social media gives me access to millions of beautiful women. Now I know you are reading this and saying to yourself, "Meeting women is not the only thing the Internet can be used for." But for a young, handsome, and horny dude like myself, there is nothing better.

I was home chilling one day, scrolling through Instagram when I see a post from the Bro 'POP', who's known for taking pictures with the baddest strippers in the tri-state area. As always, Pop is in the pic standing next to this bad Caucasian with an ass like a mule. She's wearing a skimpy outfit, I figure, "She's got to be a stripper!" So, I do what I always do, I click on her page since her picture is tagged. She had only 7,000 followers, which was good, because I don't fuck with chicks with more than 10,000 followers. I scroll through her photos and click 'LIKE' on eight of them. Her page wasn't private, and neither was mine, so I followed her. I waited to see if she would return 'LIKES' on my page, and like clockwork she 'LIKED' five of my photos. I didn't waste time playing games, I in-boxed her, sending a heart emoji. She responded with a blushing face. I can't front, I was a little hyped. Shorty was thicker than a snicker, and I doubted she knew her worth. I slid in her DM (Direct Messages) and got her info. Her name was Britney, she lived in Boston, Massachusetts.

We started talking on the phone regularly, and the more we talked, the more I realized I had the juice. She loved my New York accent and was feeling my young boy swag. One day I got a text from her saying she was coming to visit family in New York and wanted to meet up. The timing was perfect, wifey was on vacation with her mom's, so Britney and I made plans to hook up the following day. I got up early the next morning to get ready for that meet & greet. I got my hair trimmed, making sure shit was tight. I slipped on a pair of Double Stitch True Religion Jeans, a pair of Constructs (Timberland Boots), and a Billionaire Boys Club Hoodie. Shorty pulls up in a minivan. I'm saying to myself, "Really!" With a body like hers I assumed she was caking (making a lot of money) at the strip club. I was expecting her to pull up in something foreign, but it was cool. At least she had her own ride.

Britney hopped out of her van wearing baggy jeans, a college sweater, and a pair of Reeboks. I was not impressed but knowing what was underneath had me excited. I gave her a hug and felt her curves. She had plenty potential, all she needed was the right coach. Too bad I didn't have the time, nor the patience to turn this snow bunny into a star. I had my own girl to worry about, and she was a handful.

After our embrace, I asked her, "Ma, you smoke?" She smiles nodding her head, "Yeah." We walked to the corner store where I cop a few Dutchies. Poppy behind the counter kept staring at shorty like she was Kim Kardashian, acting like he never saw a phat ass white chick. Come to think of it, maybe he hadn't. I paid for the cigars and we headed to my crib.

I told her to kick back, take off her shoes and relax. She did exactly that, getting comfortable on the living room couch. "What kind of shows you like?" I asked her. I had that jail-broken Firestick by Amazon. I could pull up any show, any movie ever made, old and new episodes. She wanted to watch Love & Hip-Hop Atlanta, so I put that on for her, then lit a blunt. We both got lit and was feeling the effects. She inched her thick body closer to me then placed her head on my chest. I used that opportunity to try my hand and kissed her forehead. She kissed my lips in return, and we started to tongue kiss. My hands caressed her body. It was so soft it made no sense. I kissed her neck, pulling out her left titty, licked and sucked on it. She moaned, encouraging me to go further. I unbuttoned her jeans, she grabbed my dick, stroking it through my pants. I slid my hand down her panties, sliding my middle finger inside her. She let out a soft moan, grinding and rotating her hips. Her juices soaked my hand as I slid another finger inside her. I was hot, feenin to taste her. I pulled her pants and panties off her, then got up to remove my clothes. I look down at her, she's laying on the couch with her legs spread. I'm staring at her thick, white thighs. The sight drives me crazy. I dive between her legs face first and begin eating her pussy like it's my first meal of the day, giving her something to remember me by.

"Aaah fuck, aah fuck!" She yells out loud. I knew I was eating it right, sucking on her clit. She squirmed, grabbing my head trying to pull me away, but I was locked onto her pussy like a

Pitbull… "Oooh my God, stop, stoop. I'm about to…" She pulls my head into her, grinding her pussy on my mouth. She shakes and shivers, busting her first nutt. I lapped up her juices like a thirsty puppy. I was feeling myself. I get up feeling like a sex don…You know me, I position my dick in front of her face so she can return the favor.

"I'm not giving you any head!" I stare at her like, "WHAT?" This girl got to be joking. My thoughts were written all over my face because she looks at me and says, "But we can have sex!" You damn right we having sex… I just ate this bitch's pussy, I sucked her juices, and now she is talking about she ain't giving me no head. Bitch you should have said that from the jump! I was in my feelings.

"TURN OVER!" I said with a touch of gangsta in my voice. She rolled over in the doggy-style position. I watched her ass spread like wings on an eagle. The sight was amazing. I got behind her, and as soon as I entered her, she let out an erotic moan.

"Shake that shit!" I commanded her. She did as she was told, twerking on my dick. Her ass shook in waves like a tsunami. I wasn't sure if I could get any harder, but the sight of that phat ass moving in waves put me in beast mode.

"I'mma fuck the shit," in my mind I'm saying, "out of this white girl!" I went in going slow, enjoying the softness of her plump ass. She kept moaning, "Oh fuck, ooh fuck" and I wasn't all the way in yet. After a few strokes, I edged in deeper and deeper until I reached her bottom. Then my strokes gradually got longer, and harder. I wanted her to feel that shit. "Fucking bitch, you wanna play games!"

I was still hot about not getting any head. I grabbed her long hair and pulled on it while I thrust in and out of her. She screamed "OOH my God!" I slapped her ass and she screamed, "OOH SHIT, OOH SHIT" So, I slapped her ass harder, leaving my palm print. "You like it?" I asked her. She moaned, so I slapped her ass even harder as I thrust into her. "YES, FUCK ME,

FUCK!" She moaned over and over. This bitch must be a freak for pain. I yanked on her hair forcing her head back as I commenced to fucking her harder and faster, while at the same time smacking her ass. My dick went in and out of her like a piston. Her ass was smacking and waving, it looked like a scene from a porn movie.

"You love this dick, don't you?" She answered with more moans. I slapped her ass again, "YOU LOVE THIS BLACK DICK DON'T YOU BITCH!"

"OOH FUCK, ooh fuck, yes, yes, fuck me, fuck me!" I wanted to choke this bitch out, but instead I fucked her harder and faster trying to kill the pussy instead. The bitch finally came, and I came too.

I was done. I got up, went to the bathroom and flushed the condom down the toilet. After wiping myself off, I looked in the mirror and said, "You the Man!" I walked back to the living room, and shorty was laying on the couch sound asleep. I knew I punished the pussy. I tapped her on the shoulder, "Yo love, I got a few moves to make, get dressed." I know I was being petty, but fuck that shit, she played herself. It was time to dismiss this bitch.

I walked her to her car, she was talking about how much she enjoyed herself. "You better call me later." I smiled knowingly; this snow bunny would never hear from me again. I replied "I got you ma, we definitely need to do this again." In my mind I'm saying, "Bitch please!" Shorty jumps in her whip and leans out her window to give me a kiss. "Don't forget to call me," she says before driving off.

It was good while it lasted. Her ass was definitely phat, but it was on to the next one, plus wifey was on her way home. And no, I did not call. I clicked "Delete!"

# 16

# LOVE LOCKDOWN

Shawn Covington
Dannemora, New York
Winter, 2015
Social Media: WriteAPrisoner.com
Username: Caged King

If you think finding love in prison is impossible, my story may change your mind. When I met her, I'd been incarcerated for 11 years on a 20-year sentence for possessing 750 grams of cocaine. I was housed at the maximum-security prison 'Clinton Correctional Facility,' in the state of New York. The same prison Marion Suge Knight infamously persuaded 2Pac Shakur to sign a recording contract with Death Row records. The rapper Shyne was also incarcerated there.

At that time, I was going through a tumultuous period. My wife and I officially ended our marriage. She relocated to California, started a new life, found a new man, and birthed new children. I wasn't bitter. She and I had issues prior to my incarceration, so her departure from my life was inevitable. Nevertheless, the divorce affected the bond I shared with my children. Despite my line of work, family was paramount to me, so being separated from them was a heavy burden to bear and a price too high to pay.

To keep from losing myself to despair I took to exercising both my mind and my body. I was coming in from the gym one day when I happened to bump into my homie Mike. Mike was coming from the visiting hall. "You down there on the regular Son!" He looked over his shoulder and smiled when he noticed who it was.

"What's up fam?" He responded holding a package his visitor left for him.

"Who came to see you, that shorty you were telling me about?" Mike shook his head still wearing that Kool-Aid smile. "Yeah, that was shorty I met on Write A Prisoner." He reached into his breast pocket and handed me five photographs they took together that day. I shook my head in approval, shorty was pretty. Creamy brown complexion, long shoulder length hair, black with honey blonde highlights. Her eyes were warm with a radiant smile. She was around his height, 5'8"-5'9" tall.

"You caught yourself a winner, she got any friends?" We both laughed at the same time. "I don't know, I'll ask her when she comes through next week." I didn't think much more about it until a week and a half later. I was sitting outside of Mike's cell when he passed me his photo album. As I'm going through it, I come across a picture of this attractive woman with a short Halle Berry hairstyle.

"Who's this?" I asked him. Mike glances at the photo and responds, "That's Wifey's sister." I flip the picture over to see if there's a name on the back. Sure enough, "My sister Denise!" is written on the back. I flip the photo back over and stared at it. Her eyes were inviting, sensuous, and seemed to be reaching out to me. Her lips were full, juicy and looked soft. The small button nose fit her face perfectly. Where Mike's girl had an angular profile, her sister's face was oval, and fuller. "What's up with shorty, she got a man?" Mike gave me this look, then shrugged his shoulders like, "fuck it!"

"She told me her sister can't find a good man. Give me a picture and I'll send it with the letter I'm mailing off tonight."

"Say no more!" I replied and ran up to my cell to retrieve a recent photo of myself. I jotted my information on the back and headed back to Mike's cell.

I forgot about the photos I sent and continued my daily routine. Two weeks later I received a letter in the mail. The name on the envelope was "Sabrina Moore." I racked my brain trying to remember if I knew a Sabrina. I opened the envelope and a picture fell out. I picked up the picture and stared at the image of a curvaceous sister with long braided hair. I turned the picture over on the backside.

"Shawn, I hope you like what you see, Sabrina Denise!"

I read her letter over and over laughing every time. Sabrina described how she had to sneak into her sister Yvonne's dresser drawer in order to get my info from the back of my picture. Apparently, her sister Yvonne was not happy about Mike trying to play matchmaker with her younger sister.

"My sister showed me your picture and the little note you wrote, commenting on the picture of me that Mike showed you. She was pissed with Mike for trying to hook us up. I'm 27 years old and grown, I can make my own decisions."

Although I had her by eight years, I was feeling her energy. But I felt bad about possibly being the cause of any riff between Mike and Yvonne. In my reply I expressed the fact that I totally understood her sister's concerns. I was all too familiar with the negative stigma associated with people who are incarcerated. I reassured her that I had my own money and wanted for nothing except a sincere friendship. She immediately replied to my letter and our friendship blossomed.

After several months of corresponding, I decided to send her some travel expenses to visit me at the prison. I'm not gonna front, I was anxious, and nervous in anticipation of that first face-to-face meeting. We exchanged photos, opened our hearts through the pen. We had become budding lovers, and were fast becoming best friends. Yet there was that possibility our first date could be a bust. Nevertheless, I made sure my haircut was tight, waves spinning, my beard was trimmed to perfection. I wore a cream knit sweater over the state-issued green pants, and a pair of construction Timbs.

When I entered the visiting room, the officer directed me to the table we were assigned. Sabrina was nowhere in sight, but her coat was draped over one of the chairs at our table. I figured she stepped into the ladies' room. I moved her coat to the chair on the opposite side. I wanted to sit as close to her as possible. I sat there waiting, nervous as hell. Don't get me wrong, I'm not bad looking at all. I'm 5'10" tall, with a muscular build. I wore my hair close cropped, in waves and a trimmed beard. I'm not light skin, nor dark skin, I'm somewhere in between. I never had difficulty attracting women, but it had been a minute since interacting with a woman. My nerves were on edge, but I played it cool.

Roughly five minutes passed before Sabrina entered the visiting room. She carried a few snacks and soft drinks. I thought that was thoughtful of her. We immediately made eye contact with each other. I watched her as she approached our table. She strutted in a pair of black suede ankle boots, with a 2½ inch heel, black wool pants that hugged her hips and thighs. I stood to greet her, pulling out her chair like a gentleman. She smiled, then gave me a hug after placing the drinks and snacks on the table. I inhaled her sweet fragrance. Her body felt soft against mine. I placed my hand against the small of her back, pulling her into me. "Damn you smell good!" I whispered in her ear. "So, do you," she replied. We took our seats, sitting at the corner of the table. "Thanks for the snacks and drinks. That was thoughtful of you."

She smiled, "I brought that for me, a bitch be hungry." We both bust out laughing, breaking the ice. This chick had jokes. I was feeling her. We sat there conversing and I just listened to the melody of her voice. It was smooth, syrupy, and seductive with a slight drawl, like a female version of Ma$e the rapper. Yet I could sense her nervousness. She could not hold my gaze for more than a few seconds. "You make me feel naked, like a little girl when you stare at me." I thought that was cute and grabbed her hands to put her at ease. "Relax Ma, you good. Don't mind me, I'm just absorbing your whole aura." She blushed again, and I was feeling her whole vibe and energy.

We took pictures together and I made it my business to stand behind her, pressing myself against her phat ass. I know she felt me rising to the occasion. The six hours we spent together that day went by quick, yet it was memorable. What we christened "Our First Date!" When it was time to leave, we stood facing each other. I pulled her into my embrace, wrapping my hands around her waist. She pressed her body into me, wrapping her arms around my neck. We tongue kissed and my hands roamed the contours of her ass. I wanted to fuck her right then and there.

From that point on, our relationship was a whirlwind of letters and visits. I made it a point to show my affection with little surprise gifts. For her birthday, she received a gold chain with a diamond encrusted key pendant. Shorty had stolen my heart.

As our relationship blossomed, Mike and Yvonne's had struck a roadblock. Yvonne was a devout Jehovah's Witness, Mike practiced Islam. Their respective religious beliefs became a source of strife, driving a wedge between them. I felt slightly responsible, because as I said, Yvonne didn't appreciate Mike hooking me up with her sister.

Things between Sabrina and I were developing nicely until she approached me about my profile page on Facebook. Months earlier before she and I got serious, my peoples decided to create a page and post my photos on Facebook. Like I mentioned earlier, I'm not bad looking, and I'm pretty much a workout fanatic. I lift weights six days out of the week, and jog 3 to 4 miles a day. My waist is slim, stomach chiseled, and when I stand in front of a mirror, I look like a cobra. Not bragging, facts! A couple of shirtless photos got posted and the ladies online went crazy.

Soon after, I started receiving letters from random women around the country. White women, Asian, Latin and sisters. It got so bad I started giving away some of the addresses, most of the women were lonely housewives. I figured I was doing them a favor passing their info to someone who had the time and desire to correspond with them.

Although Sabrina and I were pretty transparent, I didn't tell her about the Facebook page. Stupid mistake, but technically I wasn't responsible for the page. Plus, it was created before she and I got serious. I agreed to have it deleted, and we got back to doing us.

The winter months flew by, then came spring. However, I was looking forward to the month of July. Every summer the prison holds an annual festival. For the prisoners it's an opportunity to experience time with family, friends, and loved ones in a less restrictive setting. They are usually held outside with picnic tables, grills, etc.... I knew something wasn't right when I stepped out into the picnic area that day and Sabrina had this strained look on her face.

"What's up babe, what's wrong?" She looked at me with an expression I had never seen on her face before. "Who's Monica?" I looked at her with a blank expression on my face. I knew several Monica's, so I hadn't a clue which Monica she was referring to? "I'm lost babe, I don't know who you're talking about?"

"Oh, you don't? Well, the bitch is outside waiting to come in here to see you." Now I was tripping because the only Monica I could think of was my ex, but she lived in Atlanta. It couldn't be her! Shit this wasn't a good look, shorty was fatal attraction, that's why I broke up with her in the first place.

"That might be my ex, babe, the one who tried to beat my kids' mother's ass."

"Oh, so you do know the bitch?"

"Ma, chill, you bugging right now. I know a lot of Monica's. The only one crazy enough to pop up unannounced is shorty I told you about."

Sabrina was pissed, and I was getting agitated. "Why you mad at me? I ain't got nothing to do with her popping up." She rolled her eyes, crossed her legs and turned to face away from me. I stared at her legs under the summer dress. I was feening to feel up under it, but that expression on her face made it obvious she was not in the mood. Then out the corner of my eye I noticed everybody looking towards the entrance. I shook my head, mumbling under my breath. "This shit is crazy!" All eyes were on her as she strutted down the aisle, literally, as if she was a runway model. Her long silky hair ruffled in the breeze under a straw beach hat. She wore white Chanel sunglasses, a pair of white linen capri pants that hugged her wide hips. Her belt was blue, accentuated with gold Chanel monograms on a wide gold buckle. Her blouse matched the pants, and her 3-inch heel, ankle-strapped sandals completed the outfit. I'm not gonna lie, she looked stunning.

In her over-the-top fashion, she walked right up to our table. Putting her back to Sabrina, she placed her hand on her hip, tilted her head to the side to add a lil sass and said, "You just gonna sit there? Get up and give me a hug!" Typical Monica, thinking the world revolved around her.

"Monica, what are you doing here? I didn't invite you." She took a seat on the bench next to me, then replied, "I wanted to surprise you, don't you miss me?" leaning in trying to kiss me on my cheek.

"A-YO stop! You bugging right now, don't you see me sitting here with my visit?" She feigned surprise, then turned towards Sabrina extending her hand. "Hi, my name is Monica, I'm an old friend of Shawn's." If looks could kill, Monica would be dead, and I wouldn't be alive to tell this story. Sabrina ignored the hand offered to her; I could tell from the tone of her voice that she was two seconds away from catching a case. "Shawn, you better tell your bitch to leave before I put my hands on her!" For all her prissy ways, Monica wasn't no slouch. I've witnessed her start and finish numerous cat fights with other women I dealt with in the past. It's one of the reasons I cut her off. Shorty was extra!

"Who you calling a bitch? Bitch!" I stood up quick and got in between them. I had to defuse the situation before the C.O.'s got involved. "I got this babe, chill!" I told Sabrina, while grabbing Monica by the waist and directing her away from the table. It took a lot of persuading, but I got Monica to leave with the promise of allowing her to visit the next day. Monica was the first to crash a visit, but she certainly was not the last. Sabrina blamed it on my Facebook page, but I didn't agree. If someone wanted to find out where I was, they could Google me. I'd show up on the prison data base regardless. To prove to her that I was committed to our relationship, all of my exes and a few of the random pop-ups were placed on my Visitor Rejection List. And of course, my Facebook page was deleted.

As things got better between us, Sabrina and I started discussing the possibility of going through the process of getting married. We were ready to take things to the next level. However, both of our families were against it. My family thought I should wait until my release before committing to another marriage. Her family was adamantly opposed to her marrying an inmate. But the more our peoples were opposed to our relationship, the closer we got. We became Bonnie and Clyde, us against the world. She was quickly becoming my ride or die.

Getting married meant qualifying for conjugal visits. We made our request, got all the paperwork done and got a date for December 11, 2015. I'd been married and divorced, yet on the day we were scheduled to get married I was nervous. Sabrina looked classy that day dressed conservatively in a cream business suit, and a pair of cream and black riding boots with 3 inch heels. She wore her hair long with a simple part in the middle.

We stood facing each other, the Justice of the Peace was administering vows to another couple. Sabrina grabbed my hand sensing my nervousness. "Look at you, your hands are sweating. Let me find out you're scared!"

"I'm not gonna front babe, I'm nervous as shit." I said staring into her eyes. She looked so happy, smiling like a schoolgirl. She was glowing, and I felt good about being the source of her happiness.

We took our vows in a small room adjacent to the visiting room. After the exchange of vows and that kiss, we stepped out of the room holding hands. Other inmates and their visitors congratulated us. Sabrina held up her wedding and engagement ring. "I can't believe we did this babe. I'm so happy. We're married now and that dick officially belongs to me." She reached under the table, grabbing my manhood for emphasis.

Our first conjugal visit was scheduled for the second weekend of March, 2016. I could not sleep the night before that first conjugal. I stayed up packing the items allowed for the two days we would be on the visit. The following morning, myself and two other guys were summoned on the intercom to report to the "FAMILY REUNION PROGRAM" for processing.

The conjugal visit units were situated on the other side of the prison in a secluded area up on a hill. Me and the other two guys were processed then escorted in a van up to the units. We arrived before our visits (wives) and had 30-40 minutes to clean our assigned units before they arrived.

There were six units divided in three individual homes. Each unit consists of two bedrooms, a full bath, kitchenette and living room. I opened the windows to air it out. Cleaned the refrigerator and bathroom before Sabrina arrived. The other guys and I helped the women with their belongings once the van arrived. Sabrina and I unpacked her things, placing the food and beverages in the cabinets and refrigerator. Soon as we were done with that, I grabbed her around the waist, taking her into my embrace. "You know your ass is in trouble right," planting a kiss on her lips while palming her ass. She wiggled out of my embrace and ran into the bathroom. I started laughing and called after her. "Your ass can't run from me all weekend!" I heard her running the shower. She yelled back, "Let me freshen up babe. You know the ride up from the Bronx was long. Plus they took like hours to process us."

I wasn't trying to hear all that, I grabbed the door handle shaking it, "Oh, you locked the door on me!" I could hear her laughing over the sound of the shower running. I figured I may as well finish unpacking her things. She brought bed sheets and a comforter, so I made the bed, lit some incense, and threw on a Maxwell CD to get the mood right.

Sabrina emerged from the bathroom 20 minutes later wrapped in a towel, immediately dipping into the bedroom and locking the door behind her. I shook my head saying to myself 'women'!

I decided to step outside. There were swings for the kids to play. Picnic tables situated in front of every unit with barbeque grills for cooking out in the summer months. I headed to the half basketball court set up for us to use. For 20 minutes I shot free throws before I got bored and headed back inside. I was greeted with the scent of fried fish when I entered our unit. My mouth watered immediately. I didn't 't realize how hungry I was until that moment. I hadn't eaten since the night before. But the sight of Sabrina standing in front of the stove in purple lace Victoria Secret lingerie with a black garter belt, stockings and pair of black stilettos took my breath away. Her smooth chocolate skin was the perfect contrast to the purple lace. Sabrina looked over her shoulder and giggled at the shocked expression on my face. I stood, stuck at that spot staring at her. The sight of her voluptuous body sent a rush of steaming hot blood straight to my crotch.

"You like what you see?" She teased, twirling her body 360° giving me a peak of her crotchless panties. I walked up to her, palming her ass, then leaned into her.

"What you cook Ma, red snapper?" She nudged me and replied, "No this is Whiting, but I got some Red Snapper between these legs for you." I wrapped my arms around her waist, pressing myself against her. I kissed her neck and whispered in her ear, "As long as your snapper don't bite and smell like fish." She jabbed me in the ribs with her elbow. "Boy don't play; my shit always smells fresh."

"I'm just fucking with you Ma...you look sexy as hell!"

She adjusted the knob on the stove to low, turned to face me kissing me on the lips, then grabbed my dick through my pants. "I want you to fuck me in your Timbs babe, go put them on." She didn't have to ask me twice. I replied, "Say no more," patted her on the ass, then headed to the bathroom. I took a quick shower, and when I emerged from the bathroom, a black silk pajama set was laid out across the bed for me. The Timbs were right at the foot of the bed. I lotioned up, a nigga can't be ashy. I splashed on some Blue Nile cologne, slipped on the silk pajamas and Timbs, then stepped out of the room.

The curtains were drawn, lights were dimmed. Soft music was playing in the background. I found Sabrina laying on the sofa bed in the living room with her legs spread wide open. She was sucking on her titties while playing with her pussy at the same time. When she noticed me, she spread her pussy lips exposing herself to me. "The darker the berry, the pinker the pussy," was the thought that came to mind. Her fingers glistened with her juices. "You wanna eat me, or eat your lunch first?" She purred.

I was mesmerized, stuck, I had no words to reply. I walked towards her. She sat up and reached for my crotch, fumbling with the slit at the front of my pajama pants. She freed my manhood and stared at it in wonder and amazement. She started stroking it while staring up into my eyes. Then she kissed the tip. "Your dick is fucking huge!" She said in a sultry voice. Then ran her tongue down the shaft. "I fucking love you Shawn. I'mma be whatever you want me to be... your cum-drinking whore, your slut, whatever!"

I palmed the back of her head, guiding her mouth to my dick. "You were talking all that shit right, stop talking and suck this dick!" She took me into her mouth. I closed my eyes as her warm mouth engulfed the head. It felt so hot, so good. I wanted to see if she could live up to all her boasts. Claiming her head game was on 1,000. She swallowed half before gagging. I smiled, knowing she couldn't swallow me whole. My dick matched my shoe size, 11½. "Suck it like you love it," I said, forcing myself an inch deeper. She choked, drooling saliva down her chin. I released my grip on her head so she could recover. She pulled back, then lubricated my dick with her saliva by running her tongue up and down the length of me.

"Wait a minute." I said, pulling my pajama pants down to my ankles, stepping out of them. I stepped back in front of her with my dick pointing directly in front of her face. She reached up and started fumbling with the buttons on my pajama shirt. I helped her with the top two buttons. I shrugged the shirt off and stood there naked with my Timbs on. She pulled me closer to her, running her hands across my stomach. My shit was chis-eled, washboard. I looked down at her with my hands on my waist feeling like the king of New York as she admired my body. Then she resumed, grabbing my dick, spitting on it with plenty saliva. She took me into her mouth again, going beyond the halfway mark before gagging. She had her own lil technique of forcing my dick deeper down her throat until she gagged before taking it out completely, then going deeper and taking more of me. I didn't think she could do it until she took me into her mouth with her tongue sticking out like a dog. I grabbed the back of her head and forced my entire dick down her throat. My balls hung low and heavy with cum. I hadn't touched myself in months. I was saving myself for this occasion. I was momentarily lost in the warmth of her mouth as I began to fuck her face, my nuts slapping the bottom of her chin with every stroke. "Damn!" Sabrina definitely had skills. Any women who could deep throat me had extraordinary gag reflexes. She must have sensed me coming to a climax as that feeling of pure ecstasy was erupting from deep inside me. She pulled away and looked up intently into my eyes. "Cum in my mouth baby, cum for me." Opening her mouth wide, sticking her tongue out as I erupted like a volcano. A long stream of sperm shot onto her nose, forehead and eyes, nearly covering her entire face. She grabbed my dick, guiding my nutt into her open mouth. I wanted to cover her tongue, milking my dick, swallowing every last drop. I stared at her in amazement, "I married a fucking porn star!" I said to myself. She drank my cum and smeared it all over her face as if it was youth cream.

I got down between her legs as she reclined on the couch. Her legs were spread wide, and I started eating her pussy like a starving lunatic. I slid my middle finger in her ass while sucking on her clit. I could tell by her moans and how she pressed my head into her that she was loving it. So, I slipped another finger in her ass and finger fucked her ass while sucking her clit. She started grinding her pussy against my mouth.

I picked up the pace, finger fucking her asshole and applying more pressure to her clit, sucking it with intensity. I could sense her coming to an orgasm as her asshole started to contract, squeezing my fingers tight, so I finger fucked her faster and faster still sucking her clit at the same time. She started to shake and tried to pull away from me, I held on tight until her climax was spent. I removed my fingers from her ass. It was glistening with a clear liquid. I sniffed, curious, I thought it could be shit but it had no scent. My baby's ass was good enough to eat. But I wanted to see what that pussy was like. My dick was harder than stone. "Turn around," I said to her. She was breathless and I hadn't fucked her yet. She rolled over placing her knees on the floor, the top half of her body on the couch. The sight of her brown skin had me amped. I was going to murder the pussy and that's exactly what I did. I smacked her ass and grabbed a handful of her hair. "Spread your ass for me!" She looked over her shoulder. I smacked her ass harder. "You heard what I said!" Then I yanked her hard pulling her hair. "Okay daddy" she replied, spreading her ass cheeks wide for me. All I saw was asshole and the pink of her pussy. I guided my dick into her waiting pussy. The pussy was hot, tight and wet. I slid inside of her until my dick head reached her cervix. Her walls hugged my dick like a latex glove. I began to pump into her slow. I leaned forward and whispered in her ear,

"You love me?"

"Yes daddy."

"Don't lie to me!'

"No daddy, I love you!" She purred.

I smacked her ass hard. Then began to drill her at a steady medium pace. Her pussy juices foaming white on my dick. I wasn't in the mood to make love. I wanted to bruise her. Beat the pussy up.

"Whose pussy is this?" I said smacking her ass in between strokes.

"Oh, fuck me daddy!" She moaned.

I smacked her ass harder. "Bitch, who's pussy is this?"

"Your pussy daddy, ooh it's your pussy." She gasped.

I started fucking her harder, going deeper, and deeper. I knew she was in pain, but it was the pain that brought her pleasure. The sight of my dick sliding in and out of her pussy mixed with her ass bouncing against my pelvis was enough to make me cum. But I was on a mission, she was going to cum before me. She reached underneath and grabbed my nuts every time I stroked into her. I was about to erupt so I pulled out, giving myself time to recover. I wasn't ready to nutt just yet. I bent down and started eating her ass. She reached behind me and pressed the back of my head deeper into her ass. I spread her cheeks wider so my tongue could go deeper. She was moaning with intensity.

I was in that freak mode... I positioned myself behind her, sliding my dick into her pussy. I pumped a few times, lubricating my dick with her pussy juices, then I slid out of her pussy and entered her ass. Her asshole felt so tight, it felt like a rug burn on the side of my dick. I spread her ass wide so I could go deeper with each stroke...then I leaned into her and reached under her so I could massage her clit at the same time. "Oh, fuck me, fuck me!" She moaned. And I did, going all the way in and out. "Smack my ass, smack my ass!" She begged and in between every stroke I smacked her ass.

"Fuck me, fuck my ass harder." She repeated over and over.

"Oh, fuck me, don't stop, fuck me, fuck me, don't stop..." I fucked her ass until I was about to cum, she took my dick fresh out of her ass and sucked all the cum out. I collapsed on top of her.

That entire weekend was a fuck marathon. But we did make love the last night together.

The feeling was so intense. Our bodies were in the missionary position. Her soft moans were like an erotic melody that plunged me to depths of emotions I didn't know existed.

As much as we enjoyed our conjugal visits, the last night was always the most difficult because we're forced to part ways until the next visit.

Being in a relationship on lockdown isn't easy, but Sabrina and I make it work. She's still rocking with me today. So, don't believe what they tell you, finding love in prison is possible…. I'm a believer, … I found love on lockdown!

17

# FOR MY MAN

**Samantha DaSilva**
City/State: Laurel, Maryland
Social Media: Snapchat
Fall, 2018

Whoever said love will make you do the craziest things knew exactly what they were talking about? I'm no Terry McMillan, and this isn't a "Stella got her groove back" story. My story and hers is only similar in that I found my love during my two years living abroad in Jamaica.

I'm an American woman through and through, but growing up in the DMV area, I was raised in a Caribbean culture so naturally I was attracted to Caribbean men. When I met Damion, I was not looking for love. I'm a Hotel Resort Manager who was tasked by the corporate heads to manage one of our locations in Jamaica for one year. That year turned into two years, and when my stint was through, I returned to the states with a new husband, and a whole new attitude.

Like most newlyweds our marriage started off beautiful.

Damion didn't take long getting adjusted to life in America. He flourished, and with success came a wondering eye. I'm not a super jealous woman but I'm very territorial. The first incident I found out about was him meeting a woman on a dating app and inviting her to our vacation home in Jamaica for two weeks. Yes, I said it correctly. And while they were down there, she posted numerous pictures of herself and my husband kissing and lying in our bed together, in our home, and in my car with my stepchildren. That was just one of his many online dating scandals. After our latest break-up experience due to his infidelities, I came to the conclusion that I needed to do what I had to do to make this marriage work. I was willing to please my man. So, like the open-minded person I am I figured if my man wanted excitement, I'd be the one controlling the narrative, and bring that excitement home to him.

After months of testing the waters, I finally decided that if the opportunity presented itself, I would run with it. And that's exactly what occurred on this one particular night. It was 10:30p.m. and I'd been sitting behind my desk at work, putting in overtime as usual, finishing some paperwork when my phone buzzed on the desk. I checked the screen and saw it was this chick who I'd met on Snapchat who called herself "Tasty-Cake." To be clear I don't consider myself gay or bi, but I have dabbled on an occasion or two in the past. I'd been planning to invite Tasty Cake over for the past three months to try out some new games with me and my husband but hadn't gotten around to it. Maybe I was putting it off due to a subconscious fear. But her call that night put me in a different mood.

After two rings I answered the phone, "Hello! Wassup lovely?" Yeah! I could come off smooth like a dude if I needed to! I got skills.

"I'm feeling horny tonight and thought about what you proposed, I want to fuck! Will you come for me?"

In my mind I'm saying, "Oh yeah?" I replied, "Go take a shower and get that pussy right, I'll pick you up in an hour."

It was around 12:00a.m. when I pulled up to Tasty's house. She hopped in my car and we headed straight to my townhouse. On the drive there, I reached over to check her pussy to make sure she was on point. She didn't have on any panties, so I parted her pussy lips, this bitch barely passed.

Tasty Cake was also from Jamaica. She stood 5' tall even, weighed about 130 lbs. She wore a nude, skintight tube dress that hugged her slim yet thick frame. Her skin was smooth milk chocolate that contrasted with her long blond dreads which reached down to her thick firm ass. Her butt and thighs were nicely toned by all the squats she did regularly. Her ass reminded me of a juicy plum.

We pulled up to my house and entered it to find Damion laying on the living room sofa sound asleep. I directed Tasty Cake to the kitchen to get us some liquor, then I went to run the water in the jacuzzi.

Back in the kitchen Tasty was sitting on the bar stool with her legs open. I popped open a bottle of D'usse VSOP and we both took two shots to the head. I told Tasty to follow me into the shower. My mind was made up. Any chick I'm putting my mouth on, I'm washing myself. I took off my clothes, wiggling out of my bra and panties. I stood a few inches taller than Tasty, at 5'4" tall, my skin tone is sort of a light cornmeal color. I'm super thick with big 40DD titties, thick thighs and a juicy plump phat ass. A real junk in the trunk booty.

While we were in the shower, I washed my ass, pussy and the rest of my body then turned my attention to Tasty as she focused on washing her pussy. I used my sponge to soap her from head to toe, rubbing her nipples gently. Her titties were little with big areolas. I could cup her breast with one hand. They sat nicely and looked succulent.

I rubbed her breasts repeatedly then started sucking them

while my sponged hand made its way down between her legs and began washing her pussy. I rubbed between her pussy lips with the soap, then massaged her clitoris with my index finger. I felt my pussy getting wet as she let out a soft moan. My warm pussy juice started to run out of me and down my thighs. She started sucking on my breast while I continued rubbing her clit with my left hand, and with my right I slid my finger between the crack of her ass, fingering her ass crack. The water ran over both our bodies, then we started kissing each other, rubbing our bodies together passionately. I replaced my two fingers back on her clit, rubbing it in a circular motion while kissing her at the same time. In our intimacy the bathroom got really steamy.

In her pictures, Tasty's pussy print made her pussy look small. Her frame was small, but her tunnel felt deep when I slid my middle finger inside her. Tasty returned the favor sliding her fingers inside my slippery pussy. I removed my fingers from her pussy and placed it in her mouth. She continued to slide two fingers inside me and we both brought each other to a climax. Soon after it occurred to us that my husband was in the living room. We cut it short, finished washing up and got our fine asses out of the shower.

I entered the living room wearing a robe, while Tasty had on nothing but a wife beater. Tasty went into the kitchen for another shot before placing herself on the couch opposite from the sofa where my husband laid. I called out to him in a low tone, "Babe wake up, wake up babe." Damion roused from his sleep to find Tasty staring at him. "This is Tasty babe; she came to visit." Damion stared back at her as she sipped on her glass of D'usse. I sat on the loveseat sipping on Hennessey, straight no chaser, because I knew my mind was made up, I was going to blow Tasty's mind. Damion said hello to her. I got up and sat next to Tasty pulling her shirt over her head. I asked Damion, "Did he like her breasts?" He replied by shaking his head up and down in the affirmative. I knew my husband well, he's a shy sneaky freak. The kind that played innocent in your presence but will bend a strange chick over and eat her ass in a heartbeat.

I started to rub her breasts and told him to come rub them too. He got up, his lean 6'2" tall frame momentarily hovered over us. I could make out that 10 inch thick, pelvis punishing dick of his bulging out of his sweatpants. I swear every time I take his dick, I have to adjust my mind and my pussy. The dick pressure was always unbearable, I sometimes wondered why I kept him around, I guess I loved the pain, it came with the pleasure. I could tell he was nervous, so I got up and told them I'd be back. I proceeded to dim the lights throughout the house. After I returned, I stood by the dining room and watched him kiss her, and without my consent, he proceeded to go down on her, eating her pussy. That's when I entered the room to join them.

I directed Tasty to get on her knees so she could suck him off because if he ate her pussy, she was going to suck his dick in return. She started to suck him slowly and the more inch she took in, the more her gag reflexes got louder. I got behind her and started licking her pussy from the back. It didn't take long for her pussy to soak up my tongue with her juices. She came moments later all in my mouth. I didn't stop there, I then spread her ass cheeks as wide as I could and started pushing my tongue in the hole of her ass while she was sucking my husband's dick.

Damian must have wanted to sample her pussy because he stopped her from sucking his dick, got up and maneuvered himself onto the couch and gestured for Tasty to climb on top of him. She turned in the reverse cowgirl position facing me and started riding his dick. I placed my face between their legs and sucked on her clit while she was riding his dick. I glanced up and her facial expression told me she was in pain. I rattled my tongue on her clit, and she started cumming so hard I could see it running down his dick. I tightened my lips together, blowing and sucking on her clit making wet whistle sounds. She started riding his dick faster and faster bringing herself to an orgasm.

We switched positions. I laid on the floor and Tasty climbed off his dick and got on top of me. I spread my legs and pussy lips to expose my fleshy inside. Tasty placed her pussy on top of mine and we were clit to clit. The sensation felt so good I started rubbing and whining up against her waist. My husband got behind Tasty and between my legs with her still on top of me. He started fucking her doggy style. Tasty and I continued grinding our pussies together while Damion was fucking her, and we kept fucking in that position until Tasty reached another orgasm. Afterwards we all took a break and drank a couple more shots of D'usse.

Twenty minutes later we headed to the jacuzzi. It was always my fantasy to watch a live porn scene, so my intent was to chill. I was enjoying the experience, but I knew my husband like the back of my hand. He nicknamed me suction pump by the way I gave him head. I knew what he wanted so I started to stroke his dick under the water with one hand while I played with Tasty's pussy with the other. I pulled her closer so we all could kiss together.

Damion stood up out of the water. I grabbed his penis and begin to suck it, locking my lips together like a tight vagina. I put the entire 10inches into my mouth until it reached the back of my throat, then letting it rest there. I could feel his penis throbbing at the back of my throat as Tasty licked and sucked his balls. I loosened my grip on his dick and began to move my head up and down, twirling my head around as I had his dick in my mouth, working it with no hands. Then I lubricated it with saliva, licking and spitting on it before swallowing his entire dick deep in my throat.

Tasty begins playing with my pussy. I reach for my double-headed dildo sitting on the side of the jacuzzi and rubbed it against Tasty's pussy, while I'm still sucking Damion's dick. I took his dick out and slapped it against my jaw over and over again before placing it back into my mouth. His dick grows harder in my mouth, I know he's ready, so I stand up and bend over. He doesn't hesitate, he slides his dick inside me. Ahhhh, it felt so fucking good. I grab Tasty and bend her over and slide the dildo inside her while Damion is fucking me. After 10-15 pumps, he's cumming inside me. Damian then climbs out of the jacuzzi leaving me and Tasty alone together.

Tasty and I begin kissing. I climb on top of her while she still had one end of the dildo inside her. I put the other end inside me. We start fucking and kissing in the jacuzzi. I'm rubbing her clit while riding her. My titties are bouncing up and down, then she grabs them and starts to suck on both of them squeezing them together. After a while our pussies are super soaked, we change positions with her on top. She's riding me with the double-headed dildo. I'm holding onto her waist as she continues to ride me. I feel her body start to tremble, I take the dildo out of her and start to suck her pussy while I'm playing with mine. We both have an orgasm at the same time. Moments later Tasty and I climb out of the jacuzzi drenched in sweat. We head to the bedroom and lay across the bed taking another break. We sip Hennessy while we build the mood back up.

After a while Damion enters the room, he's carrying a cup of ice looking over at Tasty who was laying on her back. I watched as he flips Tasty over and pulls her to the edge of the bed by her feet. I take out my bullet sex toy and sat in the recliner chair opening my legs to allow the vibration to massage my clit.

I observe the scene play out as Damion arches her ass in the air. He takes an ice cube from his cup and slide it down the crack of her ass then inserts the cube into her asshole. He begins slurping the melted ice water seeping out of her ass. Tasty moans and moans until her moans turned into cries. I got up, walked over and placed my hand under her and started rubbing her clit. Then I climbed on the bed, slide underneath her and started sucking on her pussy. We lay in the 69 position with her on top. Damion comes to the edge of the bed and starts slapping my pussy with his dick while Tasty is sucking on my clit. I place the bullet in Tasty's pussyhole and continue sucking on her clit. Damion pushes an ice cube as far as he can inside my pussy then takes another ice cube and inserts it inside Tasty's pussy.

Damion begins fucking my hole with the ice cube inside me. I could feel it melting and hitting against my pussy walls as he power drills inside me. At the same time, I'm sucking the melting ice water from Tasty's pussy. He sinks his dick deeper inside me and it felt so good I begin sucking harder on Tasty's clit. I take the bullet out of her pussy and push my tongue as far as I could in her. She's fucking my face letting me know my tongue is hitting her spot. She cums all over my face as I continued to rattle my tongue inside her.

Damion rotates Tasty's body while she's still on top of me. I'm lying flat on my back; she lays back flat on top of me. Both of our legs are open exposing our pussies. Damion grabs the dildo and fucks my hole with it. Then he works his dick in and out both our holes, going back and forth while massaging our clits. He works that dick in and out both of our pussies then pulls his dick out and bends down to start licking and sucking both our pussies. Using his fingers and tongue he plays in our vaginas at the same time. Then he slides his middle finger deep in my ass while tonguing Tasty's asshole, licking up all the cum that was pouring out her pussy. He gets up, pulls Tasty off me and flips her onto her stomach. Then he spits in her asshole and slides his dick in it. He begins fucking her ass with a lot of thrust and force until he came in her ass. I laid there playing with my pussy until I came. We were all beyond satisfied. All three of us hopped in the shower and afterwards I took Tasty home.

It was two months before I finally got a text from Tasty. "Hey wet-wet, call me!" I smiled and returned her text. "Hey lil pussy where you been?" Her reply was "Call me girl we need to talk." Okay this sounded serious, so I stepped out of the office and into the bathroom, locking the door so as not to be disturbed.

"Hey girl what's up?" I spoke into the phone as soon as she answered.

"Hey Sam, how are you doing?" I stared at my phone like bitch I didn't call you for idle conversation! So, I spoke a little more urgently. "What is it you needed to talk about?" She hesitated then exhaled… "Sam I'm pregnant!" I looked at the phone like what the fuck. Then said, "Okay and why are you telling me?"

"You know why Sam, I'm pregnant by your husband!"

"Oh no you ain't bitch?" I replied hanging up the phone. Who did that bitch Tasty think she was fooling? Ain't no way in the world she was pregnant by my husband. My anxieties went on overload. My heart was beating out of control. If she was truly pregnant, it didn't mean it was my husband who impregnated her. I paced the bathroom back and forth for 20 minutes before splashing water on my face to clear my mind… I stared at myself in the mirror and said out loud, "Samantha if that bitch is pregnant by your husband, she better get rid of it… I'll do a homemade procedure on that bitch myself…"

Two months later I drove up to Tasty's house to see what her update was. I looked through the window before knocking and to my surprise she was in the living room getting fucked sledgehammer position on her couch. I knocked! She came to the door with just a sheet wrapped around her. She told me the pregnancy was a false alarm and offered an invitation for me to join the fun…

18

---

# BREAK UP – NO MAKE UP

**Leslie Andrews**
Social Media: Hi 5
Silver Spring, Maryland
Summer, 2019

It's been over 11 months, two days, and 3 hours since breaking up with the love of my life. I've been moping around the house trying to figure out what's next. Not to mention, I haven't had sex in over a year. Prior to our break-up I stopped giving up the pussy to my partner. As much as I wanted the pain I was feeling to go away, I could never see myself starting all over again in a new relationship. Meeting new people is never easy, especially when coming out of an 18-year relationship like mine.

Walking away from who I believed to be the love of my life was not the easiest thing to do. But, after years and years of lies, infidelity and insecurities, it was surely time for me to move on.

The straw that broke the camel's back was catching my life partner in the car sucking on another woman's pussy. I'll never forget the sight of her head buried between that hoe's legs, literally going in. That was it for me, I called it quits right there on the spot. Closing that chapter in my life was devastating, and the heart repairing process was taking way to long.

During our break-up I consumed myself with work and exercise. I did anything to avoid thinking of the heartache and pain. One day my best friend Amy popped up at my house unannounced. She was concerned because for weeks I hadn't taken any calls.

Amy was one of the few people who knew where I hid the spare key to my house. She entered after knocking on the door for five minutes. Why couldn't she just simply leave me alone?

When Amy entered my house, she found me laying in my favorite spot, the leather sectional in the living room. "Bitch get up!" She said, pulling back the curtains. I covered my eyes from the bright rays of sunlight, "It's a new day, and way past time for a NEW ATTITUDE. You need to stop tripping over Tamara because you best believe she damn sure ain't tripping over you. You're better than this Les!"

I forgot to mention, my name is Leslie, Les for short. I'm not your average female by far. I grew up in the "Barry Farms" section of south-east, Washington, D.C. where more likely if you were a female, you were a freak, dyke or both. And if you grew up in the church you were down to give a guy head before giving up your virginity. But for me I was a girl who grew up loving the smell and taste of pussy. Clean pussy that is!

I love pussy. Sweet pussy, tight pussy, loose pussy, phat pussy, wet pussy, deep pussy, slim pussy. I even loved a girl with an ugly pussy. Just as long as the pussy is juicy, I'll love it. I just love women. Short women, tall women, thick women, I even dated a super BBW. But I prefer those I.G women (Instagram models). They're the freakiest and wildest. However, I happened to meet Tamara, my ex, on Hi 5, aka, "the jump off site."

Tamara was a P.G. county girl. After about two weeks since

connecting online, we both decided on a date to meet up for dinner. The plan was to meet at the Eastover Shopping center. Tamara was sitting in her wine color Nissan Maxima near the Popeyes when I pulled into the parking lot. We were at the center of the hood, off Indian Head Highway. I walked up to her car after parking my Ford Expedition. She was leaning against the hood of her car, and greeted me with a hug. After our embrace she opened the passenger door for me. I got in her car, and after she climbed behind the wheel, we drove out to Tyson's Corner, a large shopping mall in Northern Virginia.

We stepped into the 'Long Horn Steakhouse' for our first date. I ordered a house salad because I don't eat red meat... except pussy of course. Dinner turned out nice, and afterwards we sat in the parking lot talking, getting better acquainted with each other.

Tamara was what we in the LGBTQ community considered to be a "Dom" (Dominate Female). Her hair was cut short in a fade tapered near her temple and back neckline. Her clothes were cut close in the European males' style. She reminded me of the WNBA player, Kristi Toliver, even with her smile and round face. Now I'm what you'd call a "Fem" (femine female). A true glam doll with big titties that sit pretty. My titties are so huge they take away from my narrow, plump ass. My booty may be small, but this thang can shake and jiggle.

About an hour into our conversation we started kissing. Tamara smelled like cherries. Her lips were so soft and tasted like cupcakes, I couldn't contain myself. The intensity grew so strong that I wanted to sample her pussy, eat her out in the front seat of her car, but I kept my desires in check and allowed her to take the lead. She must have felt that deep sexual energy between us because she started rubbing my thigh with her hand, slowly making her way up to my nipples. She found them erect and poking through my shirt.

"Oh, my fucking goodness, that's my spot. I caaann't...., oh I caaan't...., stooop!" I moaned breathlessly, pulling away from her embrace. "Let's head back," I said, trying hard to resist her touch. She kissed me again, then we pulled off and headed back to D.C.

When we got back to Eastover Shopping Center Tamara asked me what did I have planned for the rest of the night? She invited me over to her place in Landover, Maryland. I was a little hesitant. Her place was across town out of my neck of the hood. But my juices were still soaking up my thong, and I secretly wanted to see how far things would go. I shrugged my shoulders, "Sure, I'm game!" I jumped in my vehicle and followed behind her.

It took us 25 minutes to reach her townhouse. I parked in the space next to her then followed her inside. After entering her home, I discreetly looked around to make sure there were no signs of another woman living there. Tamara's place was very nice and clean. A three-level townhouse. Tamara offered me a seat in the living room and excused herself saying she would return shortly. I took it upon myself to search for the bathroom to freshen up. I found one in the hallway near the front door.

In the bathroom I pulled out my baby wipes to clean my private parts, then another to wipe my body down. Tamara had a his/her sink. I sprayed on some body spray, took off my thong and bra, placing them into my purse. When I stepped out of the bathroom, I'd decided to ruffle through her kitchen cabinets and took it upon myself to pour both of us a glass of Remy Martin. Ten minutes later while I'm sitting on the couch sipping on my drink and scrolling through my phone, Tamara enters the living room wearing nothing but a bow tie and heels. Her titties were small, perky and pretty. Her stomach was flat, ripped and chiseled into a six pack. Her pussy was waxed bald with only a thin landing strip of hair down the middle. I'm staring at her. She walked towards me and placed her left leg on the arm of the couch.

"You like what you see?" My eyes were glued to her pussy. "Liking is one thing, but tasting is another!" I took my two fingers and part her pussy lips, exposing her clitoris. I leaned forward, taking a closer look at it. Her clit looked like a small bean. I wanted to flick it with my tongue, and as soon as it met her pussy, I found it dripping wet.

I blew softly on her clit and swiped her pussy lips with all tongue. I moved front to back, back and forth like a surfboard on water. Her pussy was so hot, sweet and juicy, just the way I liked it. I was determined to make it erupt like a volcano, feenin to taste her lava.

I took her left leg and placed it on top of my shoulder and continued to suck her pussy. I stuck two fingers inside her, she was sticky and wet. I fingered and tongue fucked her pussy at the same time while using my thumb to rub her clitoris. Tamara let out a deep sinuous moan grabbing my head as more of her juices started to pour out of her onto my tongue. I stopped, turned her around and bent her over the coffee table. Then I spread her ass cheeks and thighs so I could suck, and finger fuck her pussy from behind.

Tamara was loving it, moaning, and panting as if she was out of breath. "Oh, I love you, I love you, I love you," she repeated over and over again on that first night. I sucked up all her juices, massaging my thumb on her clit, while my tongue was buried inside her pussy, tongue fucking her until she reached her second orgasm.

I stopped to take a sip of my Remy, then spat some into her pussy. I sucked it out of her, then laid back on the couch, spreading my legs wide like wings on an eagle. Tamara turned to face me, positioning herself in the 69 position. Her pussy was in my face and mine was in hers. We sucked each other into a frenzy, ejaculating in each other's mouths.

The intimacy was at a high level. I felt so connected to her. We switched to the scissors position. Our legs were intertwined, our clits rubbing against each other's. Our breasts were mashed together rubbing against each other's. We started kissing with deep intimacy. The sensation was incredible. I could feel her clit grow stiff against mine. That's when I took my fingers and began to rub her clit real fast. Tamara started moaning and breathing heavy, grinding and humping into my hand. I started tapping her clit over and over until her cum squirted out spraying my hand.

We laid on the couch catching our breaths. Then Tamara stands, grabs my hand and led me upstairs into her bedroom. I immediately noticed a swing hanging next to her bed. She places me in the swing, securing both my hands and feet in buckle straps. My legs are spread far apart. I'm completely nude at this point. My heart is racing, I don't know what to expect as I watch her enter the closet. She emerges wearing a super large strap-on dildo. My heart beats faster as she walks towards me with this devilish grin. I'm helpless and have nowhere to go with my wrist and ankles buckled to the swing. Tamara begins pouring oil on the head of this 14-inch, strap-on. She stands between my legs and begins fingering me. And real smooth like, she slowly guides the head of the dildo into me.

Omg! It's so big, but that big dildo feels so damn good. She humps in and out of me with the motion of the swing. The feeling is so bomb I feel myself erupting into an instant orgasm. Tamara seems to know my body because she pulls me in close to her and starts drilling into me using the motion of the swing. She's holding my waist with both hands. My moans get louder and louder, I erupt and cum so hard I can feel it running out of my pussy down the crack of my ass. Tamara pulls out of my pussy with that super large dildo and sucks the rest of the cum out of my pussy. The flow is so heavy that she follows the stream down my ass hole and licks it up.

I barely recovered from that orgasm when Tamara reinserts the dildo back inside me. She then places a vibrating bullet on my clit. She takes two small clamp vibrators and clip them on my nipples. She begins to fuck me with the strap-on, the bullet is on my clit, and the vibrating clamps are on my nipples. To top it off, she leans into me, reaches around and inserts her middle finger into my asshole, all while she's tongue kissing me. I lose control, the sensations are too much to control. I shake, shiver and convulse into a deep gut-wrenching orgasm. I squirted so hard it sprayed out like a shower head.

For the rest of the night Tamara and I drank, sucked, fucked and made love, experiencing more orgasms than I could count. Around 5:30 in the morning we were passed out from that previous night wrapped in each other's arms and awakened by the morning sun seeping through her parted curtains.

That was the thought running through my mind when Amy parted the curtains in my living room that day. It felt like déjà vu. In that moment I was reliving the joy of that magical first night with Tamara.

I'm not going to lie, I was tempted to call her right then and there. I missed her so bad it ached. The connection we once shared seemed like it would never and could never be broken. Eighteen years of love was a long time, and here I was lost and alone without her.

Amy stared at me, she seemed to read my thoughts. "Bitch snap out of it and get her out of your mind, because tonight we're going out to have fun!"

I was not in any mood to party. I wasn't interested in meeting new people. I wanted to be left alone. I rolled over and covered myself with my blanket.

"Oh no you didn't!" Amy yanked it right off me. "Les, get your ass up. We're going out and this time you're going to find some real dick to get you right."

I thought to myself "Real dick?" I hadn't experienced a man

in nearly 20 years. I doubt I would find one packing like that 14-inch, strap-on Tamara used on me regularly. I looked up at Amy and whined, "Leave me alone, I want to go back to sleep." But of course, annoying ass Amy would not take no for an answer. At that moment I really, truly hated Tamara for doing this to us. This was it, our final break-up. There would be no make-up just to experience another breakup. Reluctantly I got up and got ready for what Amy called my NEW BEGINNING!

THE END?

19

# ONLYFANS

Kyreese_the_beast
  Social Media: Onlyfans.com
  City/State: Miami, Florida

I am a fitness trainer and I also model on the side. I have a decent following on the Gram, but when the Covid pandemic shut down the country it affected my ability to make money. Fortunately for me I stumbled upon another source of income.

One day I received a direct message on my IG account that caught my attention immediately.

"My wife is a fan of the video you posted, which was impressive. How can I arrange something similar in a private setting? Set your price."

I knew exactly what this person was referring to. Since the Covid lockdown I created an Onlyfans account and started posting exclusive live streams for paid subscribers. The exclusive videos were strictly adult content. Well, I can't take full credit for the success of the Onlyfans account. I have a twin brother, and we share the same Instagram and Onlyfans accounts.

I'm Kyrese, and my twin brother's name is Sadiek. Yeah, I know, real ethnic, but it's the names given to us by our parents. We both stand 6'2" tall. Our dreads hang down beyond our shoulders. You can distinguish us by our tattoos and the blond highlights Sadiek sports on his dreads. Otherwise, we are identical from our heads down to our toes. We're both chiseled and pretty much workout fanatics.

We grew up in Liberty City, a section of Miami, Florida, infested with drugs, murder and poverty. Fortunately for us, we escaped our environment winning football scholarships to an S.E.C. college, got our education and never looked back.

Anyway! The video this guy was referring to depicted Sadiek and I double penetrating a tall, voluptuous Brazilian woman with a strong appetite for black men with huge dicks. The video was one of our highest viewed thus far. Our subscribers commented on the contrast between her milky white skin and the deep, black complexion of Sadiek and I. We did to her what the white guys in Evil Angel Ent. porn series have done to women in their movies.

I replied back, "Talk to me, what's the proposition?" I wasn't expecting an immediate response, but when he pinged me right back my interest grew.

"I'm no weirdo, just willing to fulfill my wife's desires." I read the details of his proposition and decided to do a little research on this guy. A quick Google search provided me with a reasonable amount of information. This guy was a wealthy, middle-aged Cuban national. He owned several car dealerships in South Florida. I could definitely charge him a premium for the proposition he was offering.

I sent him a text with my price, plus double if he wanted my brother as part of the deal. He Cashapp'd me half as a deposit, plus a date, time and location. I texted my brother Sadiek and gave him the rundown. He thought it was a strange proposition but considering the amount of money this guy was willing to pay, Sadiek wanted to know the time and place so he could clear his schedule.

Sadiek and I got tested for Covid, cleared it and two weeks later we pulled up to the guard booth of a gated community in Punta Gorda, Florida.

There were three exotic cars parked in the circular driveway of our client's home. I wondered if all three automobiles belonged to the homeowner and his wife.

We were met at the door by the client. He looked the part of a successful businessman who took care of himself.

"Buenos dias." He greeted us under his mask. After checking our temperatures, he removed his mask and gave us a warm smile full of pearly white teeth. His skin was evenly tanned with a few wrinkles appearing on the corners of his eyes. We entered his home, I gave him a firm handshake, and in doing so he handed me a manilla envelope. I peeked inside, looked up at him, then we followed our wealthy client to the living room. He walked to the bar and poured us a drink from a decanter.

"That is the balance amigo. Please have a drink, and in a moment, we can get down to business."

I passed the envelope filled with big faces to my brother and took a swig. The liquor burned my throat, but it was good.

"My wife is upstairs. I explained to her that we were entertaining guests tonight. However, I want to surprise her, so follow me upstairs gentlemen."

Sadiek gave me this peculiar look. I shrugged my shoulders, "Whatever man, this dude is paying, so fuck it." We followed the client up the oval-shaped stairs and into the master suite. I could hear the shower running in the master bathroom. The master suite was set up like a loft with high ceilings. Our client directed us to a set of high-back cushioned seats, which were positioned in front of the 75-inch plasma flat screen television.

To our left was a terrace/balcony with its glass doors open. A soft breeze was flowing through. There was a tripod stand with a camera set up a few feet in front of the king-size bed. This man was about his business, and I realized at that moment I should have drawn up a non-disclosure agreement with this guy. Those thoughts were pushed to the back of my head when he emerged with his wife from the bathroom.

To use the word 'stunning' to describe this woman is an understatement. She was beautiful in the posts on their Instagram page. But I rarely pay Instagram photos much attention because everyone puts on for the Gram and usually looks totally different in person. Our client's wife looked 10x better in the flesh. Sadiek and I glanced at each with a look of amazement.

Our client was leading his wife down a flight of stairs holding her hand. She was blindfolded wearing a pair of red 3-inch heels with matching red lingerie, black stockings and garter belt. She was tall, shapely with long luxurious blond hair. If our client was 50 years old, his wife had to be at least 20 years younger.

There was a sense of excitement in the air. The feeling you get in the pit of your stomach when you know something incredible is about to happen. Our client's wife was giddy with anticipation. I don't know if they did this sort of thing on the regular, but something told me that this was different for her.

She was giggling like a schoolgirl and her husband led her towards the bed. He looked over at Sadiek holding his index finger to his lips. He laid his wife on the bed, kissed her on the lips, whispering something in her ear that caused her to laugh. He motioned Sadiek and I towards the bed, directing us to lay on the left and right side of his wife. I watched as he walked towards the camera sitting on the tripod. His wife was still blindfolded, but she could sense our presence as I watched her breasts rise with each breath of excitement.

"Touch her!" Our client instructed us like a movie director. I chuckled and began to run my hands up her right leg. Sadiek did the same from his side of the bed. Her breathing got

heavier at our touch. Her skin was soft, and the scent of jasmine emanated from her body. I was aroused by her delicateness. She reached over feeling blindly towards my crotch with her right hand, with her left she did the same to Sadiek. She gasped at our stiffness.

"Take off your clothes!" The husband directed us. Sadiek was getting a kick out of this, stripping down to his socks with urgency. I, on the other hand, took my time. I wasn't accustomed to this sort of arrangement. I kept reminding myself that we were being paid for this. As long as he didn't ask us to do some weird shit, I was going to give this rich motherfucker his money's worth.

Sadiek and I laid on each side of our client's wife. Her heavy breathing had increased when she felt our hands roaming her body in unison. We moved as one, giving the effect of one person having four hands. This was not our first time tag-teaming a woman. As teenagers we had plenty of practice running trains on the neighborhood 'hood-rats'. But we perfected our skills in college and when I say we did some things, we did some things to those college co-eds.

To my surprise the husband didn't cut in with some off-hand instructions. My hands continued to explore her body. Sadiek locked her left leg between his while removing her left breast from her bra. Without hesitation I did the same, trapping her right leg between mine. While Sadiek sucked on her breast, I slipped my hand down her panties. She was shaved bald making it easy to part her lips. I inserted my middle finger inside her. She let out a deep, erotic moan, then turned her head to face me. I took the cue and kissed her. She returned my kiss, tilting her body towards me. We were tongue kissing while I continued to explore her vagina with my fingers. Sadiek moved in closer, sandwiching her between us. Her body temperature seemed to rise to a feverish pitch. Sadiek lifted her hair and started sucking and kissing her neckline. She reacted to his touch by grinding and rotating her hips against my hand as I continued to finger fuck her. Then she reached down, taking my dick in her hand. "Oh my God!" she let out breathlessly. That's when I felt Sadiek's finger inserted into her pussy from behind. We were both finger fucking her at the same time. Suddenly I felt her husband tapping my leg. I looked down, he was holding the camera to his face pantomiming Sadiek and I to adjust our bodies in order for him to angle the camera for a close-up. I was slightly irritated but once again I had to remind myself that this was a job, and the customer was always right!

We did what we were directed to do and resumed. Her pussy was hot, tight and wet. I inserted another finger, and Sadiek did the same. She squeezed my dick harder, stroking its length.

"Oh my God, your dick is huge!"

I've heard that my entire life, it was nothing new to me, but it was something about the way she said it, that caused a deep arousal in me. I could feel my dick pulsate and grow stiffer in her hand.

At this point her juices were flowing out of her vagina as Sadiek and I continued to finger fuck her vagina in unison. The wife was whining and grinding her hips back and forth. I knew she was ready by the sound of her moans, and the forcefulness of her tongue kisses. I glanced down and her husband was at the foot of the bed zooming in closer with his camera "Rip the bra off of her!" He said to me and Sadiek. I wasn't sure if I heard him correctly. Sadiek, however, was already removing her bra, unsnapping it from behind.

"Remove her panties!" Was his next command. Sadiek started pulling them off her while I continued to tongue kiss her and finger fuck her.

We were all laying on our sides, I was still tongue kissing

and finger fucking the wife when she started to reach her first orgasm.

"Oh, oh pappi, pappi, oh, oh, my God it feels so good!"

The client's wife was in the midst of that first orgasm when Sadiek reinserted his fingers inside her, along with mine.

My brother was always more aggressive than I. He was eager to penetrate the client's wife. His dick was in his hand ready to stab into her while we were all laying on our sides. "Hold it!" Her husband said, holding up his hand like a traffic cop. He placed the camera on the tripod and walked to the foot of the bed. He grabbed his wife's foot and pulled her to the edge of the bed. He grabbed a handful of her blond hair, then pointed to Sadiek, motioning him over. Sadiek slid to the edge of the bed then stood to the left of her. Then the husband gestured for Sadiek to take hold of his wife's head. The client resumed his position behind the camera, then said "Action!" I wanted to laugh. The expression on my brother's face was priceless. He was standing there holding his dick in one hand not sure what he was supposed to do. The client's wife knew exactly what "Action!" meant. She blindly reached for my brother's penis. She seemed amazed, mumbling incoherently under her breath, massaging and stroking the length of his dick.

"Kiss it!" Her husband called out from behind the camera. His wife did as she was told. My brother wrapped a handful of her hair around his hand and forced his dick into her mouth. She gagged in reflex. "Yes, fuck her mouth amigo, fuck her mouth like the dirty whore she is." Sadiek took that as his cue to defile this man's wife. The husband gestured for me to join in the action. I got up and stood to the right of his wife. She felt my presence and blindly reached for my penis, stroking it while she sucked my brother's. As she stroked me and sucked my brother, I reached down to fondle her breasts. They were soft, her pink nipples were hard and erect. My brother was getting aggressive with her, forcing his dick further down her throat. She moaned and groaned with saliva dripping down her chin.

"Fuck her face!" Her husband directed. Sadiek grabbed the back of her head with both hands driving his dick in and out of her mouth as if he was fucking a pussy. His balls hung low, slapping against her chin with each pump. She let go of my dick to concentrate on the face drilling Sadiek was giving her. I continued to fondle her breasts. Then I positioned my dick against her face.

Sadiek knew that was my indication for him to pass her mouth over to me. I grabbed the back of her head and stuffed my dick in her mouth. The tip reached the back of her throat. The sound of her gagging turned me on. I was lost in the moment, pumping in and out her mouth relentlessly. I looked down at my dick, I was fucking her face with so much force and intensity that tears were falling from her eyes. I felt myself about to explode, reluctantly I let up.

With my hand wrapped around her hair I guided her into the doggy position. I was ready to fuck this man's wife. But my brother was more eager than I was. He positioned himself directly behind her. The husband called out from behind the camera, "Give her pussy a lick!" Sadiek had a look of frustration on his face. I could tell he was getting tired of the commands. I gave him a look, silently saying to him, "Bro, this is the deal we agreed to. Just go along with it."

Sadiek bent down, spreading the wife's ass cheeks and began licking her from behind. She moaned in pleasure. That's when a thought came to mind.

My brother and I had been tag-teaming women for so long that our moves were synchronized. I got underneath the wife in the 69 position. Sadiek instinctively began licking her anus, while I took her clit into my mouth, sucking on it. The husband got excited and brought the camera close to get a clear view of us eating his wife's pussy and ass at the same time.

"Oyee, oyee, poppy, oy, oy, poppy," she moaned, while stroking the length of my dick, then licking the tip. She began sucking on it. And the harder I sucked on her clitoris, the harder she sucked on the head of my dick.

The husband moved to the head of the bed to get a shot of his wife sucking and slobbering all over my penis. She reached down to my balls, massaging them, then stroking my penis up and down. She licked the length of my dick then took it into her mouth. She was in heat. I could tell by the intensity in which she pumped and stroked my penis.

Sadiek was licking the rim of her ass, while I continued to suck her clit. Then without notice he slid his middle finger deep inside her ass. The wife moaned then took me deeper into her mouth, sucking me with eagerness. It was feeling so good I began to gyrate my hips in-sync with the up and down motion of her head. I sucked and licked on her clitoris. Then I parted her pussy to slide two fingers inside her. I could feel Sadiek sliding another finger inside her ass through the thin layer of tissue that separated her vaginal wall from her anal cavity.

The wife continued to gyrate her hips to the motion of our fingers as we finger fucked her ass and pussy at the same time. The sound of her slurps and gagging filled the room. I was losing myself in her mouth. It was feeling so good that I couldn't hold back any longer. I ejaculated in her mouth. To my amazement she continued to suck my dick, swallowing my semen to the very last drop.

The husband was urging her on, "Yes Maria, suck it, suck it harder." Then he placed the camera on the tripod and made a beeline to the closet. He returned with a box of condoms and a burgundy velvet rope. Sadiek looked at him and blurted, "What the fuck you doing with that?" Pointing at the rope.

"My wife likes to be tied up and dominated. I want you guys to defile her in every way imaginable." I didn't see the devilish grin that appeared on my brother's face, but I could sense it from the chuckle he made in response. That was my cue, it was time to change positions.

"You already know what it is Bro!" Sadiek said as he slipped the condom on his dick. "Look at this shit Bro, it don't fit!" He looked over his shoulder at the husband, shaking his head, he mumbled under his breath, "Lil dick motherfucker!" Then he proceeded to take the rope and place it around the wife's mouth. With each end of the rope he wrapped them around his hands and pulled on them like a horse jockey straddling a racehorse. Sadiek was positioned behind her. The wife was on all fours in the doggy-style position. He slid his dick inside her.

"Adios mios, adios mios!" was her muffled cries. My brother slapped her hard across the ass. "Oyeee," she let out in pain. Sadiek looked over at the husband and said, "Get a clear shot of this," and proceeded to long dick his wife with all his strength.

Maria's ass bounced and jiggled with the force of a battering ram. Sadiek's dick glistened with her vaginal fluids. The client had his camera focused on Sadiek's dick as it went in and out of his wife's pussy from a side view. The sight of my brother pounding the client's wife in the doggy position had me stroking my dick to an erection. I was eager to sample that pussy for myself.

Out of the two of us Sadiek was the vocal one, talking dirty while he ravaged the women we fucked together. "Yeah bitch, take this dick, take this big, black dick. Yeah, you love it right?"

"Smack, smack, smack!" Sadiek repeatedly slapped her ass. The wife's cries were muffled as the velvet rope was still wrapped around her mouth. Sadiek was pulling hard on the rope, straining her head back while he continued to slap her ass. He looked over at the husband and said, "You like this shit, don't you?" The husband was mesmerized by how hard my brother was fucking his wife.

"You ready to fuck this bitch, Bro?" My dick was standing in full attention. I was staring at her ass bounce every time my brother slammed his dick into her... "Hell yeah Bro, flip her ass over," I said. Sadiek loosed his grip on the rope and gave the wife a few more pumps before slapping her hard across the ass one last time for good measure. Then he flipped her on her back. I took the rope and wrapped each end around her ankles. Then I pushed her legs back until her knees touched her breasts.

Sadiek positioned her head, facing me. He grabbed the rope holding her legs in place, and with his knees he pinned her arms to the bed. "Eat this dick!" He said, shoving it in her mouth. I was at the other end, rubbing my dick against her open vagina, lubricating my dick head with her juices. Then I plunged deep inside her. "Ummmm, ummmm!" was the muffled moans coming from the wife as I buried my dick deep in her guts.

"Fuck her harder Bro. Sledgehammer that pussy!" I was giving her the full length of this foot-long log. But when my brother said 'sledgehammer' I got in the squatting position and began to pile-drive down into her pussy. We had her pinned down, her knees pushed back to her breast, her arms pinned to the bed. She couldn't do anything except take what we were giving her. While my brother was the shit talker during sex, I was the silent one. I let my dick do the talking. I was more a silent killer, a pussy assassin. When I get in that mind-set, I fuck until I murder the pussy.

The sight of my foot-long, charcoal black dick pile driving deep inside Maria's pussy drove the husband crazy. He was getting more excited... "Punish her amigo, punish her. She deserves it. Yes, go deeper, faster. I want you to hurt her with your big black dicks." He had the camera so close to my ass I stopped in mid-stride and said, "Back up man, you're too close." This dude was a weird, perverted freak. What type of man gets excited watching two men fuck the shit out of his wife? There was no way in the world I would ever allow another man to fuck my wife. And as gorgeous as his wife was, I would beat a nigga's ass for even trying. This dude was throwing me off with his camera.

In and out, hard and fast, I pile-drove my dick into her pussy until her body started to convulse in an orgasm. She was cumming so hard that my dick was coated in foam. I didn't let up, I picked up the pace and drove into her harder, faster and deeper. My brother was on the other end with his dick still in her mouth urging me on. "That's right Bro, murder that shit, fuck her harder bro, harder!" The husband was catching all this on video from different angles. I continued to pile drive into her for a few more pumps, then I pulled my dick out completely giving the husband an opportunity to capture her gaping pussy hole on camera. "Oh my God amigo," he said with amazement.

"Hold her still Bro," I said. Her asshole was calling out to me. It looked tight, but it wouldn't be for long. I spat on her butthole and smeared it with the tip of my dick. The husband was directly

behind me holding the camera. I could hear his heavy breathing. He seemed to get extra excited in anticipation of me fucking his wife in the ass. She was really tight back there. I pushed the tip of my dick into her slowly and gradually. Instinctively Sadiek removed his dick from her mouth. He bent down to kiss her. She was obviously in pain, moving her head from side to side, mumbling,

"No, no, no!" The wife was still pinned down with her legs bent back to her chest. Her husband started speaking to her in Spanish. she yelled back at him, "Nooo, no mas, nooo mas!" I knew exactly what that meant and pulled out of her. Her husband yelled, "NO!" He stood up from his crouched position behind the camera and spoke a few stern words in Spanish to his wife, then looked at me with a devilish grin, "You may continue amigo!" Then immediately returned to his crouched position behind the camera.

My dick got soft from the husband's constant interruptions.

It was affecting my ability to concentrate and enjoy the experience. I gestured for Sadiek to move out of the way. He lost his hold on the rope and her legs came down from the bent position. I laid on top of her in the missionary position and started kissing her neck, ear lobe, then lips. I wasn't aware of the tears that ran down her face until I tasted it. I wanted to console her and pleasure her at the same time. I reached down between her legs and started rubbing her clitoris. She responded to my touch by wrapping her arms around my neck and her legs around my waist. My erection was growing stiff. I was fully aroused and hard by the time I reinserted my dick into her pussy.

"Ohh papi, oh papi, ooooh papi, papi, papi!" She moaned into my ear with every stroke. I felt her vaginal walls pulsate and contract, gripping my penis. It felt as if my dick was being milked. I became lost in that sensation, oblivious to the husband's presence, the lights and the camera. I could barely hear my brother in the background saying, "Yeah Bro, dig her back out dig her motherfucking back out Bro!"

My mind and body were lost in the wave of that euphoric sensation you feel building up from deep inside you. The wife was feeling what I was feeling. We were both riding that wave of ecstasy. She was digging her nails into my back as I plunged deeper and deeper. She started sucking on my tongue, pulling at it with so much force I thought it would be ripped from my mouth. We both reached our orgasms simultaneously. It was so intense that we continued to kiss with deep passion. The sensation caused a chill to run down my spine. I know she felt it too.

With her arms and legs still wrapped around my waist I rolled onto my back. She was now on top of me and I held her close to my chest. My dick was still hard, and I continued to grind and hump into her, palming her ass. Sadiek climbed onto the bed and sandwiched her between us. I could feel him positioning his dick at her butthole. She shook her head from side to side, "No, no mas, no mas!" She repeated over and over again.

Sadiek ignored her pleas, pushing deeper and deeper inside her. It was a tight fit with my dick still inside her pussy. But Sadiek didn't care, he was determined to get his entire dick inside her ass.

I continued to kiss her while Sadiek worked his penis in and out of her ass, inch by inch. Once he was fully impaled, we started to fuck her in tandem. The close proximity of our bodies caused us to build up sweat really quick. The wife no longer resisted, her cries went from, "No mas!" to "Adios mios, adios, mios, oyee, oyee, papi, papi, oyee, papi!" The combination of pain and pleasure was driving her crazy. I could feel her vagina contracting again, gripping my dick tighter and tighter.

Sadiek started picking up his pace. Drilling in and out of her faster and faster. He was on the verge of ejaculating. I started to hump fast to match his pace. All three of us were caught in the rapture. Maria reached her orgasm first, screaming out loud in ecstasy... "OYEEEEEEE,

OYEEEEEE!" Then Saidek pulled out, removed the condom and shot his semen all over her back. I picked up the pace of my thrusts, fucking her harder, and faster until I finally reached my climax. I heard clapping... then "Bravo, bravo! Very good, very good amigo!" I looked up to find the husband standing over us with a big smile across his face. Sadiek had climbed off the bed and was putting his clothes on. It was most definitely time for us to go. The wife Maria rolled over onto her back then removed the blindfold from her eyes. She sat up and gave Sadiek and I this look of astonishment. I was mesmerized by the color of her eyes. They were a deep shade of ocean blue. She pointed at me, "It was you I was kissing, no?" I smiled and shook my head yes. Sweat was rolling off her brow. She was still panting from the sex.

"You guys are amazing. Enrique, you must invite them over again." She said to her husband who was busy fiddling with his camera. She jumped off the bed and bounced over to him, still completely nude. Her breasts rising and falling as she spoke.

"Enrique, do you hear me? You have to invite them over again!" He looked up and pointed at the camera. "Why Maria? I have it all on video!"

They were still going back and forth when Sadiek and I gathered our things and exited the residence. I was shaking my head as we pulled away from the gated community. My only regret was not getting a copy of that video...!

20

---

# REVENGE IS THE SWEETEST JOY

Ladoria Dexter
Social Media: Facebook
Location: Negril, Jamaica

When a man cheats on a woman the woman is expected to forgive and forget. Most of us stay in the relationship out of love, the kids, or for the sake of the marriage. Many of us stay hoping that our partner will change. We make excuses for his infidelities, blaming ourselves for his actions. Telling ourselves "If I do this better, love him more and be the best wife, partner or girlfriend I can be, things would change." But when all the lying and cheating gets tiring, it comes to a point in your heart when the well runs dry and there's no longer any room for forgiveness, and the only thing that can make you feel better is doing to him what he's done to you. And that is exactly where this story begins.

I met Kwame online. We were a part of a West Indian culture group on Facebook. One of the administrators of our group asked all the ladies to drop a selfie. I dropped mine and soon after Kwame, along with several other guys, sent me the exact, same message,

"Hello Beautiful!"

I'm thinking, "Is this the only pick-up line they know?" I never respond immediately to random messages. I allow the message to linger in my inbox for several days before I decide on who I would ignore, and who I would reply to. I sent Kwame a reply. "Thanks for the compliment and how may I help you?" His response was immediate.

"I liked your picture and was wondering if I could get to know you?" He looked young, so I asked him his age. He stated he was 24. I told him that I was too old for him, and what could he possibly offer me? Kwame lived in Jamaica and was in the Jamaican Military Force. He lived with his mother and that alone was a red flag for me, not to mention the 9-year age difference between us. Despite that I was curious to learn more about him, yet still I was a little wary about continuing to communicate with him due to our age difference.

When I think of younger guys, I think their sex technique is strictly "Jack Rabbit penetration." All about humping hard and fast. Getting my vagina banged out and beat up wasn't my style. I did that when I was young. I had to make sure I wasn't setting myself up for constant fast body jerking.

My preference is older men who are attentive to a woman's body and needs. But there was something about Kwame's vibe I was feeling. He was 6'4" tall, slim with a muscular frame. His chocolate complexion was a plus. I love dark-skin men.

For the next six months Kwame and I talked on the phone every day and night. We talked so much we would fall asleep on the phone with each other. We even video sexed each other a few times.

One time during our video call he did the weirdest thing. We were both strip teasing and he pulled down his boxer briefs, turned around and shook his ass in the camera. Then he smacked himself on the ass. I thought, "What the fuck?"

Kwame's favorite nickname for me was "Sweetsop" and after eight months of talking, texting and video calls, Kwame and I made plans to meet up at the Caves in Negril, Jamaica.

Kwame picked me up in Kingston and he was sexier in person. I couldn't stop lusting over him. He hired a personal driver to take us the 3.5 hours' drive to Negril. During the drive we held hands and talked. We were both nervous. The driver made a stop at the supermarket where he picked up some champagne. While we waited for the driver to return, I leaned in and began kissing Kwame softly on his lips. As the passion slowly began to rise within me I became more aggressive, over-powering him with my tongue while my hands rubbed the print of his dick. I let up from the kiss and he stared at me in shock with his eyes wide, all he could say was "WOW!" I placed my hand down his shorts and pulled out his dick. I locked eyes with him, then started kissing him again and stroking his dick at the same time. I wasn't worried about anyone seeing us, the car windows were covered in dark tints. I stopped kissing him and looked into his eyes again. "Is this what you've been waiting for?" Before he had a chance to answer I placed my mouth on his dick. I took him halfway to the back of my throat. I didn't move. I allowed my lips to wrap around his dick and my tongue to lay flat on the head, and my saliva to run down his balls. Moving my head around softly and gently, Kwame started to moan and the more he moaned the more I sucked. I continued sucking and sucking and causing him to rotate his hips, then he let out a loud "Aww" and immediately pulled me up. I got his ass!

When I looked down at his crotch his body was twitching. While he continued to let out that "Aww, aww, aww" sound, semen erupted out of his dick like hot lava from a volcano. "Oh gosh he's a weak one." I thought.

Once the driver had returned to the vehicle, we continued down the highway to the resort. We made a few more stops for food and we even made a pit stop at a bar where I needed to use the bathroom. Kwame walked me towards the restroom, but I changed my mind when I realized there was no toilet or running water. Suddenly Kwame grabbed me by the throat and started

kissing me and pulling out his dick in an attempt to get some more of these lips. I looked around the bathroom and was turned completely off. I told him no and his grip got tighter. I yanked myself out of his grip and told him "Fuck no! Don't ever grip me like that again!" He apologized and we headed back to the vehicle.

When we finally made it to our suite, Kwame shut the door behind us and started kissing me. We wound up in the bedroom. He then took a few steps back and sat on the bed, pulling me on top of him. I told him I wanted to freshen up, but he insisted on having my pussy right out the package. He pulled my shirt over my head and I did the same with him. We were both topless. I climbed off his lap to pull his shorts off. I will admit that his dick was clean and had a nice taste to it. No after smell either so my mouth went straight to work. With every head stroke of my mouth on his dick my body moved slowly in an erotic motion as if I was ready to fuck, but not just yet. I needed to show him I wasn't all talk. I continued to suck him like I'd just won a million dollars. I was going so hard he couldn't keep his mouth shut.

"Oh sugar, oh sugar, oh really, oh really, oh, oh, ouiiiiii!" I paused and looked up at him. "What? What? I can't hear you. Talk, talk!" I gave him this deep look into his eyes, then said "You want this pussy? Huh? Then take it." I still held his dick in my hand then took him to the back of my throat, squinting my eyes at him at the same time. He jumped up and screamed "BUMBOCLAAT!!!!" I looked him in the eyes and said, "Yeah!" I pulled my shorts off, cocked my thick legs up on the dresser, and slid my thong to the side exposing all my phat pussy. Then I spread my ass cheeks and thighs, pushed my ass out and told him to come take this pussy.

Kwame did as I instructed and began to fuck me, but he couldn't handle how hard I was throwing my ass back on him. He lost his balance and I became irritated, so I told him to stop. I turned around to face him, fully looking at him. I hopped on the dresser, spread my legs wide apart and used both hands to keep them open, exposing my wet pussy. Then I parted my pussy lips exposing the pink inside and my small pussy hole. He looked at me with a lost expression plastered all over his face. I reached for the whip cream in my bag, opened the top and sprayed it all over my pussy. With two fingers I instructed him to come to me. He went face first into my pussy, sucking, licking and fingering my pussy as he ate me out.

After licking my pussy clean of whip cream, he inserted his dick back inside me. This time it felt better. He was more relaxed, so I allowed him to lead the strokes and control the tempo. When I sensed him about to cum, I said "Stop! Walk around the room, take a shot of rum, do anything to make the cum go back down."

I remained on the dresser with my legs spread wide-open playing and tasting my own pussy juice while he sat on the bed watching me. When he got ready, he got off the bed, walked over to me, and picked me up off the dresser. I wrapped my legs around him and he carried me into the bathroom. He placed me on the sink and started fucking me. There was body oil on the sink supplied by the resort. I poured some and rubbed it down his back. His dick was stirring around inside me, whirling around my walls until his body clenched tight. I rubbed his back faster and faster, allowing the oil to sink into his skin. He did two more pumps, pulled his dick out and nutted on top of my pussy. Then he grabbed a towel, wiped me off and slid back inside of me.  We continued to fuck, changing positions. I got off the sink, and placed my upper body over the bathtub. I was on my knees, and he got behind me kneeling over my ass and started fucking me in that position. While his dick was going in and out of my pussy, I took one hand and spread my ass. The way his dick moved inside me felt so good I wanted to moan, but instead I bit down on my bottom lip and pushed my ass out further. His speed increased, and I contracted my pussy muscles gripping his dick. Kwame took one last pump then pulled out and ejaculated all over my butt cheeks.

Afterwards we got in the shower and washed each other's bodies. Once we were all washed up Kwame sat in the tub, I stood up to lift my leg on the rim of the bathtub. I stared at him as he began sucking my clit and fingering my pussy. The shower water ran down my body splashing on my ass. My body began to jerk and shiver as I came in his mouth. When he finished, he stood up, grabbed the sponge and resumed washing my body and kissing me at the same time.  He continued to rub my pussy with the soapy sponge then fingered me to another climax. He sucked my juices off his fingers and said, "Let's get out now."

The next morning, we laid in bed for a bit. Kwame started kissing the back of my hand, telling me how beautiful I was, and how he enjoyed the previous night and didn't want the time to end. I started caressing his dick under the sheets. His manhood grew in my hand and he leaned in to suck on my nipples. His tongue swirled around my areola. I became so turned on I started jerking his dick faster and let out a moan. I climbed on top of Kwame, took his dick and directed it into my hole. I rested my pussy on his dick and locked eyes with him, then started contracting my pussy muscles. I rubbed his strong tight chest over and over then leaned in and started kissing him.

Slowly I bounced on his dick as if a rollercoaster was taking its time to take off. My waist dipped in and out as I continued to kiss him. I whispered in his ear "Is it good?"

"Yes!" He replied.

"Is it good?" I repeated

"Yes Sugar!"

"No, it's not!" I said, then sat up on his dick with my feet planted on the bed and knees pointed up. My pussy was exposed. I used two fingers to rub myself while his dick was still inside me. He took my two fingers and sucked my pre cum. I parted my pussy lips exposing my clit and rode him.  He moaned so loud it could be heard in the next suite. I talked dirty to him, while still riding him. "Come fuck me, come fuck me... Nahhh you don't want it. You don't like it." I taunted him, pressing both my palms on his chest. I hopped up and down on his dick froggy style. Faster and faster I rode him going rough, trying hard to bruise his dick, making my pussy hurt. I felt he was about to cum, so I got up quickly, stood over him and told him to stop.

"I fucking said stop! You better not fucking cum." He shook nervously and his sperm started to pour out his dick. I immediately went down on him and started sucking the rest of the sperm out of his dick, jerking it soft and gently. I continued to suck his dick until he pushed me away. He couldn't take the tingly sensation these lips and mouth was giving him. I walked away laughing as I headed to the shower and I blurted out "You can't fuck with this!"

Later in the day Kwame and I took a stroll on the beach, talked and smoked some weed. We went to a bar and made a bet on who could out drink who. Of course, I won that competition.

Kwame was twisted as we headed back to our room. He sat

down on the couch and I walked over to him, undressing him then myself. I stood in front of him ass naked, he wrapped his hands around me palming both ass cheeks, and he started kissing my thighs. He felt my body heat, turned me around and I bent over in front of his face touching my toes. He started to finger fuck me with two fingers then leaned in to suck my pussy. His tongue felt so good going in and out my pussy, the feeling made me want to cream all over his tongue. I felt myself about to cum, but I needed to feel that dick to complete my explosion.

I stood up, turned around and pushed him back onto the couch, then sat on his dick in the reverse cowgirl position. I placed my feet on the couch, held on to his knees and bounced up and down on his dick. He started to fuck me back. I placed my hands on the floor in the wheelbarrow position, throwing my ass back on him. Suddenly he stops in mid pump, jumps out the pussy, runs to the bathroom and threw up all over the sink. At that point he had lost some star ratings. Here we are in this 4.5-star hotel resort and his fuck game was a 2.5. I lost interest and didn't want to fuck anymore.

The following day was our last morning together. I decided I would leave him with something to remember me by. Kwame got out of the shower and apologized for the previous night. I told him not to worry about it. I had him lay on the bed and gave him a full body massage. I kissed him on his back while rubbing my hands all over his back. I used my tongue and licked from his shoulders going down to his spine. When I got to the crack of his ass I stopped and took a sip of fruit juice from the nightstand. I continued to rub his back holding the juice in my mouth. When I got back to the small of his back I licked at the crack of his ass. He didn't respond so I used my tongue going deeper down the crack of his ass. He let out a "Mmm" sound. I took another sip and resumed licking the crack of his ass, but this time I spit the fruit juice in the center hole of his ass. He flinched, then relaxed when he felt my tongue licking and sucking in every drop of the fruit juice and rubbing his back. His dick was rock hard and wanted to fuck, but I told him "NO, next trip." There would be more trips, and my revenge would lead me down a crazy love feud involving Kwane's significant others…!

2 1

LOVE, LIES & BETRAYAL

Eric Jones

Social Media: Instagram

Atlanta, GA

November, 2020

EVERYBODY HAS TRUST ISSUES AT ONE POINT IN THEIR LIVES. IT'S even more compounded when a man is incarcerated, and his woman is out in the free world. This was the case with my right-hand man Avon. We called him Avon, because he kept himself fresh and clean inside the penn.

Avon was my running partner. I met him at the United States Penitentiary Lee County in Virginia. He got into something, got shipped to another prison, and 10 years later we met up again in another Federal prison in Victorville, California.

It's hard leaving good men behind when you go home... You have a sense of regret and guilt that your partner is being left behind as you walk out those prison doors. That's exactly how I felt the day of my release on January 10, 2020.

It didn't take long to get my feet planted on the ground. I

went home to a nice nest egg and started a van service. When the country went on lock-down due to Covid-19, I thought my business would fold, but instead I had more deals delivering for Amazon than I could handle. I hired a staff, purchased more vans, and drivers. My business flourished to say the least.

My man Avon stayed in contact with me. I owed some of my success to him. He was the one who encouraged me to start the van service. So, when he asked me for a favor, it was automatic that I would look out and do whatever I could for him.

"Yo 'E', I need a favor from you." My response was, "Anything homie, what you need?" I was caught off guard when he replied, "I need you to holla at my girl." At first, I was thinking he simply wanted me to speak to her about sending him some money or whatever. But when he said, "Nah, I want you to shoot at her, holla at her like you're trying to smash." I looked at the phone and thought to myself, "The homie is tripping!"

I know how it is being incarcerated. Dudes will front like they don't trip over their woman, but the truth is we all do.

What Avon asked of me, I was not trying to be a part of. I valued our friendship way too much to fuck it up over a chick. Avon was persistent though. "Why would you want me to holla at your girl homie?" And when he broke it all down to me, I understood where he was coming from. He said, "E, I need to know I can trust her. I'm about to come home and I need to know that my girl can be trusted. Because they'll tell you whatever you want to hear while you're behind the wall." I understood his rationale, yet I was reluctant to go there.

A few days later Avon shot me her Instagram and told me to follow her. I looked her up. She was the same pretty, light-skin joint he had plastered all over his cell wall. Porsha stood 5'11" tall, small waist, wide hips, little 'B' cup breasts, and wore her hair natural and crinkly down to her shoulders. You could see she was mixed. She had freckles plastered on her cheekbones. I reported this to Avon, and he instructed me to slide in her DM.

"Hey beautiful, what's up with you?" She replied with a cordial response. And I left it at that. Several days later I got an email from Avon asking me for an update. I told him, and he responded, "Nigga stop bullshitting, you playing, shoot at her like you want that pussy my nigga!"

It was clear that Avon wanted me to go as far as she was willing to go. So, I shot my shot. I hit her up and sent her a dick pic with a quick message, "What can you do with this?" Her response was "Oh my!" I'm not bragging, I've been blessed with a pussy pounder, Facts! I knew once I sent her a dick picture, she would either curse me out, block me, or be intrigued. The pic of her laying on the bed with a thong on told me she was definitely intrigued. And so was I. Her long legs went on for days, she was what we called an Amazon.

I told Avon about her response to my dick pic, and he instructed me to go harder, so I did. I sent her a video of myself hitting this phat bubble butt chick from Savannah, Georgia, in the doggy style with a text, "You up for that back-shot action?" She replied immediately with, "I'm faithful and in love with Avon!" I replied back, "Shit, we got something in common, I got love for him too. That shouldn't stop us from doing what grown folks do."

"I don't want to hurt my man!"

"I promise you we won't!"

Avon hit me up a few days later and I gave him another update. He said, "Oh, this shit is a movie. Go at her harder. She's definitely with it. She hasn't said anything to me about you hitting her up on the Gram. She's with it homie. Fuck the shit out of that bitch, and make sure you video tape it."

I didn't expect Avon to respond like that. I thought he had enough to go on, but he seemed to be more determined to prove without a doubt that she was unfaithful. I shrugged my shoulders and pursued Porsha with that purpose. I texted her on a daily, sending videos of myself working out. She would comment on my physique and our flirtation began to expand. Occasionally she would bring up Avon and her misgivings of us flirting with each other. But I would constantly reassure her that he would never find out.

After weeks and weeks of trying to tear down that wall she had up, it finally came tumbling down on New Year's Eve. I was not expecting it. I checked my messages and saw that I had an email from Porsha. Soon as I opened it, I was shocked, and became excited. There she was bent over on all fours looking back at the camera. "Is this what you want Eric? You want this tight, thick, yellow ass?" Then she smacked her own ass with a foot-long dildo. "You keep asking me if I can take dick, does this answer your question?" And begins to take every inch of that dildo up her ass. I'm not going to lie, I hadn't masturbated since my release, but the sight of Porsha taking that dildo all the way up her ass, had me harder than King Kong, and ready to jerk off.

I shook my head, "Bitches ain't shit!" Here it was, this woman knew that Avon was my homie, yet she allowed me to send her dick pics, sex videos, etc. And now she did the ultimate by sending me a video of herself taking a dildo up the ass... I sent Avon an email on Corrlinks about the video she sent me. Avon's response was, "Oh, she loves it up the ass bro. Shorty is a good time. Hit that shit and let me know how it went." I couldn't help but chuckle. Porsha was off the wifey list in Avon's mind. To him she was just another slut he would pass on to his friends, and I was happy to be the first.

Porsha and I finally met up in Atlanta at an Airbnb I rented in a high rise on Peach Street. The apartment was laced, everything modern, floor to ceiling windows, you could see all of downtown Atlanta from the 22$^{nd}$ floor. I couldn't wait to get between those long yellow legs.

Porsha wore a blinged out Luis Vuitton face mask. Her long legs strutted down the hall. I was staring at her ass from behind.

All I kept saying to myself was, "This nigga Avon done lost his mind. Ain't no way I'd tempt this fine Amazon!" She was bad!

We entered the apartment together. She seemed a little nervous. This was our first time meeting face to face. I told her to go ahead and put her bags in the bedroom. While she was settling in, I got the mood right, lighting scented candles, dimming the lights and putting on some "get the mood right" music. Ten minutes later Porsha walked into the living room wearing nothing but a black fishnet outfit. I stood there stunned. Her perky little titties were peeking out in between the fishnet. She chuckled at the shocked expression plastered across my face. "I know you ain't over here on some Barry White shit? Take them clothes off, I've been craving that big dick of yours since the day you sent me that dick pic."

Porsha wasn't shy at all. I could see the lust in her eyes as she walked towards me. She grabbed the wine glass from my hand and placed it on the glass coffee table. Then she reached up and cupped my face in her hand pulling me into her. We started to tongue kiss, "Fuck Covid!"

Her tongue was like a slippery, cherry-flavored snake exploring my mouth. She was aggressive with her shit, unbuckling my Louie belt, then came the button to my Balmain jeans. She reached into my pants and pulled out my meat-stick. I heard her gasp, "Oh my God!" I chuckled from the look of amazement in her eyes. I could see fear in them. "Don't worry, I'll take it easy on you." Now that I had her in my grasp, I did not want her to back out of the situation.

"I don't think I can take all of that." She was shaking her head stepping back away from me. I pulled her into my chest and began to kiss her again, while whispering in her ear between kisses. "I promise I won't hurt you."

Her skin was feverish as I held her in my arms. I wanted to connect with her sensuously, to fully arouse her body deep down to her soul. I massaged her perky little breasts, feeling her nipples stiffen between my fingers. She wrapped her arms around my neck. Her kisses were becoming more intense. I wanted to get her to the point of no return, so I guided her towards the couch while still kissing her. We collapsed on top of it. I slowly began to suck on her neck. She let out a soft moan. I proceeded down to her breasts, taking one into my mouth, sucking hard on her left nipple. She arched her back and let out a deep moan. I continued to suck on her nipple while my right hand made its way down her waist. I was tempted to tear at her fishnets but decided to pull them down to her ankles as I continued to leave a trail of wet kisses down to her belly button.

Porsha's skin was smooth, soft, like a newborn babe's. The little reddish-brown hairs glistened with the sweat that was beginning to form on her belly. I started to kiss her inner thigh and she moaned deeply. She cupped the back of my head in her hands. I knew what she wanted, and I was happy to oblige.

The lavender scent from her vagina tingled my senses. I wanted to take her into my mouth instantly. I flicked my tongue around the edge of her pussy lips. She was shaved bald. It's true what they say about a woman's lips, that the lips on her mouth usually matched the ones in between her legs. Porsha's was thin, yet long, protruding out of her vagina. I took her lips into my mouth and immediately she began to gyrate her hips while still cupping the back of my head, pulling me deeper into her.

Porsha's juices flowed into my mouth. I parted her lips with my tongue to get at the insides. She grinded and rotated her hips, moaning at the same time. I glanced up at her. Porsha's head was tilted back with her mouth open. I knew my tongue was hitting the right spot.

I never shared this with anyone, but years ago while getting a tattoo, the lady that did piercings at the shop convinced me to cut the tendon-like tissue on the underside of my tongue. This allowed my tongue to extend down past my chin. Simply said, "I have a long ass tongue."

Porsha was in for a surprise as my tongue entered her vagina. I explored her insides, sticking my tongue as far as it would go. Her body reacted to it. "Eric, oh Eric, oh my God, oh Eric your tongue feels so good!" She moaned and panted. By now she was squirming trying to pull away, but I held her in place, holding on to her waist. In and out my tongue continued to go, exploring, penetrating her vagina. I could feel her vaginal walls contracting, hugging my tongue. Her juice flowed out and down the crack of her ass leaving a little puddle on the leather couch. I started rubbing her clitoris in a circular motion. She reacted by grinding her pelvis against my mouth with greater intensity. I curved my tongue to massage her G-spot. I found it four inches past the entrance.

Porsha had her legs wrapped around my neck, humping and grinding on my face. She was loving the sensations my tongue delivered. I could sense her orgasm about to erupt. My tongue was buried deep inside her, reaching far to her cervix. Her vagina started to contract around my tongue. I continued to massage her clitoris. Then suddenly she arched her back and locked my head in a death grip and started shaking with her mouth wide open, with no sound coming out. Suddenly I felt a spray of liquid soaking my tongue. She was in the midst of an earth-shattering orgasm. Finally, she let out a deep, guttural scream. "Ohhhh, ohhhh, ohh my God, ohhh my goooddddd! Eric, ohhh Eric I'm cummmmming. Please, please stop!" She moaned, panted, then convulsed.

I'm not going to lie, having my tongue buried deep inside her pussy aroused me. I continued to tongue fuck her for a while, until I was ready to stretch her out, literally. I slowly worked my way up her body, kissing and sucking on her clitoris, then her belly button, and to her perky little breasts. I sucked on her neck while my hands explored her body. I wanted to beat the pussy up, but I promised her I'd be gentle. With my right hand I guided the fat head of my dick to her entrance. She flinched, placing her palm against my chest. "No Eric, stop. We can't do this!"

"The hell we can't!" There was no turning back now. I kissed her lips, her neck and whispered in her ear, "I'll be gentle baby, I promise!"

My dick was hard, I could feel it pulsating in my grasp. I needed to get in that pussy, and fast. I rubbed the tip against the entrance, parting her lips to lubricate the head with her vaginal juices. She let out a sensuous moan. Then slowly I began to force the head inside her. She flinched, digging her nail into my right arm, the one that I held my dick with.

"I got you baby!" I said, forcing the tip inside her. She held her breath, and clenched her eyes shut as I continued to slowly, and methodically work the head inside her. Once the head penetrated her insides, I was able to go deeper.

We were in the missionary position on the living room floor, laying on top of a beige fluffy rug. I tongue kissed Porsha's nipples, then proceeded to kiss her neck, her ear lobe. I did that to distract her mind from the pain. I knew I was stretching her vagina beyond its normal limits, but once I reached her bottom, her vagina would adjust to my width and length.

We were completely naked, her breasts were against my chest. I could feel the heat emanating from her body. I started to kiss her with deep passion. Our tongues danced and inter-twined with each other's like a perfect pair. I was slowly working my way deeper and deeper inside with each stroke. Her hips began to gyrate, meeting my every stroke. It was as if our bodies were in-sync with each other's. She caressed the back of my neck while we kissed, and I continued to stroke in and out of her. When I finally reached her bottom, I just held her in place, savoring the feeling. Her vagina gripped my penis like a baby's strong grip. I wanted that feeling to last forever. Porsha had some good pussy, and for a brief moment I thought about Avon. Then just as abruptly as the thought came to mind,

I forced it out. I wanted to enjoy this experience of conquering new pussy, yet I knew that although this was our first time making love it most certainly would not be the last.

I stroked in and out of her while our bodies were held tightly together. We kissed and made love, rolling around on the living room floor. I stared up into Porsha's eyes as she straddled me and rode me like a cowgirl. Her eyes captivated me. It was as if she could see into my soul and read my thoughts. She bit into her bottom lip and wined on my dick in an attempt to get it all inside her. Then she started to ride me faster and faster. Sweat was dripping off her brow. Porsha was in a zone, bouncing up and down as if she was trying to hurt herself. Then, as if I was reading her mind she started to moan and say, "Oh oh, this hurts so good. Oh Eric, oh fuck me, fuck me, beat this pussy up. Bruise this pussy with your big fat dick." I leaned forward to wrap my arms around her, pulling her down onto my chest. I held her as I began to hump up into her. She wanted me to bruise her pussy, so that is what I did.

I fucked up into Porsha's pussy with so much force that my balls slapped up against her ass with every thrust. She was strictly moaning now. Moaning in pain as I fucked her relentlessly, smacking her ass hard in between strokes.

"You love it? Huh? You love this dick?" I was talking shit into her ear. "You love it? You love this dick? Say you love it!"

"Oh, I love it, I love it!"

"Say you want it." She panted as if she was out of breath. "I want it Eric, give it to meeeeee!"

I did, fucking hard and fast. Amazed at her ability to take this dick beating I was giving her. She reached her orgasm moments later, and I followed right behind her. We were both out of breath. She laid on top of me, drenched in sweat.

We were silent for a while. Both of us lost in our thoughts. Then she turned her head to speak into my ear. "What about Avon?" I didn't know how to answer that question. What started off as a scheme to seduce my best friend's woman had turned into something completely different. I was falling for this woman, and she was falling for me.

I felt the tears on my chest before she wiped them from her eyes. "I can't believe we did this. Avon could never, ever know." She was crying in shame, and grief. And I was feeling like the scum of the earth. Porsha didn't deserve what Avon had put into play. Yet I was just as guilty as him. I was a willing participant in his scheme. But what choice did I have? I either continued with the lie or tell her the truth. Either way I was fucked. If I revealed to her that Avon had set this whole thing up, I would betray my friend's trust and lose him as a friend. Porsha would not only feel betrayed by Avon, she would feel betrayed and played by me as well. I had no other choice but to continue on with this charade.

My desire for Porsha grew with time. I kept telling myself, "Eric you are out of line! How could you fall for your best friend's woman?" Yet another part of me kept saying, "It's not your fault, Avon brought this on himself!"

Porsha and I traveled to Miami, Vegas, and later to New York together. I knew I was completely out of line and falling for her when I stopped responding to Avon's emails and ducking his calls. Porsha and I were on a return flight from California one day when she turned to me and said, "When was the last time you spoke with Avon?" I had to jog my memory because it had been a few weeks. I shrugged my shoulders, "Last month!" She was quiet for a moment, then replied "I think he knows something."

"Avon definitely knew something. He knew you sent me those pictures, and that video." But I kept those thoughts to myself. I grabbed her hand and squeezed them with reassurance. "Don't worry about Avon he won't find out about us, and if he did, so what!" she snatched her hand away, "Eric, don't say that. You promised me that you would never, ever tell him about us. He could never know."

I'm not going to lie; I was hurt by her reaction. And she read it in my face. "Baby, I care about you. I'm attracted to you obviously. You do things to my body that no man has ever done before. That tongue, your dick, it's amazing. If I wasn't with Avon, I would probably be with you, but my loyalty is with him. I love Avon!"

"You love him but you're on this plane with me. You love him but you're fucking me." I replied.

"Don't talk to me like that. I'm not one of your T.H.O.Ts Eric."

The rest of the flight was relatively quiet with both of us lost in our thoughts. When we landed at LaGuardia Airport in New York, Porsha grabbed my hand and turned to face me. "Eric, I'm sorry, I didn't mean to snap at you. We both knew what we were getting into. I'm not going to lie and say my feelings for you haven't grown but I love Avon. I don't want to lose him!"

I played it off cool and smiled. "Avon is the Bro, I got mad love for him. I won't come between you and him. This was fun while it lasted." I grabbed my carry-on bag and headed for the exit.

Porsha was on my heels, tugging at the back of my coat tail. "Eric, Eric, wait a minute." She caught up to me at the curb where I stood waiting for a taxicab to pull up. "Eric, I didn't say it was over between us. I'm just saying we need to be careful." I stood at the curb signaling for the next cab to pull up.

"Oh, so you're going to ignore me?" I turned to look into her eyes and immediately I wished I hadn't. There was something about them that drew me in, like this magnetic pull, like moths to a flame. Her eyes were a beautiful deep, rich shade of emerald green. I knew I was being petty and acting like a lovesick lame. I smiled then pulled her into my embrace, kissing her on the forehead.

"I'm tripping babe, you are absolutely right. Avon can never find out about us," was what I said to her, but my thoughts were somewhere else.

Here I was catching feelings for my homie's chick. She didn't belong to me, she belonged to my best friend. She was his wife so to speak. How did I allow myself to get caught in this web of lies and deceit? I needed to snap out of this quick before I lost focus completely.

We jumped into the taxicab together and headed to the "W" Hotel in Manhattan. I wanted to fuck my frustration away. In our previous encounters I was gentle, but on this particular night I was out for revenge. This bitch had bruised my ego. I needed to regain a sense of power over her, and myself.

That night Porsha took me into her mouth for the first time. As she sucked my dick, I held her head in place, fucking her mouth roughly. She gagged and gagged so bad she nearly threw up. I had my phone out discreetly filming her eyes roll to the back of her head as I forced my dick to the back of her throat.

I started talking crazy, "Yeah, eat this dick, eat that shit, eat this dick up!" The sound of her gagging and choking on my dick aroused me to the point of ejaculation. I pulled out my dick and released a load of semen that covered her entire face and mouth. I stuffed my dick back down her throat. "Yeah, suck that cum, suck all of it!" She moaned deeply as if sucking the sperm out of me turned her on.

I laid Porsha on her back and grabbed both her long legs, pushing them back to her arm pits, then I straddled her and commenced to pile-drive my dick in and out of her. Her tunnel was deep, but not deep enough. I pounded those walls until she begged and pleaded for me to stop. The tears that formed in her eyes didn't faze me. I flipped her on to her hands and knees. At that moment I hated her. I wanted to abuse her stuck-up bougie ass. I grabbed my phone and started to record again. I pushed down on her back, forcing her chest to the bed, causing her ass to arch up in the air. I slapped her ass hard before sliding this pole of a dick into her. The camera was angled down focusing on my dick as it slid all the way in, then sliding all the way out. My dick was lubricated with her vaginal juice. I felt like a porn star fucking her hard and fast. Her moans and cries excited me. I continued to talk shit while I fucked her hard, bending my dick against her back wall. Then suddenly a thought came to mind. I placed my right foot on her head, pressing it down on the mattress, restricting her movement. It was something I saw in a Buttman magazine where three white guys fucked the shit out of Jada Fire, humiliating and degrading her. At that moment I wanted to do the same thing to Porsha, humiliate and degrade her.

I set the phone on the nightstand. Angling it to get a side view of this fuck scene. I fucked and slapped her ass cheeks with my foot still pressed down on her head. In that position she got all dick. All the dick she couldn't take. I didn't care, I wanted to hurt her, bruise and beat up her pussy. Her moans were muffled with her head pressed down on the pillow with my foot. I was pile-driving her in the doggy-style position. Face down ass up, literally!

Smack, smack, smack! I slapped her ass in between strokes. "Shut the fuck up bitch you know you love it!" I didn't care, I looked at the camera and smiled, pointing at Porsha, then continued fucking her harder.

I let off her head with my foot, and leaned over, placing both my hands on her upper back. Her ass was still arched up giving me the angle I wanted to stab deeper into her pussy. I was fucking her harder, and faster. Her cries for mercy went ignored. Then without slowing I pulled out of her. And collapsed on her back. I needed to regain my composure because I almost ejaculated.

Porsha was panting. We were both drenched in sweat. I began grinding my dick in between her butt cheeks. I reached underneath her to get at the clitoris. I rubbed and massaged it. She moaned and rotated her hips to my touch. With my left hand I rubbed the head of my dick against her pussy, lubricating it. Then without warning, I stuffed the head into her ass. Porsha flinched and clinched her ass cheeks shut but the head had already penetrated at least two inches deep. I was in her ass and there was no going back. She was getting fucked in the ass whether she liked it or not.

I nibbled on her ear then slid my tongue in it. Sending different sensations throughout her body as I massaged her clit and forced another inch of my dick in her ass. I slid two fingers in her pussy. It was dripping wet. I had both my hands underneath her, one rubbing her clit, the other finger fucking her. Her hips gyrating and whining to my touch. My dick was going deeper, and deeper in her tight yellow ass.

I knew she could feel me in the pit of her stomach once I buried my dick balls deep in her ass. I humped and ground into a slow pace, gradually picking up the pace and intensity.

"Whose pussy is this?"

"Yours Eric!"

"Whose ss is this huh?"

"It's yours Eric, it's all yours!"

I repeated those questions as I fucked her ass. Making her repeat herself over and over again. After I exploded in her ass I rolled over, got up off the bed, grabbed my phone and jumped in the shower.

Porsha was curled up in the fetal position when I entered the room. I stood staring at her beautiful face. She looked so peaceful. Beautiful women like her had started wars between men. A weaker man would have fell victim to her. I was almost one of them.

I quietly got dressed, gathered my things and kissed her on the forehead. I looked back at her before exiting the hotel room, she was still sound asleep.

The following week I got an alert from Corrlinks. Avon sent me a message. It simply said "Yo homie I got my release date. I'm getting 9-months halfway house. Tell no one!"

The homie was on his way home. I should have been ecstatic instead I stood there staring at my phone, stunned.

To be continued…

# 22

# TRAINING DAY

Zaydia McNeil
  Social Media: Tagged
  Brooklyn, New York
  Summer, 2017

I was reluctant to share this particular story for fear of being judged. Although this is a cautionary tale, I know that people will read this and come up with their own perspectives. Some of you will blame me, the victim for what occurred, while others may get a perverted kick out of it all. Be that as it may and judge as you will, however before judging me, read my story and take a walk in my shoes.

It was nearing the end of summer, 2017. I was chilling with a group of friends at my home girl Lakye's apartment in the Bronx. It was me, Lakye, Seven, and her sister Monica, along with a guy named Callie and his group of friends from Harlem. A few months prior to the get-together, Lakye and Seven were scrolling through profile pages on this website called "Tagged" when they came across Callie.

Callie is slim, stands 5'10" tall with a tan complexion, and wears his silky black hair in a long ponytail, with the sides in a fade. Whenever you saw him, his hair was laid, clothes designer, footwear Prada, Gucci. He was fly. He also rapped and produced music. Lakye and Seven both wanted him. He had this exotic look, sort of Asian with cat-colored eyes, and he rocked a long china-man-style goat beard. It's the reason why my sister nick-named him Asia.

The first time Lakye and Seven met up with Callie was at a house party he hosted in Harlem. Like I said, Lakye and Seven both wanted him, so when the opportunity presented itself, they both "Bo guarded" him in the bathroom where they all got it poppin.

Callie was more attracted to Seven, so they wound up sliding off together that night and many others. But that didn't stop Lakye from hooking up with him on the low…

I often listened to them describe their sexual encounters with Callie, comparing notes etc. I considered him cute, and cool, but I never looked at him in a sexual way. Flashback to the night in question, we were all at Lakye's apartment, drinking, smoking and just politicking. Then one-by-one we all started to crash. Lakye went into her bedroom to sleep, leaving the rest of us in the living room. Callie's people left a few hours later. While everyone slept on the couch and the living room floor, Callie and I were feeling each other up under a quilt on the floor. We had never flirted with each other before, which made that occasion so intriguing. He and I eventually fell asleep.

When Callie and I woke up, it was close to 6:00 o'clock in the morning. The sun was already coming up. He and I prepared to head out, but when we got to the hallway between the bathroom and Lakye's bedroom, I pinned him against the wall and started kissing him and feeling on his dick. I stopped kissing him, then looked dead into his eyes while unbuckling his pants. He knew what was about to go down. At that moment it was clear to me I'd wanted to sample him. I was subconsciously intrigued by all that sex talk between Lakye and Seven. I wanted to know what all the fuss was about. I squatted down and started sucking his dick. I could tell he was loving it. His knees were buckling, and he was damn near as low to the floor as I was. This was a risky move, Lakye could walk out of her room and bust us in the act at any moment. Not to mention, Seven and her sister were still in the living room asleep. What if one of them caught us in the act?

Reluctantly, I cut it short and stood him up with me. We then exited the apartment quietly and proceeded to the elevator. Every time our eyes locked on each other's we got it popping... The elevator was taking its time, so I dragged him into the staircase where we started kissing again.

Callie was palming and feeling my ass, then he slid his hand down my yoga pants. I wore no panties and knew my pussy was soaking before he slid two fingers inside me. Then someone entered the stairwell a few flights above us, so we stopped and exited the staircase. When we got to the elevator, I stood in one corner, Callie stood at the other. We smiled at each other and started kissing, getting it popping again. We were so lost in lust that we forgot to press the button on the elevator, not noticing that it wasn't moving until the elevator door opened and a lady with her child boarded. We quickly stopped and apologized, then stood in complete silence until the elevator reached the lobby. Exiting the building we both agreed that we needed to finish what we started. After exchanging contact info, I told him to link up with me so we could make that happen. I walked home to my apartment not feeling any type of way about what happened.

Callie texted me a week and a half later, and the following day he pulled up in front of my building in a white Wrangler Jeep. It was super hot and humid that day in August. The temperature was in the high 90s. That didn't stop me from looking cute though. I wore my hair straight to the back hanging down to my shoulders. A pair of Chanel sunglasses shaded my eyes from the blazing sun. I wore a distressed denim vest with a matching denim skirt and a peach lycra t-shirt underneath to match my peach and blue Nike Air Max sneakers.

The denim vest fit snug, which helped push up my 44DDs. I'd cut a slit in the neckline of my ycra -shirt to show off some cleavage. The skirt was borderline mini, I wanted to show off my thighs, plus my ass was looking phatter in the skirt. Underneath, I wore my brand new, peach-colored Victoria Secret thong set. Yes, I was looking like a tasty TREAT.

Callie couldn't keep his eyes off my thighs as I climbed into his jeep. He turned to me and said, "Damn, you look sexy!" I smiled and simply replied, "Thank you." He put the jeep in gear and pulled away from the curb. "You don't mind riding down to Brooklyn, do you? My peoples got that sour diesel. I wanna grab some, is that cool?" I'm a pretty adventurous girl and down for whatever. Plus, what I had in mind for him, some weed would definitely enhance the experience. I squeezed his upper thigh letting him know what was up and replied, "Lets ride Boo!"

We were soon on the Cross Bronx Expressway heading towards Manhattan where we jumped on the FDR Drive. After crossing the Brooklyn Bridge, I was lost and didn't know what part of Brooklyn we were in when he turned into a side street full of two-family homes. Callie pulled in front of a three-story house. I wouldn't consider it a brownstone, but it resembled the type of brownstones you see in Harlem.

"Come with me," he said. I unbuckled my seatbelt and climbed out of his jeep. As soon as I stepped out, the heat and humidity hit me and a bead of sweat ran down my back. We crossed the street and headed towards the house with a black wrought iron fence. The fence squeaked on its rusty hinges when he opened it. Instead of climbing the steps to the front entrance, Callie detoured to the right and descended several steps down to what appeared to be a basement apartment. Callie pressed a buzzer and moments later, someone answered from behind the door. "WHO DAT?" A heavy accented Jamaican called out. Callie replied, "YAWH KNO AH WHO MON, OPEN DI DOOR, IT'S CALLIE!" I looked over at Callie curiously, I never heard him speak in a Jamaican accent. Then I thought to myself, "He could definitely pass for a West Indian,

Trinidadian, or something." I became more intrigued by him. Callie was more than what met the eyes.

The lock bolts on the door were undone and the door swung open. The faint sound of heavy bass was seeping out from deep inside the apartment. Standing at the door was a tall, muscular built, dark-brown man with shoulder length dreads, tucked underneath a blue Yankee cap sitting low on his head. "Wah gwaan mon?" He greeted Callie, stepping to the side to allow us in. I followed Callie into the basement apartment. It was dimly lit and the first thing that struck me was a thick cloud of marijuana smoke mixed with a musky scent.

The baseball-cap dread bolted the door behind us as Callie and I stepped past. The deep thump of the music was louder once we stepped inside. Baseball-cap dread walked in behind us and seemed to purposely rub up against my ass. We followed the dread into the apartment. He stopped and turned right into a small kitchen/dining area where two other men sat at a table with a pile of weed and guns on the table. The two guys sitting at the table looked up at us. Both guys wore scraggly beards. One had his hair in box braids, the other wore a grey do-rag on his head.

The dread sat at the head of the table and resumed bagging up weed. "Where Bigga?" Callie addressed the question to the dread. He slowly looked up at Callie under the brim of his Yankee cap and replied with a blunt between his lips. "Callie mon, how yuh suh rude?... Yuh bring one fine gyal here, yuh no introduce?" "The two other guys sitting at the table looked up, shaking their heads in agreement. Callie smiled then turned to me, "Yo Zay these my peoples, Flex, Tuna and Mikey." I smiled and said "Hi!" They all stared at me with glassy eyes. The dread, "Flex" took a drag from his blunt, blew weed smoke in the air and pointed at me. "Dis di gal yuh did ah talk bout?" Callie turned to me and said, "Ignore that nigga, he stays on joke time." Then led me further into the apartment. I could hear Flex and the other two guys at the table laughing. "BIGGA UPSTAIRS MON!" Flex bellowed from the kitchen.

Callie led me towards the living room which was on our right. On the left was a small hall with a set of rooms and to the right of that was a set of stairs leading upstairs to the main house. The living room was dimly lit. A large flat screen TV hung on the wall. A half-moon shaped brown leather sectional sat at one corner, facing the TV. A large futon couch sat on the opposite corner. A low coffee table with a large bag of weed on top was the first thing I noticed in the room. "Have a seat, I'll be right back." Callie said, then abruptly turned and headed towards the hall, disappearing up the stairs.

I took a seat on the brown leather sectional. I could tell by the condition of the leather that the sectional had seen better days. I sat there looking around and noticed a few empty bottles of that beer Jamaicans like to drink. This was definitely a man's spot, or the trap. I looked to my right and noticed a screen door. The door led out to a small yard. I could hear a dog barking and got a glance of two guys lifting weights.

Sitting on the couch, I felt a little subconscious. I closed my legs and tried to cover them as Flex entered the living room. He held a beer in his hand. "Callie rude boy yuh know!" Then he grabbed the remote from the coffee table and clicked on the flat screen. "Yawh watch TV?" He asked, and before I replied he had it turned to porn. I looked at this nigga like, "I know you ain't trying me?" He had his back to me, then he turned, holding his crotch. "You can turn that off." I said. He looked at me with a smirk on his face and replied, "Yawh nuh like?" I just stared back at him with contempt. He clicked off the TV, then offered me something to drink. I kept eye contact with him because I did not want my eyes to drop to his crotch. Through my peripheral vision, I could see the bulge between his legs. This nigga had on a pair of biker shorts. I swear it looked like he had a snake in between his legs.

"No thank you!" I replied. He stood directly in front of me for what seemed like forever, then replied with a change of tone in his voice. "What's yawh name gal?" I looked at him, confused. "What's yawh name gal?" He repeated with more force in his voice. I was getting uncomfortable and felt a little vulnerable. I didn't know this dude, or any of these other strange men in the house. Callie needed to hurry his ass up. Reluctantly I replied, "Zaydia."

He repeated my name as if trying to sound it out. "Zaaaydia!" Then he said, "Yawh American gals rude yawh know…yawh come upon a mon house. Mon show hospitality, yawh act like you better, yawh too good to drink mon beer, eat mon food." He then stormed off in the deep recesses of the apartment. The reggae music got louder as a door opened, then immediately muffled back to the heavy thump bass after the door closed behind him. I thought to myself, "This nigga's bugging! Callie needs to hurry his ass up!"

I glanced at my smart watch. It was only 3:15 in the afternoon. A few minutes later, the back screen door opened, and two sweaty, muscular dudes stepped inside. They looked pleasantly surprised to find me sitting in the living room. One of them was short, around 5'6" tall. He was not attractive. His head was big, bald, and he had a long scar that ran from his left cheek to the side of his lips. His arms, chest and legs were huge, overly muscular. His partner was a bit taller, around 5'9" tall. He was attractive in a rugged way. His waist was slim, but his arms and shoulders were ripped and muscular. He smiled and said "Hi" as he walked past. The short ugly one looked at me with a screw-face then followed behind the cute guy. "Who di gal?" He called out to no one in particular. Moments later the short scar face dude stormed into the living room, followed by Flex, the dread.

"Dis dah gal Callie talkin bout?" The ugly, short dude said, pointing to me on the couch. Flex shook his head yeah.

"Dis dah mon eater?" Ugly man said to Flex. Flex replied grabbing his crotch, "Yeah mon, Callie said she eat him good!"

I started tapping my foot on the floor, something I did whenever I got nervous and anxious. I grabbed my clutch purse and stood up. "Can you tell Callie I'm ready to go!" The short dude looked me up and down with contempt then said, "Where Callie? Him gal ready to leave." Flex sucked his teeth then said, "Callie up with Bigga." Then he called out towards the kitchen, "Mikey!" The scruffy guy with the doo rag entered the living room.

Flex turned to him, "Go tell Callie him gal ready fi go!" Mikey turned and headed towards the stairs leading up into the main house. The ugly dude walked off towards the small hall that led to the rooms. Moments later, Mikey came down the stairs. He walked towards Flex and said, "Callie say him fi make a move, and fi send di gal upstairs."

I looked at Flex and he returned my gaze, then he stepped to the side and gestured for me to head towards the stairs. He didn't have to tell me twice. I brushed between him and Mikey and headed towards the stairs. Flex followed close behind. "Callie ah rude boy, yawh know!" I didn't respond to that remark. I could tell he was trying to bait me into saying something in response. I reached the stairs and looked up into the darkness. I hesitated for a split second before climbing the stairs.

Halfway up the stairs Flex slid his hand between my legs. I was caught totally off guard and in reflex I closed my legs shut and inadvertently trapped his hand in my crotch. He palmed my pussy in a tight grip. I immediately released, then mule kicked behind me, but he anticipated it and stepped back several steps down and out of reach. He looked up at me with a smile across his face that I wanted to smack. I couldn't believe this Jamaican just tried me like that. And what the fuck did he mean by Callie telling them I'm a man eater! All those thoughts flowed through my head as I climbed the stairs glancing back at Flex. Before I reached the top, the door above me opened and a big, black, Biggie Smalls-looking dude descended the stairs blocking my path. "Where yawh going gal?" I looked up at him like, "nigga move out of my way!" Then Flex responded from the bottom of the stairs. "That Callie gal yaw know!" The big dude continued to descend down the stairs towards me. "Callie no here gal, him go take care of business. Him seh wait downstairs."

I was pissed at this point. These Jamaicans were bugging. I didn't know what type of shit Callie was on, but I was done, ready to leave. I would find my own way home. I continued up the stairs, "Excuse me." I said to the big dude, who blocked my path.

"Where yaw think yaw goin?" He asked.

"I'm leaving. Can you excuse me please?" He didn't budge, then pointed down the stairs. "Leave downstairs, yawh can't go upstairs."

Truthfully, I felt uneasy from the moment Callie left me in the living room. Now the feeling was on 10. My heart was beating fast. I inhaled a breath of air and told myself, "They are not gonna do anything to you Zay!" I turned and descended down the stairs with the big black nigga two steps behind me. When I reached the bottom of the stairs, Flex, Tuna, Mikey, the short ugly dude with the scar and the cute light-skinned dude were standing in a semicircle. The big dude

nudged me forward with his belly when we reached the bottom of the stairs. I stumbled into the short, ugly dude who pushed me against the guy with the scruffy beard and box braids who was sitting at the kitchen table when Callie and I first entered the basement. "Stop! What are ya'll doing?" I protested. "Tuna" shoved me back into the big black dude who grabbed me from behind and put me in this head lock where one of his arms was maneuvered under my right arm and his other around my neck. I dropped my clutch purse and started clawing at his arm. The chokehold he had on me was cutting off my air. I was struggling to breathe. "Stop!" I pleaded breathlessly. The big dude let up a little on his chokehold. Then the short, ugly dude ripped open my denim vest. I could hear the buttons from my vest scatter across the floor. Then he yanked at the neckline of my lycra shirt pulling it until it ripped down the middle. "Please, stop, please!" I begged as tears started to flow down my face. I could not believe this was happening to me.

"You gonna like it gal!" The big dude said into my ear as I kicked out, barely missing the short ugly dude in his nuts. The dude Mikey and Tuna grabbed my legs and they carried me towards the living room. I struggled, using my legs to kick out, but their grip on me was like iron. They were strong.

"Look at her flop like a fish!" One of them said as I continued to struggle to break free. "Let me go, let me go!" I kept kicking and struggling. Then they tossed me onto the futon in the living room. I immediately crawled backwards towards the corner. They were standing all around me, looking down at me.

"Why are you doing this to me? Why?" I asked, pleading with tears running down my face. I saw no compassion in their eyes. They seemed to be lost in some sort of blood lust as my cries for mercy was fueling their desires. The dude Flex grabbed one of my legs with his rough hands, yanking me towards the edge of the futon bed. I was about to kick out at him, but the look on his face told me not to.

He crouched down and grabbed my face. He was looking at

me face to face. I could smell the beer on his breath, he was so close. "Yawh mon Callie, he owes me big money." I looked at him in confusion. "What does that have to do with me?" All six of them started laughing. Flex let go of my face and with his pointy finger nudged me in the center of my chest. "Yawh dah pay!" My mind was in a fog. My heartbeat was racing. I felt dizzy from the chokehold. It took me a moment to register what he said.

He stood up and his crotch was directly in front of my face. He was peeling off his tank top as he said, "Callie seh you eat him good. Him say you real mon eater!" Then he pulled out his dick... the shocked look on my face caused another fit of laughter from them. I swear I have never seen a dick so long, so thick and ugly with big veins, in my life. I tried to stand. All I thought was, "Run Zay, Run!" But who was I fooling? Because, soon as I made a move to get up off the futon couch I was shoved back down. I tried to crawl away, I kicked out behind me, but somebody jumped on my back, pinning me down on the couch. I screamed, the one on my back buried my face on the futon muffling my screams. Then I felt the sneakers snatched off my feet. Then my skirt was pulled up. I felt like three sets of hands pulling and yanking at my thong tearing it into shreds as they tore it off my body. It was like an outer body experience for me. I could not believe this was happening. "Please, please, stop!" I begged and pleaded.

"Don't worry gal, when we are done with you, you will beg for more. All girls cry first, then beg later!" The one pinning me down said into my ear. Then sticking his tongue into it. I shivered in revulsion.

The weight on my back eased up, and I was stood up. Then somebody grabbed both of my hands and started wrapping them in duct tape. They dragged me to the corner wall and hooked my wrists on a hook above my head. I hadn't noticed it while I'd sat on the leather couch earlier. My back was facing them. They started running their filthy hands all over my body. I still had the torn vest, skirt and t-shirt on. They unbuckled the Chanel belt from around my waist and pulled my skirt down. I was naked from the waist down. I kept wiggling, trying to break free. The hook was so high on the wall I was forced to stand on my tip toes.

"Give it to her mon?" The big black dude said to the person standing directly behind me, I turned, trying to look over my shoulder. It was the short ugly guy. I couldn't see what he had in his hand, and without warning the two dudes standing on each side of me each grabbed my ass cheeks and spread them apart. The short ugly guy smeared something greasy, I think it was lube or vaseline around my asshole. Then he shoved whatever he held in his hand up my ass. I screamed and jerked from the sudden invasion. It hurt. They laughed as I wiggled. He kept his finger in my ass, shoving it as far as he could. "Ass tight yawh no!" The short dude said out loud, wiggling his middle finger around and around and then in and out. He took his finger out then he shoved that finger into my mouth. I was tempted to bite his fucking finger off, but I knew they would probably beat me to death if I did. "Suck yawh ass gal!" He ordered. I resisted. "Lash her!" One of the other guys said. I didn't comprehend at first what "lash her" meant because his accent was strong. I turned my head to look over my shoulder. Flex was holding a long leather strap. He gave the strap to the cute light-skin dude and he struck me across my bare ass with the strap. The sting of the strap caused me to scream out in pain.

"Look at it jiggle!" The big black dude bellowed. I was struck again and again. The ugly dude stuck his middle finger back in my mouth. "You gon suck yah ass?" I shook my head yes and sucked his middle finger that was in my ass. The dude struck me across my ass again and I sucked harder on his finger. He struck me hard over and over again, until the ugly dude told him to stop.

"You gonna act nice?" The short ugly dude said after removing his middle finger from my mouth. I shook my head yes. I could barely see with the tears blurring my eyes. The ugly short guy was smiling. One of his front teeth was missing. I was truly revolted by him.

Two sets of hands lifted me and removed me from the hook and turned me around to face them. The ugly one grabbed my wrists then cut the duct tape off, freeing my hands.

"Bitch, take this off." Tuna said. He was to my left. Him and Mikey started ripping my vest off then they tore off my shirt. I stood there in my peach bra covering myself with my hands. Then they started ripping my bra off. "Stop play around gal you eat mon good!" Tuna said, roughly grabbing my left titty and squeezing my nipple between his fingers. I squirmed in pain.

"Move, gal!" Tuna pushed me towards the futon. Somebody smacked my ass real hard, as the short ugly dude grabbed my wrist dragging me to the futon couch. I fell back onto the couch. All I felt was hands all over my body. I was completely nude. Flex was standing at my foot. He grabbed both my legs and pulled me to the edge of the futon to where my ass was hanging slightly off the edge. He crouched down on his knees and spread my legs then he buried his face between them. I laid there, stiff, telling myself they could use my body, but they would not get my soul.

He spread my pussy lips open and started eating me out. Standing above me at the head of the futon was the Biggie Smalls-looking dude. He had no pants on. His dick was pointing straight out beyond his beer belly. He straddled my chest and placed his dick between my titties and started to titty fuck me. The dude Tuna grabbed the back of my head and lifted it so that my chin was tilted towards my chest. "Eat gal, eat the mon." The fat dude scooted up until his black dick head reached my lips. I kept my lips tightly closed, so the big dude pinched both my nipples until I screamed, then he shoved his dick into my mouth. He continued to pinch my nipples until I started sucking his dick. "Suck it, suck it. Eat the mon, eat!" The guy Tuna kept saying…

The fat Biggie Smalls dude leaned over me and started fucking my mouth. I could not take all his dick in my mouth. I gagged and gagged so he eased up a little. Flex was still eating my pussy. Then I felt him spread my ass and he started to eat my ass while rubbing my clit at the same time. Then someone brushed his hand away from my clit and started rubbing it. At that moment I started to feel hot and a dreamy sensation came over me. Not orgasmic. Something different.

My whole body started to float and without me having control, my body began to tingle. I felt like I was high.

"Eat the dick, eat it!" Tuna kept on egging on as I gagged on fat boy's dick. He came in my mouth and I inadvertently swallowed his cum. Then he pulled his dick out and slapped my lips with his dick.

"My turn!" Tuna said, squatting over me after at boy rolled over onto his side. I looked down between my legs to see it was the short ugly dude rubbing my clit while Flex was still eating my ass. I was feeling myself about to cum. I closed my eyes not wanting to, holding it in.

He rubbed it fast. The friction made my clit feel hot and raw. I didn't realize I was gyrating my hips. He stuck two fingers in my pussy with one hand and rubbed my clit with the other while

Flex continued to eat my ass. His tongue was going deeper and deeper into my ass. I was crying. Why was my body betraying me?

I opened my eyes and Tuna was squatting over my face. Then he lowered himself. His dick facing my chest, his ass crack facing my face. "Lick Gal!" He said, squeezing and pinching my nipples again. I started eating his ass like Flex ate mine. His balls smelled like sweat. His ass tasted like a penny. He was grinding his ass on my tongue, then he shoved his balls in my mouth, so I sucked on those while he rubbed and massaged my nipples.

The short ugly guy started to pat my clit in between rubbing it and I felt Flex stick his finger in my ass. I had two fingers in my pussy, one in my ass at the same time, while ugly guy continued to rub my clit. I was sucking on Tuna's nuts real hard because I was cumming again. I had no control over my own body, fighting a losing battle as I reached another orgasm. This time I let out a moan. Then I grabbed Tuna's dick and put it in my mouth. I wasn't even aware of all the things I did or said after that. I sucked him hard, but he pulled out before I got him to cum.

"BOY, DIS GAL VICIOUS MON EATER YOU KNO!" He said climbing off me. I was flipped onto my stomach then yanked to the foot of the futon to where my knees were on the floor and I was bent over. Flex slapped my ass really hard and they were all fascinated by how it shook.

"Who gwan first?" I looked over my shoulder. The cute light-skin dude was stripped down below the waist, dick in his hand stroking it. "Flex gwan last." He said, and they all started laughing looking at Flex.

"Yawh meat too big Flex. Yawh go first them gal no good again. Dem walls gone!" Flex chuckled, stroking his dick." We save the best for last."

The ugly man and slim cute dude fought to get to me first. The slim dude relented, allowing ugly to get behind me while he climbed onto the futon putting his dick in my face. He grabbed the back of my head and stuffed my mouth with his dick. I started to suck him. The ugly dude smacked my ass real hard. Then he guided his dick head into my pussy. He was short but his dick wasn't, it filled my pussy. He went all the way in until his balls slapped against my clit. He started to fuck me at a steady medium speed. I had his workout partner's dick in my mouth. Then Tuna and Mikey were on each side of me. They were fondling my breasts, ugly was slowly picking up his pace fucking me harder and faster, smacking my ass between strokes, while the cute dude fucked my mouth. They were fucking me in unison. I was moaning while they cheered each other on.

"GAL EAT MON GOOD!" The cute dude in my mouth said.

"Fuck the pussy Ox, fuck the gal pussy mon, she loves it!" Biggie Smalls was saying. I knew it was him by his deep baritone voice and that's when I learned the name of the short ugly guy. His name was "Ox." The name fit him. He was built like a mule with a mule dick. He started to beat into my pussy like a crazed lunatic. His balls were hitting my clit with every pump into me. He was fucking me like a machine. I never experienced being fucked that hard and fast before. The sound of my ass slapping against him sounded like hands clapping loudly. Just as I was about to cum, he pulled out and shot semen on my back. It was hot and heavy. I looked over my shoulder when the slim dude took his dick out my mouth. The ugly nigga could fuck, I thought to myself. And before I had a chance to wipe the nutt off my back, the cute slim dude was behind me sliding his dick into me, and Mikey took his place.  But he laid on his back, so I bent forward to suck his dick, which made my ass poke up in the air. I started to jerk Mikey's dick while sucking his balls.

Then he forced my face lower to lick his ass, and I did. I licked his ass, forcing my tongue in it while jerking his dick.

Slim was fucking me hard. Taking his dick all the way out then slamming all the way in. He fucked me with his middle finger in my ass. I came on his dick and he came inside me. Then Mikey maneuvered under me and I sat on his dick.  He held me to his chest and Tuna got behind me. I felt him pushing the tip of his dick into my ass. It wouldn't go in, it was too tight back there with a dick in my pussy. So, he bent down, spread my ass and spit in the crack, smeared his spit around my asshole then pushed his dick head into my ass. I tried to resist, Tuna slapped me so hard my ears rang, and a tear flew out my eye. I was in so much pain.

I'd never been fucked like this before. They started to slowly fuck me in unison. One in my pussy, the other in my ass. Then Biggie Smalls grabbed my head and forced his dick in my mouth. So, I had his dick in my mouth. Mikey under me in my pussy and Tuna in my ass. They fucked me like a rag doll. Biggie Smalls had my hair wrapped around his fist as he fucked my face. Mikey was sucking really hard on my right breast while fucking my pussy. Tuna was on top of me, drilling his dick in my ass.

"Fill her, fill her MON, she loves it!" One of them was saying, egging Biggie, Mikey and Tuna on. Then Tuna took his dick out of my ass, I thought he was done, instead he started to stuff his dick in my pussy with Mikey's dick still inside me. I started to moan in protest, that's when Tuna punched me in the back knocking the air out of me. Biggie Smalls held my head and continued to stuff his dick down my throat. It felt like my pussy was about to rip. The pain was unbearable. I never felt that stretched out before. Tuna punched me again and again in my ribs. They were dogging me out.

Fat Biggie Smalls was about to cum. I could tell by how hard he gripped my hair and fucked my face. I was gagging as his sperm shot down my throat.

Mikey and Tuna were both fucking my pussy at the same time really hard. My body was sweaty by then. After five minutes in that position Mikey said, "Flip her around, I want her ass." They flipped me over to where my back was on Mikey's chest and I was face to face with Tuna. Mikey was under me and they forced me to sit on his dick guiding it into my ass. Then Tuna put his dick in my pussy, and they started to fuck my pussy and ass in reverse. Tuna wrapped his hand around my throat choking me while he fucked my pussy. Mikey humped up into my ass, then Tuna grabbed my legs and placed them on the crook of his arms and leaned on my chest to where I was sandwiched between them. They started to hump and grind into me in a steady pace. I was lost in that sensation and it must have started to feel good because I wrapped my arms around Tuna's neck then hooked my legs around his waist. Just like that I started to meet their strokes.

I was drenched in sweat as I reached another orgasm that came from my ass and pussy at the same time. Tuna pulled out and came on my stomach and for no reason, slapped me across the face. Mikey continued to fuck my ass and I bounced on his dick, I was scared of displeasing them. They were all clapping and cheering Mikey on as he continued to fuck my ass. He was about to cum. I could feel his dick grow and pulsate in my ass. I bounced on it faster so he could cum. He shot his sperm in my ass, rubbing my clit at the same time. I laid on his chest and he was spent.

Ox yanked me off Mikey and had his dick in my face. I started sucking his dick. Then I felt the cute dude come up next to me on my right. I was still on the futon on my knees. He had his dick out. I grabbed it and started jerking his dick while sucking Ox's dick. I was going back and forth sucking both their dicks while they massaged my breasts. Before I knew it Mikey, Tuna and the big black dude had me in a circle with their dicks out. I started to suck them off too. I had a dick in each hand jerking them off while I sucked a dick, alternating from dick to dick, gagging whenever one of them forced their dick down the back of my throat.

After jerking and sucking their dicks they started to cum one by one. Each time one of them came, he would splash on my face. My face was painted in cum when Flex stepped into the circle. All of them were packing in dick size and shape. But Flex's dick was abnormal. He grabbed my head really rough and mushed me down onto the futon. I fell face down onto the futon.

"Hold her down," Flex said, and Ox held down my head. My ass was poking in the air. I could feel Flex position himself behind me. He slapped my ass real hard, then he told Bigga, that was the Biggie Smalls-looking dude name and Ox to keep me still. I felt two hands spread my ass so wide I thought I would rip open. Flex smeared my ass with lube and started to finger fuck my ass with one finger, then two, three and four fingers. I was squirming. I could feel him forcing his thumb along with his four fingers squeezing his whole hand in my ass. I could not believe how painful it was until I felt him stuffing fingers in my pussy, OMG... Why was he doing this? They were still spreading my ass until he had both his entire hands in my ass and pussy. "I'm getting you ready gal" I heard him say as the rest of them laughed. Then he began to hand fuck both my pussy and ass. He took both his hands out of me, then I felt him rubbing the head of his dick against my pussy.

After stretching my insides with his rough hands, his dick head was too big. I closed my eyes and bit down on my lips. No way was his dick going inside of me.

He pushed in slowly and it felt as if a real cobra snake was inside me. I blacked out...

✗ ✗ ✗ ✗ ✗ ✗

When I came to my vision was blurry, it took a moment for my eyes to come into focus. Callie was leaning over me, shaking me. "Wake up, wake up stupid!" I looked around, disoriented and confused. My mind felt foggy. "Get up, get dressed." He said, holding my denim skirt, torn vest and sneakers out to me. I stared back at him with a blank look on my face. I didn't know where I was, or why he held my clothes out to me. Then slowly things started coming back to me. Sensing my distress, Callie's tone changed into a soothing one. "Put your clothes on Zay, I'm taking you home." I got up feeling as if I'd been in a car accident. My body ached all over, inside and out. Callie steadied me with his hand. I felt weak and light-headed. My mouth and throat were dry, I needed some water. He directed me to the bathroom. I looked around nervously expecting to see Flex and his crew, but the dudes who attacked me were nowhere in sight.

I stepped into the bathroom, closing the door behind me. I gasped at the reflection staring back at me in the mirror. My face, hair and neck were covered in dried semen. I looked down at my breasts, stomach and thighs. They were covered in bruises. My insides felt sore and raw as I began to wipe myself. I splashed water on my face, rubbing the caked-up semen off of me. I felt so dirty and disgusting. I got dressed and tried to cover my breast as much as I could in the torn vest. Callie handed me a grey hoodie when I stepped out of the bathroom. I stared at him with hate, and contempt. I wanted to scratch his fucking eyes out. I kept my cool, taking deep breaths as I silently followed him out of that trap-house because that's exactly what it was, a fucking trap. At that point I simply wanted to escape what felt like a living nightmare.

It was nighttime and chilly when we emerged from the basement apartment. I glanced at my wrist to check the time and realized that my smart watch was missing. Callie's Wrangler Jeep was parked at the curb. I was tempted to walk to the corner and find my way to the nearest police station. Callie must have read my mind because he grabbed my elbow guiding me to his jeep. I climbed into the passenger seat and glanced at the digital time displayed on the dashboard. It was 4:26a.m., how long had I been knocked out? I sat there silently fuming, paying close attention to the street signs as we drove back uptown.

At a red light on Nostrand Avenue, Callie started scrolling through his cellphone, then he passed it to me.

"This the type of shit you're into?"

I stared at the phone screen; it depicted a girl getting gang banged. I thought he was being an asshole. It took a moment for me to register that the girl in the video was me. But I wasn't being raped, I was a willing participant in the scene depicted in the video. I was moaning and begging to be fucked. "Oh yes, fuck me, fuck... Yes, yes, I want it. Please, fuck me, yes, fuck meee, pleeaasee!" I was literally begging for it, laying on my back, my legs were pulled back on Flex's shoulders. He was pile driving into me. His dick had to be 14 inches long at least. Sweat was dripping off his body. Bigga, Ox and the rest of them stood around routing him on yelling, "Fuck her mon, kill it, murda da pussy mon!" His dick was slamming into me, his balls hung low and slapped against my asshole with every stroke. He stretched my pussy beyond its limits. His dick was pulling my insides out with every stroke.

Flex then palmed my ass with both hands, spreading them wide, inserting his middle finger into my ass to finger fuck it at the same time. Then he flipped me onto my side and started fucking me with one leg on his shoulder and the other on the futon. While Flex fucked my pussy in that position, Ox, Tuna, Mikey, Bigga and the slim cute dude took turns fucking me in the ass until each one of them came in me and on me.

They took turns fucking my mouth, my ass and my pussy. They ejaculated in my mouth, my pussy, my ass, my face and in my hair. Flex fucked me in my ass until it bled. They made me eat their asses. They did things to me that I'd seen on ghetto gaggers, but worse. They truly violated me.

I watched that video in disbelief, not recognizing that girl. How was she taking all that dick? Moaning and begging to be fucked. There was no way I could claim I was raped.

The remainder of the ride back uptown to the Bronx was in silence, until we pulled up in front of my building. "Keep this shit to yourself!" Callie said, emphasizing with the wave of the cellphone he held in his hand. I just stared back at him as I climbed out of his jeep and headed into my building. I was so ashamed of myself. I felt so low and dirty, wondering what man would want me now?

The following day Callie shot me a message to my DM reminding me to keep things to myself. Then he attached the video to my email.

For several weeks I kept to myself, avoiding my friends, just going to work and returning home. A month went by and I was beginning to allow that fateful night to fade into my memory, then out of the blue I got a text from Callie, "Come downstairs!" I immediately felt lightheaded. My heart was racing with anxiety, I did not want to see him again. But what choice did I have?

When I reached the lobby, I could see his white Wrangler Jeep parked in front of my building. Reluctantly I stepped outside and walked to the curb. His windows were tinted so I didn't see my bestie Lakye sitting in **the** passenger seat until she rolled down the window.

"What's up bitch? I ain't seen you in a minute!" Lakye said. I was shocked and started mumbling an answer.

"Me and Callie are about to hang out with his people in Brooklyn. Come hang out with us, you ain't doing nothing." I must have looked like a deer with headlights beaming in my eyes because the look on Callie's face said, "Bitch don't say shit, get in the motherfucking jeep!" My heart was beating hard against my chest. I was hoping and praying that Callie hadn't shown Lakye the video.

Lakye seemed oblivious to the simmering tension between me and Callie as she made small talk during the ride down to Brooklyn. Every so often Callie would make eye contact with me through the rear-view mirror. When we pulled up in front of that house with the black wrought iron fence Callie looked at me silently saying, "You know what time it is, bitch!"

My stomach was tied up in knots. I was filled with a combination of mixed emotions from fear and dread, to anxiety as we entered that basement apartment filled with marijuana smoke, weed, guns and sweaty men. It was eerie watching a similar scene play out all over again. What they did to me, they did to Lakye, to the both of us, but this time it was more of them. Ten guys took turns on us. I felt bad for Lakye. I tried telling her not to resist as they beat her into submission, punching her in the ribs and back. I realized then I was drugged as I watched them shove an ecstasy pill up Lakye's ass.

I had already been broken in, not realizing I was being trained, we both were. Later, I finally got the nerve to ask Callie why he'd done that to us? He said, "I knew you were a freak, I just needed to bring that shit out of you." I asked him why he didn't do that to Seven? His claim was that Seven wasn't like me and Lakye, that she was different. I took offense to that. He was implying that she was better than us.

Seven is my home girl, I've known her for over 15 years. She was no different than the rest of us, and I went out my way to prove that point. I tricked her into coming with me down to that Brooklyn trap house where Flex and his Jamaican crew ran a train on her too.

By this point getting ganged banged wasn't such a big deal to me. I was more so wanting to control the narrative by picking the guys who fucked me.

I no longer visit the Brooklyn trap-house to satisfy my sexual urges. That shit came to an end the day Callie tried to extort me into working for him as an escort. I told that nigga to leak the video, I no longer gave a fuck. Best believe if he did, that Brooklyn trap-house would have gotten raided by the Feds!

I know this story sounds crazy and goes beyond your wildest imaginations but in every hood, there is a nigga like Callie, and a group of men like Flex and his crew who take advantage of young girls, running trains on them and turning them out. These women are victims, so don't judge us, judge them...!

After completing the manuscript to this book, a sense of relief and contentment washed over me. It had taken over two years for me to gather the stories, interview people, compose the manuscript, proofread, then submit it to my publisher. I was now an author. So, imagine my reaction to the following message I received from my publisher several days later.

"Gil, the manuscript you've submitted of your book "Love, Lust And Scandalous Hook-Ups!" (LLASH), is as what you described. However, in my opinion it is incomplete."

"What do you mean? I've submitted 22 different stories, a total of 22 chapters, that is the entire manuscript."

"Yes, I received all 22 chapters, however, I noticed that your stories are not included."

"Of course not! The book is not about me or my experiences. The book is about the social media experiences of other people."

"I get that Mr. Tu'Challa, but in my professional opinion your readers will feel cheated if the author's stories aren't included."

I stared at the computer screen racking my brain for a plausible counter argument, but my mind was blank, I had none... I logged off the computer and went to the place I usually go to gather my thoughts, the library.

To be completely honest with you, I'm not comfortable with writing about my personal experiences. Trust me, I acknowledge the irony in that statement, but it's true. However, after considering my publisher's point of view, I took her advice, threw caution to the wind, and decided to dig deep, go down memory lane to share with you some of my most intimate, past experiences.

I chose to convey three stories that occurred at a particular period in my life when my values were skewed and dominated by "the life!" Don't judge me too hard, as I know some of you will. Keep in mind that I'm not comfortable with writing about myself, which means, "I'm sensitive about my shit!"

Sincerely
Gil Tu'Challa

# 23

# BROOKLYN

THE FIRST TIME I SAW HER, I MEAN REALLY SAW HER, WAS WHEN my 'Day-one' Kev pointed her out to me. I was taking inventory of her assets. She had on a pair of tight, faded jeans that had her ass looking nice, heart shaped. She was one of those girls who were part of the in-crowd in college. You know the ones who dressed fly, kept her hair done, never out of place, gear was strictly designer. I figured she had to be from Brooklyn by her style of dress, plus she wore a pair of Gucci sneakers that day, signature Brooklyn.

Her hair was styled in that Halle Berry, Anita Baker, Toni Braxton cut, asymmetrical. It fit her face perfectly. She was a shorty, bowlegged with hips and a nice ass. I thought her cheek bones were made for modeling. If she was 5'9" instead of 5'1" tall, she would have graced the cover of Vogue and Essence magazines.

Back then we were checking for all the light-skin girls with the hazel eyes and silky hair. But shorty had that 'It Factor'. Her brown skin was smooth and devoid of blemishes. She was standing with her girlfriend Aisha, with her back to me as I approached her. My eyes were focused on her butt as I tapped her on the shoulder. She turned around in surprise.

"What's up Ma, how are you doing?"

She smiled bashfully, I held out my hand, and she extended hers. I shook it, it was soft, and she held it timidly. "My name is Gil." Then I turned and pointed to Kev who was standing across the street near the administration building on the college campus.

"My homie Kev said you wanted to meet me?"

"Oh my God, he told you that?" She was shocked, and a little embarrassed.

"Yeah, he did. Was he lying?"

"I'm so embarrassed!" She covered her face. I brushed her hand away.

"Don't be, I wanted to meet you." That broke the ice. She told me her name, "Brooke", but I nicknamed her 'Brooklyn'. She asked me what courses I was taking in school. I kept it real with her, I wasn't a student at the college, I just knew a lot of people who attended.

I don't know what it was about her. I couldn't describe the feelings that I grew to have for her. I was no sucker for love. I had my fair share of women. What I used to describe as my starting five. But Brooklyn had me on some other shit. I wanted to wife her up, give her anything she wanted.

The first time we got intimate was the day I took her home with me during a school break. I had a nice apartment in Fort Lee, New Jersey. The mood was set right with soft music playing. You know, that take your panties off, old school R&B: Luther Vandross, Freddie Jackson, Keith Sweat, a little Anita Baker, even some R. Kelly way before he caught that case. The lights were dimmed for a little bit of that red-light special. I was serious about getting the ambiance right, because for me, sex was an art form. It went beyond the physical. It was mental, emotional, damn near spiritual the way I made love. Yes, I call what I did, making love. Although I can give it to a chick rough and bang the walls out whenever the mood was set for that. But I'm more about that intimacy.

We slow danced to the music and started tongue kissing as our bodies swayed back and forth. My hands had a mind of its own, undressing her until I held her completely naked in my arms. When I lifted my shirt over my head and pressed her against my chest, her skin was on fire. I laid her on the bed and began exploring her body with my lips and tongue. That's when I discovered her birthmark. A small indentation in the center of her chest, between her breasts. I rubbed it with my fingers. I never felt or seen anything like it before. It fascinated me.

Her little, perky titties fit in the palm of my hands. Her nipples responded to my touch, going erect in my mouth as I sucked them. She was moaning and breathing heavy. I knew she was ready for me, but I wanted to explore her secret garden first. I licked her belly, going further and further south. Her pubic hairs didn't deter me from going further. She spread her legs wide for me. I could feel the heat rising from deep inside her womb. I parted the lips between her legs to reveal her secrets to me. I inhaled her aroma, and that shit sent a rush of sensations down my spine. I flicked my tongue on her clitoris and she let out an erotic moan. I was lost in her scent, her aroma, the taste of her juices, her moans and the motion of her hips. The way she pressed it against my mouth. She wanted my tongue to go deep inside her vagina and I obliged. I licked and sucked her pussy and clitoris until she creamed on my lips. Then I retraced the trail of wet kisses back up to her neck. She pulled me into her embrace, kissing me with so much passion I felt an electric current flow through my body. Her pussy was soaking, dripping wet when I entered her. I immediately felt this ridge inside her. It was a few inches beyond the entrance of her vagina. Her pussy was tight. I could feel the ridge massaging the underside of my penis as I moved in and out of her. I knew from that moment on I would crave her pussy.

Brooklyn arched her back as I went deeper and deeper inside her, picking up speed. Our bodies were in sync with each other's, she was grinding and rotating her hips in rhythm with my every stroke. We kissed and made love to the sweet melody of the love songs that played through my speakers. Brooklyn was on the brink of reaching another orgasm. She started to rack her nails into my back, nearly drawing blood. I picked up the pace, boring deeper and deeper inside her, amazed at the ability of her petite body to take all this dick I was giving her. I came inside her, then collapsed on her chest. We were both drenched in sweat. We laid in bed, breathing heavy. I found myself rubbing her birthmark. She turned to me and said, "You know you gonna have to get my hair done because you sweated my weave out!" We both burst into a fit of laughter....

Brooklyn and I became inseparable. Every spare moment I had was spent with her. On the weekends I'd take that 4-hour drive to upstate New York. We would spend those weekends off campus, taking long drives through those winding back country roads where we once came across a grass field, pocketed with apple trees. That day we laid a blanket on the grass, had a little picnic and enjoyed a day of lovemaking surrounded by nature.

During our time separated by distance we talked on the phone, often running the long-distance phone bills up to $1,200, or more.

To see us together was to witness love. You could see it in our eyes whenever we looked into each other's. And people on campus thought we made the perfect couple.

After a year and a half, a change occurred. Brooklyn's demeanor started to shift. That sparkle of love in her eyes began to dim. I noticed it the day I popped up on campus after returning from a month-long trip out of town. When I showed up at Brooklyn's dorm to surprise her, the look of disappointment on her face spoke a thousand words. She was falling out of love with me.

I kept my thoughts to myself as the distance grew between us. After 18 months she was ready to move on. I could feel it.

They say, "If you love someone let them go. If that love is meant to be, they will return to you. But if they don't then it was never meant to be!"

I had pride, and as much as I loved her. I knew she was outgrowing me. I guess she didn't see a future with a guy like me who was knee deep in the game.

I made love to Brooklyn for the last time during her Christmas break. I pulled up in front of her apartment building in Brooklyn. We drove uptown to my parent's crib in the Bronx. I knew it would be our last night together, so I made it a memorable one, making sure I hit all her spots and bringing her to multiple orgasms, leaving a mark in her mind, if not her heart... Forever!

# 24

## HARLEM

After my breakup with 'Brooklyn' I was done with love. Being in a committed relationship didn't work for me. I started dating women in abundance, Black, Puerto Rican, Jamaican, Panamanian, Dominican, Asian. But, one in particular stood out. She was from Harlem.

I was in New York hanging with my little brother taking him shopping for some school gear. We were coming out of KP-CONS, a sporting goods store on 145th Street and Broadway in Harlem when I noticed her instantly. Mesmerized by her strut, staring at her ass as she walked by... I handed lil bro the shopping bags, tossed him the keys to the truck, told him I'd be right back, and took off after her.

Shorty was strutting down Broadway in a pair of Milano Timbs. I focused on her long, jet-black hair, while I pursued her in the crowd, dodging the Dominicans on the corner screaming out their wares, "Poppi $15.00-gram, $15.00 gram, me got chu for cheap!" I ignored them keeping my eyes on her as she turned the corner on 144th Street where I lost sight of her. So, I picked up my pace, turning the corner in pursuit of her. I made her out in the crowd by the sway of her hips and her jet-black hair. She had a nice plump, ass in the tight jeans she wore. I did not want to lose her, so I started jogging a little to catch up to her. I reached her before she turned the corner on Amsterdam Avenue.

She was definitely my type. Her complexion was flawless, even toned, light brown, nearly tan in color. Her nose was narrow, lips full, with a lil sparkle from the gloss she had on it. Her eyes were light brown with specks of hazel. I stared at them in the bright sun. She looked at me as if I was crazy, twirling around in shock when I grabbed her arm.

"What the fuck?" She said with a look of surprise. I threw my hands up in the universal sign of surrender.

"I'm sorry miss, but I had to stop you. You are the most beautiful woman I've seen in forever. I could not allow you out of my sight without introducing myself." She looked me up and down, inspecting my attire. I was on point, Coogi sweater underneath a brown, butter soft, Andrew Marc leather jacket, some Tommy jeans, Technicia boots, LV belt and LV aviator shades covering my eyes.

"This what you do, run up on women all day with those corny pick-up lines?" I chuckled because I could see the smile in her eyes even though it didn't show on her face. I introduced myself, explaining that my truck was double parked on Broadway, while glancing at my watch, a diamond studded Movado. I pulled out a wad of cash, peeled of a $100 bill, scribbled my number on it, then handed it to her. I knew it was a lame move, but I wanted her to remember me, lame or not. She took the $100 bill. "Call me. I wanna take you out, anywhere you wanna go." I said back peddling as I made my way back towards Broadway.

I was on the New Jersey Turnpike heading south to Maryland when I finally got a call from Harlem. Two weeks had transpired, I was thinking that maybe Harlem wasn't feeling me. I picked up on the third ring, and was excited to hear her voice, but I played it cool.

"Hello." I answered.

She replied,

"May I speak to Gil."

"Speaking, who this?

"Harlem!" She replied in that smooth, seductive voice.

"Where I know you from?"

"Hmmn, you must hand out $100 bills to every woman you meet on the street!"

I bust out laughing. "Nah Ma, I'm just fucking with you. It took you long enough to call. What's up with you?"

"I was going through a break-up. I'm over it now, so I decided to give you a call."

"So, I'm the rebound guy huh?"

"Who said you're anything? I'm just calling to say hi!"

I could sense a shift in her tone and attitude. I did not want her to end the call abruptly, so I cut in, "My bad Ma, I didn't mean to offend you. Can I at least take you out to dinner and a movie because I really wanna get to know you?"

"Sure, I wouldn't mind."

"What are you doing tomorrow?" I asked.

"I don't have anything planned." She replied.

"You ever been to D.C.?"

"No, why?"

"I'm on the highway right now heading down there. If you like, I'll have a plane ticket waiting for you at the Eastern Airline ticket counter at LaGuardia Airport tomorrow. You can fly down, hang out with me. We do dinner and a movie, and I'll have you back in New York the next day." She was silent for a few moments.

"Hello?"

"I'm still here." She said, still contemplating my proposition.

"Don't worry Ma, you'll be safe with me. I don't bite!"

She chuckled, then said, "Can I get back to you on that?"

"Sure, take your time!" She hung up the phone, and I stared at the road in front of me wondering if I'd overplayed my hand? I was on the Baltimore Washington Expressway turning off the Greenbelt Road exit when Harlem called back.

"I don't really know you like that to be traveling out of town to chill with you. But if my cousin Lisa can come with me then cool, I'm with that."

"No problem, I'll have two tickets waiting for both you and your cousin in the morning."

I called my ex, Samantha, who worked at Eastern Shuttle's ticket counter at LaGuardia Airport and made the arrangements with her.

The following day Harlem and her cousin Lisa arrived at Reagan National Airport in Washington, D.C. Harlem was looking as pretty as I remembered. Her cousin was taller. She stood around 5'9" tall, chocolate complexion, cute oval face, shoulder length hair and a decent shape.

Lisa climbed in the back seat with my homie Jesus. Harlem rode in the front with me. We rode out to the Marriot Marque right across the D.C., Maryland line in Montgomery County. I got a room for the ladies to freshen up and 45 minutes later we headed to Houston's restaurant in Georgetown for dinner. After dinner we drove out to a movie theater in Largo, Maryland. When we emerged from the movie theater, an inch of snow had accumulated. I took the ladies back to the Marriot. Lisa was obviously feeling Jesus, they both got a room together. Harlem and I chilled that night. I learned that she lost a child to still born 18 months prior. And she was taking a break from school. We kissed, but she wouldn't allow me to go any further.

The following day Harlem and Lisa flew back to New York. I didn't want to appear thirsty, so it was three weeks before I reconnected with Harlem. I was back in New York to handle business. I pulled up to her address on 151st Street and

Amsterdam Avenue in Manhattan. She emerged from the apartment building with an attitude. "Gil don't fucking play with me. Why haven't I heard from you since D.C.?" I smiled. This was the first time she showed any emotion towards me. I'm not gonna lie, I liked it. I said to myself, "If she is acting like this right now, imagine how she'll act after I give her this dick?"

"Girl, get your fine ass in this car!" She glanced in the backseat and saw I had two of my homies with me.

"Drop them off first and come back to get me." She said.

"It will be late when I do!"

"I don't care, just come back to get me."

I returned later that night and took Harlem home with me to the Bronx. I kissed her lips that night. They were so soft. Her tongue mated with mine. We both tore at each other's clothes to get at our bare skin. Our lust for each other was evenly matched.

Harlem's breasts were a full 40DD. I rubbed them, then took her nipples into my mouth. She let out a soft moan. She had my jeans and boxers down to my ankles. She grabbed my penis and began stroking it as we continued to kiss. My hands explored the contours of her voluptuous body. I scooped her off her feet and carried her to the bedroom where I laid her on my bed. I lived on the 11th floor. The bedroom curtains were open to allow the light from distant apartment buildings to sparkle in the distance. I hit play on the remote connected to the Nakamichi stereo system, and instantly soft music started playing.

Harlem pulled me down on top of her with her legs spread. I started exploring her vagina with my middle finger while continuing to kiss her. "Put it in me." She purred in my ear. I was eager to fuck her. She had her right hand wrapped around my dick, gripping it hard. I wanted that pussy bad. She guided me into her. The heat from her vagina engulfed me. We both let out a moan. Harlem locked her legs around my waist and we began to meet each other's strokes. I wrapped my hands around her, palming her ass cheeks and continued to stroke in and out of her in the missionary position. Our hips rotated, and grinded into each other's with every stroke... I dug deeper and deeper into her, hitting her back wall. Her moans grew louder, and her grip around my waist got tighter with the buildup and intensity of the sensations we were feeling.

Harlem buried her face into my neck and let out a guttural moan, then squeezed me so tight that I could barely breathe. My middle finger was caught in the center of her ass between her butt cheeks. She clenched them real tight, trapping my finger. She was experiencing an orgasm and I continued to stroke into her until she released my finger from the crack of her ass. It was numb and felt as if it had been slammed in a door.

Harlem was breathing heavy. Then she suddenly laid still, looked me in the eyes and said, "You better not fuck them other bitches the way you fuck me!"

"What other bitches?" I replied.

"Don't fucking play with me Gil!" Were the words she would often say.

This girl had me. I was feeling her energy, but I couldn't allow her to know this. We made love until the sunrise brightened the room the following morning.

Harlem and I became infatuated with each other. For me it wasn't just about her beauty and booty, it was the feeling I experienced whenever we spent time together. She was a breath of fresh air, a sunny day in a life that could go left at any moment. I was knee deep in the game making a few coins, and a lot came with that life. It wasn't all what it was cracked up to be.

For Harlem I was what she termed 'different!' "You're not like the guys I know!" I didn't know what that meant, but nevertheless, whenever I made trips back home to New York we spent the majority of that time together.

Hanging out with Harlem was cool. It was cute the way she

expressed her affection for me in public. Or, how the store clerks would comment on her beauty and how good we looked together when we were out shopping.

The more time I spent with her the more of it she demanded. It became a challenge juggling her demands for time and affection, and my need to conduct my business affairs. One day I made the mistake of taking Harlem to an apartment I had on 16th Street in Washington, D.C. We had been dating for five months. The occasion was her birthday. We rode the Amtrak Metro liner to D.C., stopped at my apartment to drop off her bags then I drove her out to Baltimore Harbor, where we had dinner at Windows of the World. We rode the little paddle rafts, and ended the night with something special. I surprised her with a treat, aside from the gift I gave her.

Until that point, I had not performed oral sex on Harlem. Although I was no novice to eating pussy, I had given Harlem the impression that I'd never done it before.

When we arrived back at my apartment on 16th Street, I quickly undressed her and led her into the bedroom. I laid her on her back and before I had my shirt off, Harlem sat up and reached for the belt around my waist. She unbuckled my pants then roughly pulled my pants then my boxer briefs down. She took me into her mouth instantly. I closed my eyes. Her mouth felt so good. I palmed the back of her head and began to slightly gyrate my hips back and forth. This wasn't the first time Harlem performed the act of fellatio on me.

"Cum on my face, cum on my face!" She would blurt out as I reached an orgasm. This time was no different, and I happily obliged her. Wrapping a handful of her hair around my hand, I held her face still as I ejaculated all over her pretty face. Harlem loved to catch it on her face and would get upset if I didn't.

"Lay back!" I directed her, my dick still stiff in my hand. "Spread your legs," I said. I got on my knees and pulled her to the edge of the bed. It was the first time I put my tongue on her pussy. She let out an erotic moan. I teased her, kissing her inner thighs, then resumed playing with her pussy, inserting my tongue as deep as it could go inside her. She arched her back and moaned "Ooh, ooh, oooh Gil," when I rubbed her clitoris. My tongue was still buried deep inside her. I licked and sucked her pussy lips, with a whole lot of saliva, slowly working my way to her clitoris. I paid close attention to how her body reacted to my touch. Harlem gyrated and rotated her hips in a circular motion. She grabbed the back of my head and mushed my mouth onto her crotch! I began to lick and suck with more intensity.

Giving Harlem pleasure aroused me. I lapped up her juices, alternating from sucking her clit to tongue fucking her. I could sense her orgasm coming on. Just as it did, I inserted my middle finger into her ass, she clinched her asshole around my finger. I pushed in deeper then hooked my finger upward, massaging the inside of her vaginal wall. I could feel my tongue pressing against the finger I had in her ass and applied pressure on it. I continued finger fucking her ass and tongue fucking her pussy simultaneously. Harlem held my head and mushed my face into her pussy so hard I could barely breathe. She let out a moan so loud that it seemed as if it came from deep within her gut. Then she laid stiff and fell silent...

We both laid side by side for a few moments. Once her breathing subsided Harlem looked over at me, giving me a peculiar look. I asked, "Did I do it wrong?" She continued to stare at me then she said, "You a motherfucking liar, you ate pussy before Gil!"

Harlem became engrossed in me. She became clingy. So clingy that one day while I was out with a female acquaintance of mine, I got a call from one of my homies. "Yo Harlem is out here."

"Where?" I was a little surprised.

"In front of your apartment building."

I had to abruptly end the date with my female acquaintance. I dropped her off at her townhouse in Alexandria, Virginia, and headed to my apartment building on 16th Street in D.C. Harlem wasn't there when I arrived, but soon thereafter I got a call from her.

"Where you at Gil? And who is Grace?" I dodged her questions and simply asked her,

"Where are you?"

"The Holiday Inn on Georgia Avenue."

"What the fuck are you doing there?"

"Don't fucking play with me Gil, who the fuck is Grace?"

Grace was my woman. She and I shared a townhouse in Lake Arbor, Mitchellville, MD. How Harlem knew about her was beyond my comprehension. I made a beeline to her hotel room and admonished her for popping up in D.C. unannounced. When I was in D.C. I concentrated on business. Harlem's presence was a major distraction. After dicking her down that night, the following morning I put her on a train back to New York and ignored her calls for a week.

I had fallen in love with Harlem, and she was equally in love with me, but she was doing the most and I had to curb that shit ASAP.

When I finally pulled up on her at her apartment on 151st Street, she wasn't too thrilled, but I needed her to understand that she couldn't do pop-ups on me like that. Of course, she had her own views and a few months later Harlem started acting fatal.

I was partly responsible for her behavior. When I met Harlem, I was dealing with a woman I'll call Puerto Rico from the Bronx who I'd known for years and had gotten pregnant. Nine months later she had my child, something I failed to tell Harlem. I know it was a lame move on my part. I was being selfish and basically wanted to have my cake and eat it too…

The fact is I wasn't shit. Here I was in love with not two, but three women. All tugging at my arms from each end pressuring me to make a choice.

It all came to a head one summer night when Puerto Rico and I were out together. Her little brother was babysitting our child. I don't know how Harlem got Puerto Rico's home phone number. But she called and convinced Puerto Rico's brother to give her the address. Unbeknownst to Puerto Rico and I, Harlem and a group of her friends were waiting for Puerto Rico to show up so they could beat her ass. There was no way in hell I would allow my child's mother to be jumped by Harlem and her lil clique.

"What are you doing here? I asked Harlem.

"Gil don't play with me. You're not going to lay in my bed, tell me you love me and play house with her. You need to make up your mind. It's either me or her!"

I wasn't with all the drama. I told her to take her little friends home and I would talk to her later, but Harlem wasn't having it.

"Gil I'm not going anywhere. You said you love me, right? So, what's it gonna be?"

"We ain't doing this right now. Go home, I will talk to you later..."

She stood there defiant, "It's either me, or her, make up your mind Gil!"

She was looking as beautiful as ever, and if the circumstances were different, I would have made a different choice. But for me it was not about how I felt about Harlem, or how she made me feel. It was about my child, and my determination to raise him in a two-parent household.

"You lose!" I said.

She stood there stunned, as if struck by lightning.

"Wha... what?" She stammered.

"YOU... LOSE!" I repeated with emphasis.

At that moment I witnessed the gleam and the sparkle in her eyes dim. It was not the answer she was looking for.

"Bbuut wwhhat about mmmy baby?" She said cradling her stomach.

I thought she was being dramatic. Harlem never mentioned being pregnant. I was looking at her with a smirk on my face. Then the tears came pouring out and I knew she was telling the truth. Harlem was pregnant with my child… Damn, this shit was crazy!

Despite my promises to take care of our child Harlem aborted our baby. It was a decision she made without consulting me. Something I didn't want because I didn't believe in abortions.

"You broke my heart, Gil!" Was the last words she said to me. Harlem didn't deserve what I did to her. The pain I inflicted on her was unwarranted. I regret hurting her, even till this day.

It is true what they say about karma, that "what goes around comes around!" Because the same pain I inflicted on Harlem would be inflicted on me Ten-Fold…!

# 25

# SADE

THE RELATIONSHIP WITH MY CHILDREN'S MOTHER WAS GOING through one of those phases, basically holding on by a string for the sake of the children, when I met Sade. I call her Sade because she resembled Sade the singer from her prominent forehead, full lips, to her skin tone and body frame. She even wore her hair pulled back in a ponytail exactly like the singer Sade.

Sade and I were introduced through a mutual friend of ours, Tasha. Tasha was more of a sister to me than a friend. She and I were so close people often mistook our bond as intimacy, opposed to what it really was, a close friendship.

It was early fall when I pulled up to Tasha's house in the valley, a residential area in the north-east section of the Bronx called Eastchester. Prior to that day I'd met a lot of Tasha's friends and had relations with quite a few of them, but Sade, I'd never seen her before. She was standing with one foot on the bar stool in Tasha's basement. Her 6'1" tall frame instantly caught my attention. I'm only 5'11" tall, so her height advantage intrigued me. Her long legs went on for days. I wanted to see where it ended under that skintight mini skirt she wore.

Tasha introduced us and we both held each other's gaze. The attraction for each other was instantaneous. Every time our eyes met she licked her lips seductively, letting me know how interested she was in me. We exchanged contact information, and several weeks later she and I met up at a Burger joint called Jackson Hole on 85<sup>th</sup> Street and Columbus Avenue in Manhattan. I ordered a pizza burger and Sade ordered a steak and cheeseburger. We laughed at each other making a mess of the oversize burgers they served at Jackson Hole.

The night was pleasant, the sky clear when we stepped out of the restaurant, so we decided to take a stroll down Columbus Avenue and wound up on Central Park West. We talked and got to learn a little about each other. Sade was a lab technician employed at Mount Sinai Hospital. She was planning to switch careers. She wanted to be an airline stewardess. I could visualize her tall, voluptuous figure in a stewardess uniform strutting up and down the aisle of an airplane, fluffing pillows for passengers in first class.

Sade was straightforward and direct. She had no problem telling me how she felt, and what she wanted.

"I heard so much about you. Tasha always talks about her brother Gil. My brother Gil this, my brother Gil that!"

"Oh yeah, that's my sis." I replied.

"You have a reputation!"

"A reputation, for what?" I was curious.

"You know!" She gestured toward my crotch.

I chuckled and asked, "Really, what have you heard?"

"That you know how to put it down!"

She had me blushing, and it was difficult to conceal my grin. Sade grabbed my hand then said, "Come on, take me to your place. I wanna see what all the fuss is about." We walked back to my vehicle and headed uptown to an apartment I kept on Riverside Drive in Washington Heights.

When I say Sade was aggressive, I mean in every sense of the word. We barely entered the apartment before she tugged at my belt buckle unzipping my pants to get at my penis. She was a tiger in heat the way she aggressively yanked my pants down, then got on her knees and immediately took me into her mouth. I was engulfed in a warm suction cup. I grabbed the back of her head, wrapped my hand around her ponytail to control the movement of her head. She was bobbing and sucking so fast I was on the verge of cumming in less than a minute.

I slowed her down and controlled the tempo, forcing my penis to the back of her throat. I looked into her eyes, they glazed over in moisture. I could see the lust in them. We maintained eye contact until the moment I reached my peak. I shot my load of semen down her throat. She didn't stop but continued to suck the semen out of me like a Hoover vacuum cleaner.

Sade stood up and walked pass me, leaving a trail of clothes as she removed every piece from her body until she was completely nude. I stared at her long legs and the jiggle of her ass as she headed towards the living room. She looked over her shoulder, then gestured for me to follow with her pointy finger.

I followed behind her, stripping off the rest of my garments. Sade halted, standing completely nude on the white shaggy rug placed in the middle of the living room floor. Her back was towards me, she looked over her right shoulder, then bent over touching her toes. Her yellow ass was spread open for me to see. Blood rushed to my dick. I was looking for my pants, I needed to slap a condom on. I rummaged through my pockets and retrieved the pack I kept in my wallet. I ripped open a pack, rolled it onto my dick then stepped up behind her.

"Oooh shit!" I mumbled under my breath as soon as I entered her. Even with the condom on I could feel the heat emanating from inside her. Her vaginal walls swallowed and gripped me. It took only three strokes for me to determine that Sade had some fire pussy. I got pulled into that hot fire pit. The sheer pleasure of it had me sinking my dick deep, deep inside her. I was lost in an outer body experience, drilling into her nonstop at a steady, rapid pace for 10-15 minutes.

I fucked Sade in that position until our entire bodies were drenched in sweat. I had her pussy farting every time I pulled completely out of her, then plunging back in.

"Fuck me harder, fuck me harder!" she demanded, and I fulfilled her wishes. We both reached orgasms and collapsed on top of the shaggy rug drenched in sweat.

Sade stared at me for what seemed like an eternity, then without speaking a word she removed the condom from my penis then took me into her mouth again. She sucked me into a rock-hard erection. Her mouth felt like a wet oven. With her free hand she reached for a fresh condom, then with her mouth she placed the condom over my dick. "This bitch got skills!" I said to myself.

Once she got me to a full erection, Sade straddled me in the cowgirl position. I allowed her to do her thing. I laid on my back and placed my hands behind my head, staring up at her while she rode me like a horse jockey.

Sade bounced up and down on my dick leaning back on her haunches. She was bouncing on my dick like she had a point to prove, as if she held a grudge and wanted to take it out on my dick. She was bucking hard, so hard that my dick was bending against her cervix.

Her pussy was shaved bald, revealing her swollen clit. She reached down between her legs and began rubbing it vigorously while continuing to bounce up and down. She was lost in her own world. I watched the sweat glisten all over her body. Her perky C-cup breasts bounced up and down. I glanced at my dick and noticed her vaginal juices had foamed white into a froth around my penis. I leaned forward, wrapped my arms around her waist, then pulled her down on top of me. We were now chest to breast. I began humping up into her, meeting her every stroke. She was moaning and grunting, "Ooh, ooh fuck, fuck, ooh, oh, oh, fuuck meeee!" I drilled into her like a jackrabbit until she shrieked in ecstasy, then collapsed on top of me.

We laid on the rug side by side just listening to each other catch our breaths. Sade rolled over then spoke into my ear, "I see what all the fuss is about!"

"Oh yeah, does that mean I lived up to your expectations?" She giggled, reached down and grabbed my dick. "It depends on how well you perform in round three!"

For the next couple of months Sade and I hooked up whenever I made trips back to New York. One night on our way to the village in Manhattan we made a detour to an apartment she claimed was her uncle's in Co-Op City. The apartment was on the 24th floor, nicely furnished in a grey and black theme. Grey plush carpet, black sofas, black and grey lacquer dining room set. She was nervous and was ready to leave as if her uncle was bound to pop up at any moment. I suspected the uncle was some old cat she was staying with. It mattered to me none. She could have kept it 100% with me. Her having a dude wouldn't stop me from fucking the shit out of her.

On a different occasion Sade and I were returning from seeing a movie. On our way back to my apartment on Riverside Drive I noticed my children's mother's car parked across the street.

"Oh shit!" I blurted out in surprise."

"What's wrong?" Sade inquired with a look of concern.

"My children's mother is here."

"So what, just tell her to leave." I looked over at Sade sitting in the passenger seat as if she was crazy.

"You're bugging!" I said, then put my car in gear and headed uptown to Co-Op City. It was time to drop this chick off.

When we got to Co-Op City Sade turned towards me and said, "I don't feel like going home."

"So, what you trying to do?"

"I'm horny!" She seductively replied while leaning towards me. She began to unfasten my belt buckle to get at my dick. I thought to myself, "This bitch stay in heat!" I wasn't about to turn down that hot pussy…

"You wanna get a hotel room or something?" I asked.

"No, we don't have to do all that. I know a secluded spot," and she directed me to a vacant lot behind Co-Op City. The lot was large and strewn with bricks and trash. It resembled the burnt-out vacant lots of the South Bronx in the 1970s.

I looked at Sade sitting beside me in the passenger seat. "You wanna fuck right here?" She nodded her head, "Yeah, we're good!" I surveyed my surroundings and contemplated whether or not I was being set-up. You could never be too cautious. I knew plenty of dudes who got clapped with their dicks buried in some random pussy.

Sade was already removing her pants and pulling down her panties, reclining back in her seat with her legs spread open. I backed the truck into an empty space. I wanted to face the entrance to observe if anyone entered the lot. I removed my hammer (gun) from the stash box, placed it in the door jam, then slid inside her raw.

"OMG!" I said silently to myself. Sade's pussy was on 10 with a condom, without it, it was on 1,000…The truck rocked from side to side as I buried my dick in and out of that hot pussy. "Damn this pussy is good!" I kept saying to myself over and over again. Sade had her long legs wrapped around my waist pulling me deeper into her with every stroke. I was lost in the moment. The windows of the truck were fogged up. If someone decided to walk up on us this was the perfect opportunity… I was vulnerable. My pants were down, my dick was buried inside some hot, wet, fire pussy. The only thing on my mind at that moment was reaching an orgasm, but my instincts told me to keep my left hand on the butt of my gun, and my finger on the trigger just in case.

"Oh, ooooh shit!" I grunted as I released a load of semen, pulling out of her at the very last moment. I mumbled under my breath, praying I didn't impregnate her.

A moment later I rolled over into the driver's seat. While Sade pulled up her panties, re-applied red lipstick on to her full lips, and smoothed down her ponytail, I pulled up my pants and buckled my belt.

"Yeah!" She replied. I put the truck in gear and pulled out of the vacant lot, following her directions to the "townhouse" section of Co-Op City.

"Drop me off right here," she said as I pulled up in front of one of the townhouses. "My home girl lives here," answering the question I had in my mind.

It was two weeks later when I got a call from Sade. I was out of town handling business. "Hey babe, I need a favor," she said. "I'm trying to get this apartment; I need $2,400 for the security deposit." I thought to myself, "Shit, I could always use another apartment."

"No problem, I got you. How soon do you need the money?"

"Before the end of the week," she replied.

"I'll Western Union it to you tomorrow and before ending the call I said, "I know I'm getting a copy of the key right?"

"Absolutely!" She replied.

The following day I got another call from Sade. "Gil, I was talking to my cousin Cynthia about the apartment, and she made a good point. She said, "Why should I have to give you a key to the apartment? Since you fuck with me, it shouldn't be any strings attached for giving me the money for the apartment!"

I chuckled, then replied, "You're right, get the money from your cousin!" Then I hung up the phone. What she thought, that she had a lame...? Sade had me confused with the "Uncle/Sugar

Daddy" she was fucking with. Picture me paying for an apartment she would be fucking the next nigga in...

Three days later I was experiencing a burning sensation whenever I urinated. I took a trip to a local clinic, got tested and was diagnosed with gonorrhea. "Damn! Sade got me... That pussy, was literally on fire, and I got burned!"

Today Ms. Sade is doing good, now an executive at a major record company. I wouldn't be surprised if she used that hot pussy to her advantage. What is it that some women say, "Work what your momma gave you!"

Sade had that fire pussy. Pussy so good I would have fucked her again. After she cleared up that gonorrhea of course!


The End!